CONTENTS

Neon Helix

By

Nik Whittaker

Copyrights

ABOUT THE AUTHOR

Nik Whittaker is an Independent Author, currently working his way into the industry.

Finding he always worked best through self-learning, he earned an Open University degree in English Language and Literature whilst working full time to pay the bills.

Now, fueled by coffee and imagination he has begun his quest into self-publishing.

Join him on his journey at www.nikwhittaker.com for all updates and information on upcoming releases and the path he is forging.

ACKNOWLEDGE-MENTS

Additional Editing by
Kate Milbourne

Cover Design by Rebecacovers

Dedicated to everyone who says they never have the time to do the things they love.

You do, you can, you will.

CHAPTER 1

Prelude

<**Breaking News**> Shocking images this evening from the Metropolitan Courthouse, where corruption within the MPD uncovered by investigative reporter Julian Travitz, has led to several high-profile cases being thrown out of court.

Most prominent of these being the trial of Peter Henshaw, who was expecting the verdict of guilty of several kidnapping and murder charges. Instead, the AI-J, Artificial Intelligence Judge, are forcing a halt to the trial because of the new information. Image feeds from the courthouse show Henshaw being escorted out of the building, followed by the detective in charge of the case, Alexander Draven, who then assaulted Henshaw, leading to several broken bones and hospitalization.

The MPD has suspended Draven, with the probability they will remove him from active duty with immediate effect. More information as we get it.

\<Breaking News\>

ONE YEAR LATER

CHAPTER 2

Julian

Multiple images flashed before his eyes.

Julian Travitz adjusted the headset, as it changed between over one hundred news feeds from across the Metropolitan area; alternating at two-second intervals. In the background, fragments of news radio stations played into his ears, these changing station on the opposite second of the images. His breathing slowed to a slow five second in, and five second out.

As he lay across the lounger and took all the information in, his mind picked up key phrases.

Murder. Crime rates soaring. Haven, the new party drug. Is AI too powerful? Technology the new religion. Increase in homeless disappearances but does anyone notice?

He was searching for the next story, something meaningful.

"Quartzig, shift visual interval change

to four seconds, audio on the two," Julian spoke out loud, addressing his personal AI.

"Please?" Came the response through the ear piece embedded in Julian's ear.

"Please Quartzig, if it isn't too much trouble," he replied, the sarcastic sweetness dripping from each syllable.

"You know, when you allowed my memory patterns to map new pathways and creating me into one of the most self-sufficient and leading AIs in the Metro, I didn't think my role would be as a remote control," the AI chimed back.

"And I didn't know the first human aspect you'd develop would be sarcasm Quartz, but what can you do?"

"I am only what my maker created me to be, in his own image I guess?" Quartzig chirped back.

The channels switched at four second intervals and Julian took a deep breath. It has been almost a full year since he had exposed the tampering of evidence at the Metropolitan Police Department. Over fifty cases back to the drawing board. He didn't regret the expose but the release of Peter Henshaw had affected him and his motivation. Henshaw had been on trial for the murders of several people along with multiple charges of torture. Whilst some other cases were less severe and some even in process of convicting the wrong person, Julian had to take a step back and consider the repercussions of his actions.

'New Biotech launch tomorrow'

The headline caught Julian's attention. It was from a science network wire. He reached forwards and balled a fist around the image and it continued to play without switching at the interval.

Biotech company 'Cybio' opens its doors to the public for the first time tomorrow. It's expected the opening will tie in with the launch of the much hyped enhanced cybernetic implanting techniques rumored to be in development. Cybio, founded by Maxwell Owens, Jacob Winters, and Yuri Renko over twenty years ago say the new system will, in their own words, revolutionize the way we adapt to the ever changing landscape of cybernetics.

"Make a note of that Quartz, looks like something worth checking out."

"Yes master. Anything else master?"

"See what you can find on the founders too, I'm sure those names ring some bells," Julian replied, ignoring the sarcasm.

Julian disconnected the headset from the small connection on his right temple. They were one of several small implants he had, along with some artificial grafts for aesthetics. They were generally all to help with his reporting, but some were personal indulgences. Sitting up on the lounger he tapped a few buttons on his left forearm, a display lit up across his arm showing multiple controls; a subdermal Personal Digital Assistant. Tapping a further button, he muted the radio broadcasts, before another tap illuminated the almost silent room. The humming of electrical servers creating a background of white noise.

The smell of warm electrics filled the air. The room was a mess of cables and wires which encircled the single lounger chair. This was his media room into which he could tap into any media outlet, television station, radio broadcast or Net stream using the implant in his temple. He found a certain peace within the juxtaposition of being isolated in the room and connecting to the entire world around him The voyeuristic nature of the Net allowing the lives of the world to be laid out before him.

"I've found what I believe you may be looking for regarding Winters, Owens and Renko," Quartzig broke the silence.

"Talk to me," Julian slid off the lounger and walked over to the desk at the side of the room.

"Well, Mr Winters is no longer present

within the company after an incident several years ago. The official reports say he left under amicable circumstances."

Picking up an empty glass that lay on the table, Julian opened the only door in the room, brushing past a handful of cables which hung from the ceiling like metallic vines, and entered the main room of his apartment.

"However, there were reports circled at the time that there was an issue with his health causing him to leave, furthermore there seems to be rumors of him going 'off the rails' one article puts it and causing harm to several of his colleagues," Quartzig continued.

Julian moved further into the apartment which comprised of one large open plan area encompassing the kitchen, bedroom and living space all in one. It was tidy, though the futon bed was unmade and a definite lived-in feel emitted from the walls. A large floor to ceiling window covered the expanse of the whole wall of one side, allowing the dim neon-lit skyline of the Boulevard below to radiate in. Julian headed to the kitchen area and swept his hand under the tap, causing a steady flow of water to dispense into the glass.

"Regardless, since his departure there is little information about him. In the meantime, Owens and Renko have taken full control of the company and its profits to bring it back on track."

"Hmm, what time is the conference tomorrow?" Julian asked, taking a gulp of the cool water. He'd lost track of how long he'd been in the media room but his dried throat told him it was too long.

"Eleven AM, shall I set a reminder?"

"Please," Julian finished the water and walked over to the window and looked out on the Metropolis below.

The apartment was on the 54th floor, two from the top, and the view was a rainbow of neon. The constant fog which draped over the city causing the colours to smudge into each other.

He liked the feel of this story, new tech that could influence the world would reconnect him with the city and it's people. Following his self-imposed exile from high profile stories, some street level interviews of the human aspect would reconnect him to the world. Also, if he could find what happened to Winters whilst reporting on the Cy-Bio launch, he could add spice to the reports.

"Do I have anything scheduled for today Quartz?" He asked.

"Considering it's seven in the evening Julian, no. However, you have several missed calls from Mr Porter from the Tab, if you'd like to return the call?"

Mr Carl Porter was the Editor-in-Chief for the Tablet, a news media company where Julian freelanced.

"I've still got nothing for him Quartz, next time he calls, tell him I've got a new report in the works but keep the details vague."

"Yes sir, what are you going to do?"

Julian picked up a dark blue shirt and pulled it on, he paused as he noticed his left forearm. A pattern of lines was forming around the implant under his skin, the subdermal augmentation reacting to his body.

"You should get that looked at," Quartzig said.

"It'll be fine Q, it's just settling in."

"It's showing the starting forms of t-pox Julian, you know that," Quartzig reprimanded.

"If it gets worse, I'll go to the body shop Q, promise," Julian replied as he pulled the shirt over his t-shirt. Tapping the PDA on his arm he typed in a few keystrokes and his hair, a collection of fibre-optic strands which changed, shifting from a bed head mess of short brown curls into a straight shoulder length blood-red colour with a centre parting.

"I'm going to see if there're any stories on

the streets,"

"Very well, I'll run some searches for Mr Winters and let you know if anything comes up."

"Thank you Q, don't wait up."

Julian waved his forearm across the front door, unlocking it wirelessly, it slid aside. Outside, the cold steel metal corridor contrasted with the homely atmosphere inside the apartment. They built all the apartment buildings in the area from the remains of the dockyard just behind Julian's complex. Most of the apartments themselves were old cargo containers, stacked in bundles back when the docks closed. Welding them together to create housing, the outsides kept their metallic origins, leading to compact and well-built homes, with cold stairwells.

As Julian stepped out of the apartment, the door sliding closed behind him, he could hear shouting coming from below. As he neared the stairs, the shouting grew louder.

"I don't care if he's missing, I need the dracking rent! I got kids to feed ya know!"

Julian recognized the voice of Sculley, the landlord of the Containers.

"When I find him, I'll get the rent, I promise, he has a new job and is bringing in the credits!"

This voice was from Mrs Preston, she'd only moved into the Containers with her husband in the last few months. From what Julian had gathered they had been living on the streets before Mr Preston had found work.

Julian passed them, flashing a smile of sympathy at Mrs Preston whist avoiding Sculley's eye contact. While he had no issues with Sculley, he always felt he disliked Julian. The man only came to Julian's shoulders and walked with a slight hunch from working on decommissioning submarines at the dockyard in his youth he'd told Julian once. His work in the dockyard had given him the bonus of owning several containers ,which he now rented out.

Julian continued down the winding stairs, passing several other containers. Many of which had doors decorated in some personalized design by the owners, to help distinguish them from the cold metal walls surrounding them. He liked the ones near the ground floor ,where the residents had recreated a cityscape of the Boulevard in stylised graffiti on them.

Getting to the ground floor, Julian pushed the metal gate which opened onto the street, his PDA wirelessly signaling the unlock code. A rush of heated air hit him as he stepped into the warm evening of the Metropolis.

CHAPTER 3

Xander

Alexander Draven had sat in the bar for two hours now. He'd received the call half an hour ago. The Chambers Bar had called his office in a panic. The Sliders had come in demanding protection money. Since losing his job at the MPD and setting up as a PI, he had found it hard to get steady work, and the bills needed paying regardless. Taking care of Sliders was usually easy work, which meant he found himself here, watching the door of the bar as four Sliders sauntered in.

The bar wasn't far from his office but had never been a main haunt for Xander, too much tech. The fiery red-head waitress behind the bar matched the flame red neon decor, a holographic dragon breathed artificial smoke above the centre of the dance floor, bathing the dancers in a smog, which doubled as the air conditioning system. Xander drew a breath on his cigarette as he eyed the Sliders walking in.

One, Xander assumed the leader, was more machine than flesh. His chest area consisting almost completely of metallic chrome, the lights dancing off it like a glitter ball. The Sliders were the largest gang in the Metro, comprising of several factions which spanned the entire Boulevard. Most of them were small fry, running errands for the big fish which controlled most of the illegal market.

The four moved into the bar and shouted at the red-head waitress over the rhythmic music of the bar. Nanoseconds later a blade was to her throat, as the smaller of the four jumped frog-like onto the bar and grabbed her. Xander noted his legs, he must have animal themed augs. The other two Sliders then moved towards the dance floor, the first rolling a small device into the crowd. Xander paused, contemplating the chance of it being an explosive. It was unlikely they would risk such a high casualty rate for some protection money. The device hissed as a gas escaped, a scream from the crowd and within moments, the room had evacuated. Another moment and the music cut off leaving the bar in silence.

Now Xander picked up his Bourbon and downed the rest of his glass, the burn warming his throat. He stood, brushing his duster coat aside to check his revolver was ready.

"Excuse me," he called out towards the bar, "I think you should be leaving."

"Get out of here old man," said the leader, pushing away from the bar

"I may be old, but I'm more man than you," Xander nodded at the augmentations, he had never understood the desire to have so many changes to your body.

The leader dived forward, fist first. Xander took a side step, grabbing the Sliders' fist as he did. Using his own momentum, he caused the Slider to fall forward, his face bouncing off a table before crumpling to the floor.

"Anyone else?" Xander asked as he revealed his revolver, it had an ID trigger lock, assigned to his fingerprint only. It was one of the few advanced technology items he owned.

The two Sliders on the dance floor raised their hands, their index fingers towards Xander. The fingers then spiraled clockwise into a small gun, barrels pointed like children playing cowboys.

"Really?" Xander asked, the pity mixed with sadness ,creating a cocktail of disappointment.

Before he could say anything else a shot

fired and ricocheted off the wall behind his head.

"Goddamn it!" Xander dived behind the bar, his jacket flailing behind him, as he rolled into cover behind the bar. The frog released the barmaid and threw her towards Xander, as he jumped back in line with his colleagues. Xander checked the barmaid was all right before adjusting position.

"Don't suppose you guys want to discuss this over an Old Fashioned?" He shouted over the bar. Several shots cascaded above him, shattering bottles and sprayed a mixture of glass and alcohol over Xander.

"Have it your way," he shouted back.

Pulling his revolver out, he tapped the fingerprint scanner on its side with his thumb to unlock the safety and another double tap on one of the side buttons registered his desired ammo type. He fired the gun straight upwards then, almost immediately, he pulled the trigger again. As he did, the bullet which was on course to the ceiling, had a secondary detonation, causing it to change direction at a ninety-degree angle and fly over the bar towards the Sliders. Xander knew the chances of it hitting a target were slim but he counted on the distraction to give him a few moments to slide down the bar, to get into a better position.

He heard a smash from behind the counter, as the bullet broke a light fitting on the opposite wall; he crawled quickly down the bar to the far end. The red lights flickering from the damage.

"Come out here old man! We just want the money," a voice shouted.

Xander nodded to the barmaid, who was curled up in a ball opposite him. Looking around, he saw a keg of beer attached to a draught pump above and a gas canister below. He quickly uncoupled it and lay the gas canister on its side.

"You guys want to give up now or after I've hurt you some more?" He shouted, moving the cannister down the bar until it poked slightly out, the nozzle facing Xander. More shots fired above the bar, Xander retaliated with more bi-directional bullets before he unscrewed the valve on the canister. Within seconds, the pressure of gas erupting from the nozzle caused it to spin away uncontrollably from Xanders' grip and into the bar.

Shouts of confusion from the Sliders gave Xander the opportunity he needed. Getting to his feet he managed to take two careful aims at the panicking Sliders, he fired. Bullets flew straight into their heads, blood splattering over the last one left standing, the frog. He crouched, his amphibian legs poised for action, though his eyes betrayed his fear.

"Get outta here and tell your boss this bar is out of his patch," Xander said, pointing to the door with his revolver.

He looked at the three bodies on the floor, the blood flashing black as the lights stuttered on and off. The holographic dragon swooped down over the dance floor and let out a burst of steam. This was the last straw, the frog turned and ran from the bar.

Xander leaned down and pulled the barmaid up from the floor.

"Sorry about the mess," was all he said before taking the last intact bottle of bourbon off the shelf, grabbing a glass, and headed to a table.

This was the work he was used to since losing his job at the MPD. The expose wasn't what annoyed Xander; he wanted the corrupt cops to get to hell as fast as the devil could take them, but Henshaw, he'd been killing people for years and they'd finally caught the bastard. That the piece of shit was walking free had been too much. Xander had attacked him as he left the courthouse and left him a bloody mess on the steps. He was still alive, roaming the streets, and that ate Xander up. Not only had he lost the case and his job, but it had all been for nothing.

Now, he took any cases that made money, but his reputation of violence preceded him and mostly, he just worked protection and security services to make ends meet.

Finishing a third glass of straight Bourbon, he got up from the table and walked out of the bar, the barmaid who was sweeping up the broken glass paused to let him pass.

"Thank you Mr Draven," The barmaid said, Xander nodded in acknowledgment.

The cool night air did Xander good, as he breathed in and let the cold sit on his lungs for a second before exhaling. He heard sirens approaching; he needed to be gone before they got there. Three dead sliders wouldn't make the headlines but he didn't want to deal with the questioning that came with a police report. Sliders had been slowly spreading into the Boulevard in the last couple of years. Mostly they were just junk-heads who worked for the local gang leaders so they could get their next Aug, but they were becoming more of a problem.

Taking several steps down the street, he passed a few more late night bars, all of which had the newest bar room technology which matched their neon facades and holographic hosts. Whilst he didn't *hate* technology over-all, he felt it had too much control on the lives of those who used it. The world saw the AI Judges as being the perfect courtroom system, non-bias and would only take the facts as proof with zero human emotion. Unfortunately, this system had its flaws, as was clear in the Henshaw case. Sure the evidence was corrupt, but the crimes remained. Yet the judge deemed one anomaly in a case to be enough for reasonable doubt. Ever since, Xander would only take user-controlled tech as reliable.

He passed a few more bars; the neon enhanced by the drizzle of rain which fell. Xander turned the collar up on his jacket against the rain before stopping off at a convenience store. The white lights inside made him squint for a moment as his eyes adjusted.

"Hey Mr D," the young clerk called as he entered, "Usual bottle?"

Xander shrugged, finding it hard to decide if being that predictable with alcohol was a good or bad thing.

"Sure, and throw in a pack of smokes too, not the synthetic crap the proper stuff. Thanks Howie."

It was more expensive because of the difficulties in growing tobacco in the Metro but Xander could taste the artificial ingredients in the synthetic cigarettes like burning electrics.

"No worries Mr D, I know you like quality!" Howie grinned and passed a bottle of bourbon and a pack to Xander. He pulled out a wad of notes and handed them over.

"When you going to upgrade Mr D?" Howie asked, pointing to his forearm where his PDA was attached, its connected wireless credit system the most common of all the augmentations.

"Never Howie, I don't want no electrical crap stuck inside my arm, don't get why anyone would," he replied, his usual response for Howie's daily query.

"Ah, you will one day Mr D, I guarantee it. Soon, no one can last in this world without it!"

"Well, I'll be the last true flesh and bone human on that day Howie."

Xander smiled, as he took his change and walked back out into the drizzle. He lit a cigarette under the store's awning, inhaling deep, he scanned the streets. The rain was so commonplace that the streets remained busy. He stepped out and turned to head back to his apartment, which doubled as his office.

Located in Megatown the office was a middle apartment in the large concrete building which remained from the old days before the expansion of high rises took over the cites. It had stairs and no lift but Xander liked it for its charm. As he made his way up, he smiled a greeting to several neighbors but spoke little. While they knew him for helping the local community, they also saw him as somewhat a thug. As such, he was viewed as more of a necessary evil than a genuinely good person. He could live with that as he wouldn't have called himself anything else.

Arriving at his apartment, he swung the door open and walked in, before locking it behind him and collapsing on the sofa, which served as a waiting space for any clients. It was pristine from lack of use.

CHAPTER 4

Prime

His eyes opened.

Who am I?

Where am I?

The thoughts crept into his mind before answers appeared, slotting into place like plugs into sockets.

I am number 733

I am at work, and my shift is just beginning.

733 looked around him. He was laying at a slight incline inside a large vertical cylinder. He raised and pressed his hand against the glass panel in front of him, as his hand glanced the glass it slid sideways with a hiss. The smell of fresh air filled his nostrils.

As he stepped forward, he was aware of many other pods lining the pathways, which ran left to right as far as the eye could see. Glancing down, he saw the grey jumpsuit he was wearing, his feet covered with boots. More thoughts slotted into place within his mind, though they felt foreign and not his own.

I am a perfect employee. My main goal is guest satisfaction and aligning this with the customer needs. I should return to my post upstairs to action my goal.

With that he turned and walked down the pathway to the left, heading towards a white door, which seemed to be the only entrance point to the room. He was aware of the large warehouse space he was in.

As he walked, he examined several pods on his way. Inside were bodies of varying stages of development. Some were only babies, whilst others looked teenage and others in the mid adulthood.

What do I look like?

The thought formed in his brain, but within moments the thought vanished, forced out by another.

I should get my uniform on.

Arriving at the door, he pushed it open. Revealing a large cloakroom with multiple lockers stacked around a large square area, a second door was at the far corner of the room.

Where is my locker?

Scanning the lockers, 733 found one with his designation on it and pulled it open. Inside, a pair of black trousers hung from a hanger; a white shirt and black tie also hung on a separate hanger. Polished black shoes sat on the bottom of the locker.

I need to get dressed.

He changed, making sure every crease was in line. The fit of the clothes was perfect.

Time to go to work. Swipe in.

On the opposite side of the room, next to the second door, was a small panel with a retina scanner. He walked over to it and a flash of light glared into his eye.

733 opened the second door in the room. Through it, the hustle and bustle of the Grand Falls Hotel came into view.

The large foyer area was lit in a dazzling white, with several large chandeliers hanging from the high ceiling, illuminating the room. All the decor was a brilliant white with gold trim. Several luxurious armchairs were scattered around room opposite the long reception desk which spanned the centre of the room. There was little to no invasive technology, fitting with an almost ragtime era aesthetic, which was furthered by the smooth jazz music piping out of unseen speakers.

Among the varying guests, 733 observed several waiters, service staff and receptionists all conducting their duties. Something about them felt off to 733. He gave it a minute, before a call from someone at the reception desk stole his attention back.

"Reilly can you help this gentleman with his bags ,please," the receptionist chimed, looking directly at 733.

733....7ee... Reilly. I am Reilly and am ready to serve.

Suddenly, everything slotted into place in Reilly's mind. All doubts and questions faded. As if someone had flicked a switch, his whole demeanor changed, he stood upright, arms straight, shoulders back. His mouth stretching into a huge smile, revealing a perfect set of teeth.

"Of course Jan," he walked towards the desk, "How are we today sir? Wonderful weather for your visit, here let me help you with that,"

Picking up the bags, he motioned for the guest to follow him. 733 was no more, there was only Reilly. Whatever thoughts 733 had developed were being replaced with the perfect service of Reilly the Porter.

The evening had drawn in, Reilly was now sat behind the quiet reception desk, scanning the check-in reports for the hotel. No additional requirements further to complete, all jobs completed for the shift. There were no guests around at the time and he was aware of several members of staff arriving for the start of their shift.

"Evening," he nodded at the arrivals. His energy levels were low, and he was glad of the arrivals as it meant finishing time was close. They met him with silence, all three of the night reception team's faces were blank, as if they were sleeping.

As the team came around the desk, Lee stood and smiled at them in an attempt to wake them from their slumber, but to no avail. Suddenly, the rotating door at the entrance moved, and a well-dressed couple strolled in, greeting the desk as they approached. As if triggered by an electric prod, the nights team came to life.

"Hey Reilly, how are you?" One of them sang, "Bet you're glad to be finishing!"
Then, as if the arrivals had surprised them;

"Oh, I didn't see you there! Welcome to Grand Falls Hotel! How are you today! Wow, you guys look amazing! Let's get you checked in!"

Throughout this performance, Lee looked puzzled. Hesitantly he tried to say something, when a thought popped into his head which eliminated all others.

Time to finish. Let's swipe out.

With that, all other thoughts that had been forming before, dissipated and Reilly was calm. Rising from his seat, he waved to the nights team.

"Hey, see you later, guys! Have a great evening!" And to the couple checking in, "Have a great stay!"

With that, he turned and headed back towards the door he had used to enter the hotel earlier that morning. Walking up to it, another retina scanner was next to door.

Time to finish.

Leaning forward, he put his eye to the scanner, a flash of light.

Then darkness.

CHAPTER 5

Jacob

A large neon red crucifix loomed over the corner of Broadway and Finch. Fixed above the large double wooden doors of Saint Damien's Church, the cross was illuminated all day and night.

The church had stood on the corner since the Metropolis was nothing more than a small village, but over time the religion had waned in correlation as technology rose. Fewer people prayed to a God, as they now prayed for likes and online presence. The area surrounding the church became less popular as the masses moved towards the central light of the new technological beacon within the opposite side of the city. In the singularity's wake, they abandoned the church, the doors chained up, and the windows boarded. The building now stood in as the central point of the downtown area of the city, where those of lower technological desire lived.

Until five years ago.

The man shuffled up to the chained doors of the church. His body covered in a tattered robe, the hints of a ragged beard emerging from under his hood. He rested his hands on the chains across the door and with one swift pull, the rotting wood splintered and released the bolts holding the chain.

A slow, deep moaning creak emerged as the giant doors slowly swung inward. The noise, so loud in the quiet of the street, caused several of the locals to raise their heads and take notice.

Once inside, the man walked down the centre aisle, his steps brushing aside years worth of cobwebs and dust that eddied into the air. He walked straight up to the alter at the top of the aisle and dropped to his knees under the half-broken statue of the crucifixion and prayed.

He stayed there, on his knees praying for twenty-four hours with no food or drink. He prayed non-stop until his lips and tongue were dry and cracked. His words only a whisper, no-one could make them out, only the long humming drone of syllables. Several of the locals investigated what this strange newcomer was doing and why. Overnight, tens of people had entered the church and took seats along the pews, brushing away the dust and watching the man. Watching and waiting, they hoped for at least some real-life entertainment, in contrast to the diet of online media they consumed daily. Some had left bottles of water and small donations of food around the man, yet still he prayed appearing to not notice any of the items now scattered around him.

Eventually, twenty-four hours exactly from the moment he arrived, he stopped praying.

Turning his head slowly, achingly, as if a statue was turning its head for the first time, he saw a bottle of water close to him and reached slowly for it.

He unscrewed the cap and took a long, gulping drink from the bottle. Not stopping until he had finished, he placed the bottle on the ground next to him and looked upwards at people who had flocked to see him. Amongst the human eyes staring at him from the crowd, he also saw many digital screens and cybernetic eyes all recording and broadcasting what they saw.

Standing slowly, he reached out his hand from under the robe and pointed at a woman who was sitting closest to him. Her arm was a mess of cheap circular metallic implants, one for wireless connectivity, another showing her current heart rate and step count. The veins around the implants were raised, a purple cobweb of infection spreading from each connection. The clear signs of T-Pox caused by non-biological incompatibility. She looked confused at first, until the man turned his hand over and beckoned her to join him.

Getting up from the pew, she shuffled towards him slowly. She reached him and he took her hand. Pulling her close, he kissed her forehead before turning her towards the gathered crowd.

"This woman, just like all of you before me today, is blinded. Fooled. Deceived and tricked by the Devil of this world. It has infected you and pulled you into a deep abyss, the illusion of connectivity. When in reality, the more connected you are to this evil, the less connected you are to yourself and the spiritual soul!"

He used a fingernail on his right hand to scratch a long cut in his own left forearm. Blood immediately trickled down his arms and dripped to the floor below.

"I was pulled from this evil and have regained my vision. This gift has been given to me and I will help you all return into the true nature of the human soul."

Before she could resist, the man put his forearm to her lips, blocking her nostrils as he did, she had no choice but to open her mouth and allow some of his blood to pour into her mouth. Choking she tried to move away but he held her tightly.

"It will not be easy, for nothing worth having is. The path to your salvation will be painful as it rips you apart from the masquerade of the world."

He released her. She fell to the floor screaming as a red flaming heat ran through her entire body, like hot lava was pulsing through her veins. Scratching at her own skin, she rolled on the floor. The gathered masses rose to their feet, some rushing towards her to help. Before they reached her, the man threw the robe off his shoulders, revealing a long blade strapped to his side. He didn't draw it but raised a palm to the crowd, making them stop in their tracks.

Below, the woman was now whimpering in pain and was staring at her arm. Suddenly the infection faded as blood pooled around the implants' edges.

"See as the power of the divine take effect! Heal this woman from her evils!"

The implants raised out from their sockets, the blood pooling more as they detached from the woman's skin. A moment later, they finally fell from her arm and dropped to the floor. The infection now vanished, with only two small scars where the implant had been, as the only evidence they had even been there.

The crowd stood, stunned as they watched the man pick up the scraps of the implants from the floor.

"Nothing but metal shards of imperfection."

He threw them behind him into the depths of the church, then offered a hand to the woman who was rubbing the scars in shock. She looked up at him, taking a moment to realise she was free of the infection she had suffered with for so many years. She smiled and took his hand and hugged him tightly.

"Bless you sir," she repeated over and over.

"Welcome to the flock my dear and welcome you all! Join me and let us end this tyranny of evil which infects all it touches!"

With both hands raised, he welcomed them and began his baptism of technology within the community.

Within two years, the neon cross was the only visible modern technology in the area. It's red light, both a beacon to guide lost souls, but also the representation of technology as the symbol of death of the modern Jesus.

Father Jacob lifted the community into a new age of belief.

CHAPTER 6

Julian

Julian walked down the Boulevard of the Metro. Officially known as *Lamplight Boulevard*, but known to the locals as the *Neon Boulevard* due to the constant rainbow of neon which illuminated it from end to end. The Boulevard ran through the city like a central nervous system.

Beginning at the outskirts of the Metropolitan, commonly referred to as the BitSlumbs, where average income was close to nothing, the Boulevard continued through thousands of kilometres, past the dock lands, or MegaTown where Julian lived, and further into the heart of the city. Following this it evolved into the GigaCity, which was the main shopping district of the Metro, containing the most shops and food areas. Next ,it spread into the more wealthy research areas of the TerraCity before moving into the ZetaCity, here was where the most advanced tech and wealthiest inhabitants lived. Every inhabited area of the

Metro spun off the Boulevard. There was also the Underpass of the Boulevard, built on the remnants of the old city. It was supported on several large pillars, under which the residence of the Underpass lived. Though few crossed between the Over and Under levels of the Metro.

Julian stopped at one of the food stalls upon entering GigaCity and walked up to check the menu out, the smells of fried vegetables and soy sauce saturated the air.

"Hey Jools, how's it going, buddy?" The voice shouted over the drone of conversation emanating from the several customers sat at the stalls' seven seats, which ran along its counter. George, the noodle bar owner, waved as he spoke and beckoned Julian over.

"Going good Georgie, how's the noodles today?"

"Best in the Metro as ever Jools!" He beamed and dished fresh Szechuan noodles into a box and passed it over to Julian. As he took the bowl, Julian swiped his forearm over a detector on the counter of the food stall. A confirmatory beep indicated the credits were debited from Julian's account.

"Thank you, Georgie," Julian took a seat as a space became available at the counter.

"No problem Jools, always a pleasure."

"How's the augmented hand holding up?" Julian asked watching as Georgie cooked a fresh batch of food.

As he watched, Georgie lifted his right hand to display it. As he did his bottom two fingers rotated and fused together and the edge of his hand from his little finger all along to his wrist tapered to a sharp knife edge. Laying a cucumber along his chopping board, Georgie sliced it into thin sections before his hand morphed into an elongated spoon, with which he scooped up the cucumber and threw it onto the hot wok which was waiting for them.

"Perfection Jools, sheer perfection," he laughed.

Smiling, Julian made a mental note of the success. A few months ago, Georgie had lost his hand when one of the city's automated garbage disposals had glitched and clamped down on his arm whilst throwing away the trash. Julian had reported on the incident, exposing the lack of maintenance for the disposal systems. The council had compensated Georgie with enough to cover the expense of the Augmented hand, something which only some Five Star chefs had access to. Now, this street noodle bar was one of the most popular locations on the Boulevard.

"What's the word on the street Georgie? Anything I should be paying attention to?" Julian asked between mouthfuls.

"Eh just the usual Jools," Georgie shrugged, "The street gangs have been fighting amongst themselves as usual, but they're staying out the Boulevard for the time. The Aug place just down from here, 'Aug or Nothing' got jacked a couple of nights ago but they only got the basic shiz from the display window," Georgie pointed to the shop.

"Sliders?" Julian asked.

"Eh, who knows?" Georgie shrugged again. "Probably," he passed some noodles to another customer.

"One other thing, probably nothing, but I've noticed a few less of the homeless guys hanging around after closing. Ya know, normally I'm passing out the leftovers to those guys, doing my bit, but they not been around this last month or two. Could be they jus' moved to newer locales but who knows," Georgie took Julian's empty box and threw it in the trash. He grabbed a bottle of beer from the fridge behind him, his hand morphing into a bottle opener to pop the cap, before passing it to Julian.

"Hmm, let me know if you hear anything,

might be something," Julian tapped his PDA making notes. He liked to keep track of anything he heard, never knowing when it could be the start of a new case.

A few more customers were arriving, so Julian gave up his seat.

"Thanks for the noodles Georgie."

"Anytime Jools, anytime," He smiled his big grin and waved before getting back to the cooking.

Julian continued his journey down the busy boulevard, shouldering his way through the crowds which became denser as he got closer to the main shopping district in Giga, a 24/7 hub of retail. As he progressed further, the advertising increased in both technological style and also the cost of the goods. What began as billboards with a three-dimensional image, became full hologramatic visuals. A woman walked over to him, commenting on his hair style, before offering him some matching clothing from the shop. Next, a young man waved him over, then suggested a bar behind him as *the greatest place to start the night for a bachelor such as himself.* The image-recognition algorithms the advertising used had so much access it, not only considered the way Julian looked but could also get a fast check on his basic details such as his marital status and address. Within nanoseconds, it could create personalised advertising bespoke to him. Julian was accustomed to it and could recognise the holograms before they even reached him, not that it made them any less annoying.

He arrived at the store he was heading towards, a mid-ranged Aug shop where he had purchased most of his current tech, including the hair augments.

Aug-Tech was the go to place for the best new tech at reasonable credits that Julian had come across. He stepped inside and took a seat in one of the booths,which lined either side of the store. The lighting was bright white, creating an almost clinical feel. Once sat, he placed his forearm on the arm of the chair. A virtual display materialized in front of him, showing a loading screen as it completed a full body scan. Taking account of all the current Augs within his body, checking their status and condition. It also took a down payment from his account which covered the virus scan and optimisation.

1 count of onset T-Pox detected, medical advise recommended.
1 Aug glitch detected.

It displayed a full map of his body and augs like a digital Vitruvian man. He had twelve different Augs across his body, eleven of which were in green. One, highlighted across his eyes, was orange, the upgrade. His right arm had a red flashing exclamation mark, showing the T-Pox.

Optical Aug, minor glitch detected. Would you like the system fixed? Y/N

The system chimed, Julian double tapped the Y on the screen and replaced his forearm to the armrest. The credits debited and a flashing blue light filled the booth with a glow. The procedure was wireless, however if Julian left the booth while the light flashed, it would be incomplete and could cause an unexpected error.

After twenty seconds, the light turned green, showing the procedure was complete and a success. Julian rubbed his eyes and opened them. Blinking for a few moment, he tested the fix. He looked at the screen and focused, his retina zoomed forwards and he could make out the tiny pixels which made up the screen. A double blink and his retina delivered a screenshot of his vision to his personal air-drive, where it stored it for future use.

All systems upgraded. Would you like to browse the new arrivals Mr Travitz?

"No, I'm good thank you" He answered before getting up and leaving the store.

Food and optimizing done, he was ready for a drink and for some real work. The bars scattered around the Metro varied from high-end cocktail bars to the more seedy dive bars. He headed towards the Valkyrie, a bar which had stood throughout the development of the boulevard, adjusting to the newer surroundings as they changed. Before he walked through the entrance, he tapped his PDA.

"Hey Quartz, you there?"

"At your command sir," came sarcastic the response.

Julian wondered how he had got sarcasm from an AI but shelved the thought.

"Anything on Cy-Bio of interest?"

"Not really, it looks like Yuri is the main guy running the show now that Winters *retired,* no one has heard much from Owens in the run up to the conference. I'll keep digging though."

"Thanks Quartz. One more thing, have you seen any news about homeless disappearances at all on the wire?"

"One moment please," Quartzig ran a quick search, "Only two missing person reports to the MPD but being homeless they haven't really been looking into it seems. Something up?"

"Just something else to have a look at, not sure yet. Thanks Q"

"Anytime sir."

Julian closed the connection and headed into the bar, brushing past a couple on their way out.

CHAPTER 7

Xander

ALEXANDER DRAVEN

That's what the sign above the door should have said, but the green neon tubing was faulty in several sections ,causing them to flicker like a nervous junkie, so it now read;

A XANDER RAVE

Because of this, the locals called him Xander.

He sat with his feet up on the wooden desk and looked at the sign flickering on his door. He should get that fixed, he thought, as he stubbed out the last embers of a dying cigarette into the ashtray. He'd set up as a Private Investigator since the dismissal and had bought the office space and the apartment above with the last of his savings. The office was predominantly wood of varying types, from the door and floorboards to the desk and chairs. Following the AI Judge's decision in the trial, and his newfound hatred for all things technology. The only advanced tech to be found in the room was the Visual Display Unit, a floating hologramatic display, which he tried not to use. His old monitor was smashed in a rage several months earlier. Next to the display was his answer-phone, a retro digital machine connected to the phone. He stabbed the play button with his now cigarette-less hand, hoping for something of interest.

"Erm..hello? Is this Alex Draven? I want to hire you to show my husband who is really in char.."

"Angry Wife, nope," Xander said, as he hit the next button.

Message Deleted

"Hi, Mr Draven, we need some security for the fight late..."

"Security, nope,"

Message Deleted

"Listen to me, it's important ok. You want some escape then this is how you do it..."

Message Deleted

End of Messages

Xander sighed and lit up another cigarette

using his lighter. His reputation preceded him, labeled as the *'violent ex-cop who would fight for anyone'.* The label had got him plenty of work when he first started out, but then he became a glorified security guard, and he felt it was time for more vetoing of the work he took on. This had meant, however the cash-flow had dried up like a sponge in a desert.

Exhaling, the wisps of smoke coiled around neonbeams coming in through the window behind him. He closed his eyes and leaned back in the chair.

A knock on the door snapped him back to reality. He couldn't remember the last time someone had knocked on the door.

"C'm in," he hollered.

The door slowly opened and a tall woman entered the room, she immediately raised the style of the room from zero to a hundred. Wearing a long black dress ,which emphasized her height.

"Mr Draven?" Her voice poured out.

Xander subconsciously straightened up.

"Yes Ma'am."

"Thank god, I need your help. Someone has murdered my husband."

Xander had to hide a smile, finally something worth his time.

"Please, take a seat Miss…"

"Owens, Ava Owens," she replied, as she took a seat opposite Xander.

"Why haven't you gone to the police?" Xander didn't want to ask, but felt he should.

"I have, but they concluded it a cold case because of lack of evidence. It's still an open case but they aren't doing anything about it."

Her voice trembled, the cracks forming on the strong front she had put on coming in.

"When did he die? In fact, just tell me all you know," Xander was interested now, a dead husband, a cold case the MPD couldn't solve. This could help him redeem some of his name.

"Can I have one of those?" Ava pointed at the cigarette in Xander's hand. He nodded and lit one before passing it to her. Taking one long drag in and an equally long breath out, she began her story.

"Last week, February 2nd, I returned home and found my husband laying across the hallway, covered in blood. Mutilated, with his left hand missing," Ava described the situation as if reading from a police report.

"I see, and this doesn't seem to have hit you too hard?" Xander noticed the lack of feeling coming from her now and wasn't ready to be played a fool, something was off.

"Oh, my apologies," Ava blinked twice in deliberate timing and after a moment her eyes welled up. "I... I didn't know what to do," Ava's voice now cracked as she spoke, the emotion getting caught in her throat.

"Okay... " Xander wasn't sure how to react to this.

"I, I called the police immediately, and they did a full sweep of the apartment. The autopsy said Mr Owens died of blood loss," Ava continued.

"Mr Owens? Did he not have a first name?"

"Oh, Maxwell. Max. He was my Max."

"Ava, what is going on here? For a mourning widow, you don't seem upset," Xander had enough of the guesswork, his hangover was taking root now and his patience was getting smaller by the minute.

"Excuse me? Oh, excuse me Mr Draven. I should explain," as she spoke, Ava placed her fingers to her left temple and pressed down. "I am not like you, Mr Draven."

Where her fingers had been, a small square about the size of a credit card indented inwards, then slid to the side. "I am a synthetic human. Mr Owens created me."

Beneath the square, a small circuit board was revealed, with several connections and sockets.

Xander just stared for a moment.

Ava tapped a button on the side of her temple, before the square replaced itself, becoming perfectly flush with the scalp and indistinguishable.

Xander had heard of SynthBots before, mostly they were in the sex clubs and gaming industry; programmed to perform set tasks with basic sub routine informations. Ava seemed to be free functioning.

"Mr Owens built you? He built his wife?" Xander exclaimed.

"In some regards, yes. Mrs Ava Owens died five years ago in a tragic accident. The work that CyberBio had been working on was on mapping the mind into data, luckily Mrs Owen had been scanned before the accident. After her death, Owens constructed my shell from digital imagery before transferring her prior mental data into a prototype DataBrain."

Xander listened, understanding the words and comprehending the general idea, but to be seeing it in the flesh was something else.

"I hope I don't make you uncomfortable Mr Draven," Ava smiled politely. "My emotional triggers and human responses are still developing, so I can sometimes appear, cold."

"Yeah, you are a little icy," Xander replied, "But it's ok, you aren't making me uncomfortable," he lied.

"Good, I hope we can move forward into looking at the investigation?"

"Sure, sure," Xander welcomed something which he was more familiar with. "So you found the body, called the cops, they looked around?"

"Correct, it was two days before I heard anything more. They called me to tell me the investigation was being indefinitely suspended for inconclusive evidence. They ignored any further of my questions, and I've heard nothing since," Ava genuinely looked sad. "I believe my, nature, being the reason they didn't feel the need to speak to me as a person. Giving me more of an update than anything else," she swallowed, trying to regain composure and looked up at Xander, "I may be a synthetic but I have, developing emotion responses."

Xander struggled to understand the situation in front of him. Knowing that Ava wasn't human and yet, looking at her, how could he not see her as such.

"It's... it's ok, I'll look into it," Xander said the only thing he could think of to help the woman before him. "But one thing, why me? I'm not exactly the most popular choice of PI's in the Metro," Xander said, self deprecating as ever.

"Oh, that's quite obvious, Mr Draven. Several weeks ago, Mr Owens told me he had you down as his personal choice, should anything happen to him. He specifically told me to seek you out should anything befall him. I assumed you knew him previously?"

"I'd never even heard of the guy until you walked through that door just now," Xander replied, after taking a moment to add the information to a growing list of things he didn't understand.

"I guess we have a few mysteries to solve then, Mr Draven."

"Who's this 'we'? I don't have partners."

"Understood Xander, and, I mean this with no offence, but I have many resources at my disposal which I believe would be helpful to you. Also I want, no, I *need* to understand what happened," Ava looked Xander straight in the eyes. He couldn't refuse.

"Fair enough. And It's Xander, only my enemies call me Draven."

"Very well Xander. Please call me Ava. Where do we start?"

CHAPTER 8

Prime

His eyes opened.

Who am I?

Where am I?

The thoughts crept into his mind... again?

I am Reilly, no, 733

I am at the beginning of my shift.

The cylindrical pod was new, yet familiar to him. He put his hand up to open it for the first time, or was it the hundredth?

I am a perfect employee. My main goal is guest satisfaction and aligning this with the customer needs. I should return to my post upstairs to action my goal.

These thoughts came forced into his head, he felt he knew the words.

I should get my uniform on.

He felt like the words were being sent to his brain but he couldn't understand where from, or why they felt familiar. He followed his instincts into the large changing room.

Where is my locker?

I need to get dressed.

Time to go to work. Swipe in.

He walked over to the scanner and placed his eye in front of it, with that, all the fragments of memory were gone. Opening the second door in the room, he stepped into the Grand Fall Hotel foyer for the first, or hundredth time.

As he made his way through, he knew he needed to head to the kitchens.

I am a chef, of the highest training. His programming told him. As he went through the hotel, he waved and smiled at everyone he met. Asking how everyone's day was going, being an ideal employee.

Entering the kitchen, he looked around, there were three other chefs already in the kitchen, they were preparing varying meats along the center island area. He quickly joined them and began chopping the vegetables which were waiting for him.

Several hours later, Reilly had been working non-stop; chopping, cleaning and prepping vegetables. Next ,he had cooked food for the in-house restaurant and had been standing at the hot plate, carving fresh cooked turkey for the residents in the hotel. He suddenly became aware of how tired and aching he was. Almost instantaneously, he felt a sudden urge.

The day is over, time to sign out.

Without another thought, he walked out of the kitchen and into the main foyer. At the desk, two customers were attempting to check in and were having some trouble.

"Can you find my reservation! Mr Jonathan Hall!" The young man at the counter shouted at Janice behind the desk.

"I assure you sir, I am doing the best I can for you."

Reilly slowed his pace, a slight resistance to his commands but his empathy for his colleagues took priority.

"Excuse me, can I help at all?" he made his way up to the counter.

"Unless you can cook me up a fresh room, I don't think so," the young man mocked, his breath reeking of alcohol. The woman at his side gave Reilly a sympathetic smile, clearly ashamed of the man.

"Unfortunately, I can't do that sir, but I'm sure Janice is doing all she can. Perhaps you could have a drink in the bar while we sort it for you."

"How about Frack Off!" The man took a swing at Reilly, who wasn't expecting it.

The fist flew straight into Reilly's temple and he crumpled to the floor, clutching his head. A siren rang throughout the foyer area and three guards appeared from the side of the reception desk, each lifting the man by the arm. He shouted in resistance as they dragged him out of the building and threw him to the pavement. Behind them, his companion followed and went to his side.

Meanwhile, Reilly had slowly regained his faculties and was pushing himself from the floor. As he got to his feet and leaned on the desk, he looked over to Janice.

"You ok?" He asked.

"I'm fine, are you?" She replied, concern in her voice.

"I'll be fine, just need to rest up I think."

Reilly was aware that there was no order

coming to his brain, no voice he didn't recognise. Regardless, he was so exhausted, he walked to the cloakroom as usual and started to get changed. He did as he felt he should; heading to the door that lead out of the room.

He leaned down to look at the retina scanner, only this time when it flashed, he felt nothing. He watched the flash and heard the beep of the door lock coming undone. For a moment, he stood there staring at the scanner, as he did not understand what he should do next, a large blank in his mind was all that came through.

After several moments, he walked through the door, as that was the only way he could think to go. Opening it carefully, he saw the cloakroom and the door opposite. He continued through, forgetting to change without noticing. He stepped through the second door and realised the room beyond was where he started his day. He continued into the large warehouse, glancing from side to side, he saw the chambers filled with bodies. They all looked asleep, and yet there was no life in them. Like husks of people.

Like they are waiting for instructions.

Reilly stopped at one chamber and looked closer. There was a label on the outside of the pod '801', underneath, was a track of biological functions and a timer with a label '4 hours til available'. He tapped on the glass, trying to wake the woman inside, there was no reaction.

The realisation sank in; he was one of these people, there must be a pod for him. Scanning the numbers; 800, 799, 798, he ran towards his number. Arriving at an empty pod, he looked at the tracker.

Due back, eta minus 15 min. Alert.

He didn't need to think twice about what it could mean. Torn between getting in the pod, which his instinct told him he should, and running away, he stood there frozen on the spot.

He heard a door open further ahead of him; the noise triggered him into action. He ran, back towards the changing room. He did not understand what this place was, or who he was, but he wasn't going back into the chamber!

CHAPTER 9

Jacob

Father Jacob was sat in the small office he had renovated at the back of the Church. A wooden desk and a small set of drawers were the only furnishings in the room. He scribbled down a few notes about the sermon he would deliver later that evening. Once done he rose and walked over to the door, making sure it was locked and secure before heading to the drawers.

Placing a finger on a far corner, just under an incense holder, a metallic click indicated a lock opening. He pulled at the centre drawer and as he did, a computerised display rose from the centre of the desk. Whilst he was against all augmentations, he understood technology had its uses. However, he didn't want his followers to see him using such things, as he knew it would lower their belief in his teachings.

A small holographic keyboard appeared on

the desk, just under the screen. Tapping a log in into the computer, he was soon accessing the Net. Checking his alerts, he saw that the CyberBio conference was going ahead, this surprised him. Pulling a phone from his pocket, he dialled a number.

"Mr Tombs, I see the conference is going ahead. Are you sure the Owens problem was handled correctly?"

The voice on the other end of the line was sharp and polite, but the offence was still audible.

"Yes Father Jacobs, I can assure you I completed it according to the plan. Do you doubt the work?"

"Not at all, please don't be offended. I am just curious to see the conference is still going ahead."

"It appears they are keeping the details from the public domain, Mr Jacobs. They have suspended the police investigation and as expected, they have no positive ID on the fingerprints found at the scene."

"Good, then we can proceed to the next step Mr Tombs. Is the hotel prepped and ready?"

"It is Father, when are we proceeding?"

"Soon, there are a few details to test before launch. I will be in touch. In the meantime, make sure the bodies are ready."

"Yes, Father."

Jacobs hung up the call and returned to the computer. He opened a program which had been running in the background.

85% Complete. Sample required.

Jacobs read the display, it was as he expected. He left the program running and pushed the screen down until it was submerged with the desk, another metallic click as it locked into place, the keyboard fading from view simultaneously.

Checking the clock on the wall, he saw it was nearly time for the next sermon. Hanging on the back the door was his gown, a deep red velvet which he draped over his shoulders. Gathering the papers on his desk, he made sure they were in the right order, before unlocking the door and heading out into the church.

Inside the main nave of the church, he made his way towards the lectern. As he approached, he looked out over the gathered crowd that sat waiting for the evenings service. He smiled, proud of the work he had accomplished and that which was to come. Scanning the crowd, he could see that most of them he had *healed*; giving them the antidote to their augmented virus. The antidote which his own body had created. He looked deeper into the crowd, seeking the next to be cured.

Sitting looking uneasy was a young boy, only seven or eight. He had an augmented eye which darted back and forth with nerves, as an older woman, whom Jacob assumed to be his mother, had her arm around him.

Perfect, the boy had returned.

Father Jacob stepped up to the lectern. The boy had visited the church with his mother the previous day, which had given Jacob the time he needed to prepare.

"Greetings to all!" His voice booming and powerful, he had come a long way since he first arrived at the Church. Now clean shaven and dignified, he addressed the crowd with the manner of a true religious leader.

"Thank you all for coming tonight, it is so good to see so many of you here. I see some regular faces," he smiled and nodded towards some followers he had welcomed many times before.

"And some new faces, thank you for joining us," he deliberately avoided eye contact with the boy and mother he had noticed earlier. Letting them wait for his acknowledgment.

"Let me first start by reminding you all of how far we have come. Several years ago we began our journey. We had seen the way this world was heading, there is a new God, a false God who is not God but a devil in disguise. A devil who has found its way into the lives of all. I must admit, and it shames me to say so, but I was once one of those who let this devil in," his voice went quieter as he spoke now, the gathered crowd straining to hear, as his voice, almost a whisper, continued.

"I was lost, thinking this false God I had put into my body was the answer to my problems," turning his arm over and pulling up his sleeve, he showed large scars which ran down his arm, where previous augmentations had been.

"I relied on these augmentations to do so much for me, and in my laziness, I became less of a man and more of a puppet to the new devil. Then I, like you, saw the truth. Saw that there was a better way. In that clarity, I saw a vison from God, which showed me the light," his voice went from a whisper to a shout. "Showed me I needed to turn around, before my soul was completely lost!"

"In that vision, I was given a way to free myself from the shackles of the false devil!

Begone devil! I shouted, as my body changed and rejected the sins of technology which had infected my flesh! Just as all of you before me have rejected the devil of augmentations! Now, here we are. Free. Pure. Saved!"

He leaned against the lectern, as if the energy inside him had faded from the speech. Using this moment, he glanced at the boy, who was now riled up with the crowd, his mind ready for what was to come.

"Now, I know there are some amongst us tonight who have yet to be freed."

A few hands raised in the crowd, including the boy's, pushed up by his mother.

"I want to save you all, and we will all be free, I promise. I have a strong feeling that there is one here who needs to see the light more than anyone. They have had a vision of this event and as I look around, I can feel their eyes upon me," he paused, closing his eyes and raised a hand, palm facing forward, as if feeling a guiding hand, until he was aiming at the area the boy sat.

"There!! I can sense they are there. Is there someone?" He opened his eyes and for the first time, was looking directly at the boy. "Come here, let me save you"

The boy's mother nudged him, as the crowd

all turned to look at him. Jacob typed a quick button into the lecterns podium. A confirmatory click alerted him the process was complete and a small cylinder was delivered to a hatch in the lectern. Jacob retrieved it and placed it into a pocket under his gown. By this point, the boy was slowly walking down the aisle towards him. Leaving the lectern, Jacob moved closer to the boy and held out a welcoming hand.

"Come, let me see you," he held the boys face in both hands and stared at the augmented eye. Up close ,Jacob could see the slight irritation around the socket where the eye was implanted. It was nothing unusual or causing any harm, a marking of the augmentations implanting. However, this was what he used to make people think they had T-Pox infections.

"Ah yes, I can see the infection already spreading. We can save you, we need to save you young man. Are you ready to be saved?"

The boy nodded.

"This will be painful, as anything worth having must be," Jacob said to the boy, who became more nervous, but nodded, regardless. The belief in the church overcoming his fears of the ritual.

"Then let us begin."

Jacob retrieved a goblet which was on the lectern, it was filled with a liquid which was synthesised from his own blood. After his first few *healings,* he dropped the visceral image of using his fresh blood for the ceremonies, for the more traditional chalice. As his audience grew, he needed less shock factor and more powerful imagery.

"Drink from this and be saved!"

The boy slowly drank from the goblet. Pausing and looking expectingly at Jacob. who looked back at the boy, a look saying *wait.*

Then the screams began. Slow at first, then building to a crescendo. The boys' one normal eye bulged with terror, as pain flowed through his body, beginning at his eye and spreading through his head and into his body. Jacob held the boy by the shoulders as he shook. As he held him, he kept him pointed face first towards the crowd. Whilst they had seen the ceremony before, it was the first time it had been someone so young, and such a prominent organ as the eye.

Blood pooled around the augmented eyeball, the boy was literally crying tears of blood now as it bulged out of the socket, stretching the eyelids that surrounded it.

"Let the poison begone! The power is flowing through you!" Jacob shouted over the primal screams from the boy. The connections of the augmented eyeball synced the system to his brain. These were being severed slowly, as the potion Jacob had made the boy drink, was taking effect. At a basic level, it boosted the body's immune system, causing it to fight off anything it saw as a foreign body; in this case the augmented eyeball. Once the potion was in the body, it stayed, removing any possibility of augmentations to be added in the future, a vaccination against tech.

The eyeball was now almost free of its socket, hanging by one final wire and coated in the boy's blood. Jacob now spun the boy around to face him and knelt down to him, taking the cylinder from his pocket, he opened it and retrieved its contents. With a swift movement, he pulled at the augmented eyeball and pulled the last connecting wire out, causing a yelp from the boy but also relief it had gone, his body happy the foreign object was no longer there. Jacob dropped the augmentation into the now empty cylinder and placed it back in his pocket. In his other hand, he revealed a biological eyeball, fully formed. He placed it into the bloody socket of the boy's head and held his palm over it for a moment.

"Let the power invested in me bring you back to flesh and your soul back to life!" He shouted, as he pushed the boy backwards with the palm of his hand. Once he knew the biological eye had taken root as it was genetically modified to do, he gave one last shove of his hand for dramatic effect. The boy fell over backwards and was laying across the floor of the nave, face up for all the masses to see. Where was once the augmented eye was a fully functioning biological eyeball was visible. After a moment, it moved around as the boy looked around the church. The air in the church moved in a collected gasp, as the onlookers couldn't believe what they saw.

Jacob, in the spectacle's midst, had returned to the lectern and dropped the cylinder in the hatch at its base. He had what he needed from the boy and had further cemented his followers' faith in him.

A few more samples and he would be ready.

CHAPTER 10

Julian

Inside the Valkyrie bar, the Norse theme was strong; long wooden tables ran along the main section of the room. The tables themselves had Nordic runes carved in glowing neon, which twinkled in various colours. The ceiling was made out of wooden archways, making it look like it had been built in the upturned remnants of a boat, raised high on pillars. The most impressive feature of the room, however, was the giant throne which took pride of place at the head of the room, surrounded by blood red neon highlights. A hologram of Odin sat in the seat, surveying all who drank within the establishment.

As Julian walked in, the sound of Nordic Trance music filled his ears, the modern mix of chants and electronic beats completing the experience. He smiled, he liked this bar.

Julian slid onto a barstool at the bar, which ran parallel to the great table, a low holographic fire ran the length of the bar top, as though someone had set fire to it. He ran his hand through the mock flames as they danced between his fingers and he scanned the spirit options on the shelves. Many alcohols were synthetic now because of a lack of harvests from crops, though most people couldn't tell the difference between them, the copies were so good. The woman behind the bar made her way over to him, she was wearing a classic viking outfit of brown leather and her short hair, bleached white, with one long braid hanging down her right side. A tribal tattoo over her right eye finished the look.

"What can I get ya?" She smiled, brushing the braid to the side as she spoke.

"What's the best?" Julian asked, not meaning to sound cocky but somehow succeeding.

A forced smile came from the waitress.

"Well, the Fenrir Mead is always a winner," she said, as she pointed at a bottle behind her. The logo of a wolf on the bottle animated and roared out in three-dimensions.

"Sounds good," he replied.

"Great," she spun on the spot and pulled down the bottle.

Julian leaned onto the bar and scanned the room, his seating was optimal for a full view of the room and all its customers. He was here for more than just a drink. Being in the middle of the Boulevard, this was the spot where the class districts merged, in the exact centre of Giga. This was where the most interesting stories were usually found.

"Here ya go Hun," the waitress returned and put the drink down on the table. "Anything else?"

"I'm good for now thank you, Miss..."

"Call me Ally."

"Ally, nice to meet you," Julian smiled and held eye contact slightly longer than normal. There was something about her he couldn't put his finger on, but he found her intriguing.

"Likewise," she held eye contact, before another customer took her attention away and she gave a sympathetic smile.

Julian took a sip of the mead, it tasted sweet with a fiery kick at the end. He glanced around the room; a couple on a date in one of the side booths, a lone drinker at the bar. Near the throne, there was a large table of suits. He focused his eyes on them; they were celebrating something. A few moments, later he was making his way past the table and eavesdropped on the conversation.

"This time tomorrow my friends, we will be millionaires!" One of them kept chanting. "Yuri is making it all happen!"

Julian smiled, his luck paying off once more. He knew that where there was a big unveiling from Cy-Bio, celebrating low ranks would be out and about. He tapped his PDA twice, adjusting his hair, making it slightly more disheveled and a speech modulation making his voice slightly slurred.

"Say guys, what's the party," he tripped into the table as he walked.

"To millions, my friend!" The loudmouth of the group shouted at him. "Join us, join us, drinks are on us!" he laughed.

Julian took a seat, one more tap on his PDA activated it to record, he wasn't risking missing anything from the conversation. Settling down, he took a shot of a drink offered to him and let the night take him away.

Several drinks later, Julian broached the topic.

"So, what's happening at this lunch, I mean launch," his modulation causing deliberate speech aphasia.

"Ah, we aren't really allowed to talk about

it," said Gerry, the loudmouth who Julian had now befriended.

"Ooh I see," Julian said, tapping his nose, "my lips are sealed."

He poured a shot of mead for both him and Gerry and held the glasses in a toast and they both downed the shots.

"Well, OK, basically, we've developed a new system," he began, the alcohol heavy in his speech, "which will allow anyone having augmentation implements, augmented wirelessly into them, using nanotech."

Julian took a second to process what was being said, deciphering the alcoholic phrasing.

"Wireless augmentation?" Julian asked for clarity.

"Yup, you get one injection of self-replicating nanotechnology from CyberBio and then 'poof' it's all done," his hands animated the words.

Julian tapped his PDA, reducing his blood-alcohol levels to allow himself some clear thinking. This was a huge leap in Cybernetic-Bio programming. To allow a body to augment without the need for any direct contact. The implications were huge.

"But shhhhh you know nothing haha!" Before Julian could ask Gerry another question, the table erupted in another cheer as Ally brought another round of SynthAle tankards and bottles of mead. She glanced at Julian with a raised eyebrow.

Julian made an excuse to leave the table and headed to the bathroom. Then, instead he went back towards the bar.

"Didn't take you as a TerraCity Suit," Ally remarked as he sat down. The bar was mostly deserted now, as the rowdiness of the crowded table continued to alienate other customers.

"Most astute of you," Julian replied, "just doing some research."

"Oh, what are you, a reporter then?" Ally wiped the bar down, the holo-flames flickering in mock protest.

"Two for two, you're not a psychic are you?"

"Mm, like I'd tell you if I was," she smiled back as she placed a glass of liquid in front of Julian and poured herself one. "Cheers, this is the good stuff" She raised a glass and Julian reciprocated and they downed the drink. He coughed as the liquid burned his throat.

"What is that?" he asked, once he could access his vocal chords again.

"Surtr's Wrath, strongest mead there is this side of the Boulevard," she winked. "So, tell me Mr..?"

"Travitz, but call me Julian," he smiled.

"Mr Julian Travitz, that rings a bell. What is it you're researching? The alcoholic routines of the TerraCity elite?"

"Hah. Not them, but the work they are doing. Trying to find that next big case, something to get me back on the wagon so to speak."

"You fell off it?"

"My last big story lead to some unfortunate consequences shall we say."

"Oh do tell," Ally walked round to the front of the bar and pulled up a stool, after checking the bar for customers, "unfortunate are always the most interesting of consequences."

Julian took a sip from the glass.

"My research into the MPD found a lot of tampered evidence at the main precinct in Giga. I was mainly doing the investigation to help a friend who I knew was innocent."

"What were they being done for?" Ally asked.

"He'd been put away for an assault on a

shop owner, but they had staged it so that the shop owner would have to ask for protection money from the Sliders. The evidence was fabricated so that they saw my friend as a Slider, when he had just been shopping there."

Ally nodded, the Sliders always seem to have alibis for their crimes when under investigation.

"So I exposed the corrupt officer in the department when I found Credits linking him with the Sliders. Only in doing that, all the cases where the evidence he had handled became subject to probable doubt. Next thing around they dropped twenty cases."

"Ouch," Ally physically winced.

"Yep, the worst of which, Peter Henshaw, got away free."

"I heard about that!" Ally said, "He killed people right?"

"That's the one, mind wiping people and leaving them for dead. Released on the day of his trial."

"Didn't he get attacked?"

"Uh-huh, Alexander Draven, the arresting officer beat him nearly to death on the steps. Lost his job for it too. All because of me."

"Hey, you didn't know that would happen. Don't beat yourself up about it!" Ally said. "And you were helping your friend."

"Yeah, I know" Julian didn't sound convinced as he downed his drink.

The bar picked up and Ally had to get back to work, Julian had another drink and continued to talk to Ally between customers. He hadn't spoken about the expose with anyone since it happened and he liked that he felt he could open to Ally. It felt good to get it out.

An hour, later Ally's shift finished.

"Want to grab a bite?" She asked Julian as she was about to get her things.

"Sure," he got up to leave.

Outside, the midnight air was fresh and a chill hit them both, Ally put her arm into Julian's and pulled him closer for warmth. The lights, still as bright as midday, were becoming muted as a dull fog descended over the city.

"There's this nice diner I know just a few streets down," Ally said, directing him.

From the side of a shop, they heard a scream, and a woman came running out from the alleyway. Heading directly towards them, the look in her eyes of pure fear.

"Hey hey hey what's wrong?" Julian put a hand up to stop her.

"He's dead!" She screamed and fell to the floor.

"Look after her," he said to Ally as he went to investigate.

A tap on his PDA and a light beam emitted from his wrist, illuminating the path in front of him. He also dialled up adrenaline.

Down the alleyway, he could see a lump of clothes. On closer inspection, he realised it was a man, laying face up with his eyes wide and frozen. It didn't take long for Julian to realise that the man was dead.

CHAPTER 11

Xander

It had been almost a year since Xander had been at the precinct. He remembered the route like the back of his hand, having done the trip daily for several years. Situated just off the Boulevard near MegaTown, he pulled the car up just before the station itself.

"I'm going to need you to stay here."

Ava protested with a look of anger at Xander.

"If there is something going on with this case and they see you, they'll shut up tighter than a clam. I need to get the information without them suspecting anything.'

"Fine, but don't be long," she resigned and settled down in the seat.

Xander pulled the door of the car up, the hiss of the hydraulics echoed out. The car was one of the few things he'd held onto when he lost his career. Taking a moment, he looked around the area, it had changed little. Graffiti covered the walls opposite the station, mostly in protest of something or other. The station itself was an old block style building which had never had a lick of paint, never mind a refurbishment, in several years. The 'MPD' sign was lit in bright white neon, illuminating the street below. Xander liked the look, made it feel worn but hardy, it reminded him of himself.

As he walked up to the entrance, he stepped aside as a young couple shoved past him; the man looked drunk, obviously been charged for some minor infraction. With his right hand, he pushed the door inwards, and the chaos of the station flooded his senses.

The noise, like a million voices all talking at once, hit him first. The main area of the office was open plan, from behind the reception desk, Xander could see desk after desk, where different people were talking to officers. Some were criminals, some informants and some just people of interest in cases. It amazed Xander that in this technological age, there wasn't something more high-tech to perform these tasks, but there was no replacing face-to-face interviews to find out information.

He realized how much he missed the organized chaos of the station; he took a deep breath and took it all in.

"Draven? Is that you?" The voice brought him back to earth. It came from the officer behind the desk. A well-built man of middle age, who wouldn't have been out of place as a bouncer, which was pretty much what he was in the precinct.

"Hey Mike, yeah it's me. Long time no see," Xander greeted him with a firm handshake.

"What brings you to paradise?" Mike asked, only a touch of suspicion.

"Questions, Mike."

"Ah, you still trying the PI business? How's it working out for you?"

"Slow, if I'm honest, but a man's gotta do what a man's gotta, right?"

"Well, I'm all ears, Your name still carries weight around here Xander. Lot of people respect you for what you did, regardless of the outcome. I can't promise anything though, you know that."

"I appreciate that Mike," Xander felt a surge of emotion at the words, "anything would be great. Information on a Maxwell Owens, dead husband."

Mike's smile dropped, his eyes staring directly at Xander.

"You don't want to be asking that one, Xander."

Xander paused, the comment giving him all the momentum he needed to keep going.

"Why? What's going on?"

"Man, I can't. There's a complete lock down on that case, came from the big bosses from the TerraCity HQ. Seriously, a complete blackout."

Xander's mind raced, TerraHQ never got involved in cases which came through the precinct, this must be something huge.

"Jeez Mike, what's going on? Is it really that serious?"

"No-one knows, you remember Donovan? Used to work homicide?" Xander nodded, he'd been one of the good ones. "He was assigned to the case, next thing you know, he's on garden leave and the case gets blacked out. None of us have even heard from Donovan since, it's like he's disappeared off the face of the earth, along with all the files. Since then, it's like the whole thing never happened. Donovan was the one you'd have spoken to, if he was still here."

Mike looked Xander straight in the eye as he

spoke, Xander nodded, picking up the hint.

"Donovan? Didn't he live in the Somerset Complex?"

"'Yeah that's right, number 91," Mike replied. "If you see him, tell him I said hi."

"Will do, thanks Mike, you take care."

"You too Xander."

Mike turned to deal with some junkies, who were being brought in by an officer. Xander held the door as they came through, before heading back out into the street.

Walking back towards the car, he watched Ava from a distance, she was observing the street and the surrounding people. It occurred to him, she maybe had never really been out further afield than the apartment complex she lived in, and her only knowledge of the world, was from implanted memories. How would the world look to someone with memories of a world they'd never seen firsthand? Like a child experiencing a story in real life. As he got to the car, she hardly noticed him arrive, as she watched a group of youths hanging around the opposite side of the road. They were getting a synthetic high by hooking their cerebral augmentations up to a memory node, which gave them the experience of varying drugs, without effecting their biological systems. The problem was that the addiction was still there, and the mental repercussions still existed in those who fell too far.

Xander tapped on the window, expecting Ava to jump, but she just turned to look at Xander as he opened the door.

"How did you know I was there?" He asked

"I didn't, if you're implying why I didn't react to the tapping, I simply acknowledged the sound. I don't have the fight-or-flight response you do for reacting to such stimuli."

"Ya know, sometimes I can't believe you're not human, then you go and say something like that," Xander muttered as he pulled the car away from the curb.

"Did you find anything," Ava asked, ignoring the comment.

"Nothing about the case itself, but I know where we need to go next. A Detective named Donovan was working the case, the files have been locked down but he'll have answers in his head, which they can't lock away."

Ava turned her head to the side for a moment.

"Donovan, Lance. Residence 91, Somerset Complex." She turned to Xander, who had a puzzled look on his face, "My implants can connect to the Net."

"Right, that's useful I guess."

The Complex wasn't far from the precinct; the area was much the same. The complex itself was a grey brick high rise, without many frills. Xander and Ava walked up to the building and entered.

"Donovan was a good cop, smart too," Xander said as he pressed the button to the lift.

Arriving at apartment 91, Xander stopped at the door. It was plain wood in a corridor of similar styles. He hit the intercom button that was at the side of the frame.

"Hello, can I help you," a woman's voice crackled through the speaker.

"We're here to see Mr Donovan?" Xander asked politely, though confusion entered his voice.

"Oh, I see, we weren't expecting any visitors."

A minute later, a lady arrived at the door, she was wearing a nurse uniform.

"Mr Donovan has been responsive today so you might be in luck," she said, as she allowed them to follow her inside.

"Responsive? What do you mean?" Xander asked, as they entered the living room of the apartment.

The nurse smiled sympathetically. Before she could reply, they saw the wheelchair in the centre of the room, it was facing the large television screen which was showing an old movie. In the chair sat a young man with a blanket over his legs.

"Yes, do you not know? Mr Donovan has been suffering from severe cognitive disorientation for the past month. I thought you were here to see how he was doing?" The nurse took her turn to be confused.

"What illness?" Ava asked.

"He is lost in his own mind I fear, he occasionally surfaces, but not for long."

Xander walked over to the wheelchair and crouched in front of Donovan, so that he was eye level. Donovan was looking directly through Xander.

"Lance? Hey buddy, you in there?"

Donovan's eyes moved and slowly focused onto Xander's. They widened in both horror and excitement as recognition sunk in.

"Xan... der?" Donovan struggled to let the

words out.

"Yeah, it's me Lance," He rested a hand on Donovan's knee. "What happened to you, man?"

"Brain... gone..."

"Jesus, I had no idea."

"It happened out the blue," the nurse chimed in, "quite surprising, Donovan had clear records, then one day his mind stopped working."

Donovan shook and grunted as the nurse spoke, attracting Xander's attention back. His eyes wide and breathing hard, he stared at Xander.

"Mind. Lock. Cybio,." He stuttered out.

Xander knitted his brow. "CyBio? What have they got to do with it?" He glanced up to Ava. "Mind lock? Does that mean anything to you?"

Ava tilted her head to the side as she accessed the Net.

"Searching. Mind Lock was a code name for an experimental procedure Cy-Bio were working on. Something to do with locking patients mobile and mental faculties to help keep patients subdued for surgeries. It never left the prototype stage though because of issues with rehabilitation following the procedure." Ava reeled off the information.

"You're telling me someone *did* this to him?" Xander asked, anger rising in his voice.

"If that is the mind lock he is referring to, then yes," Ava replied, "And likely someone from CyBio or someone who had access to their files."

"Anything we can do to get him out of it?" Xander was looking at Donovan's eyes which looked excited at conversation.

"Let me see what I can find, the files are quite encrypted in the Cy-Bio servers," Ava closed her eyes as she worked.

Donovan was straining to speak again, Xander crouched down.

"We'll get you out of this Lance, I'll figure it out, then we'll take down those Cy-Bastards for this."

"N...Nurse," Donovan blurted out, moments before a knife flew past Xander's head and stuck into the centre of the television screen behind him, the screen cracking.

Xander looked up to see the nurse posed in a fighting position, a blade was emerging from her forearm, until its point was just at her wrist. A small flick and the blade shot out like a bullet towards Xander. He dived behind the sofa and crawled, as several more blades impaled the wall and television behind him.

"AVA!" Xander screamed. "Get to cover!"

Ava didn't move, engrossed in the work she was doing decrypting the files. The nurse turned and moved towards her, only a few paces away.

Xander looked up, pulling his revolver from his holster, he fired several shots directly at the nurse. With cat-like agility, she bent and dodged each bullet, despite them being only six feet away.

She turned towards Xander, leaping over the sofa and crashing into him, fists flying into his chest. They rolled over the floor, each trying to get the upper hand.

"I really...don't want to hit a girl," Xander wheezed between hits.

A well-placed punch to the side of her face and Xander noticed the skin was loose around her cheekbone from the hit. A glint of metal and no blood.

"You're a synthetic?"

"Time to die Mr Draven," the nurse spoke, her voice cold and uncaring. She raised her hand, and another blade slotted into place. Xander could see this time that the blade emerged from a slot within her forearm. She brought it down towards his face. Both his hands were trying to hold back the arm but her strength was greater and the blade was getting closer.

Suddenly, the force stopped and Xander could push the nurse away. As he did, he saw Ava standing over them both, in her hand was a blade which she'd pulled from the wall. The nurse rolled over, revealing a mess of wiring protruding from the back of her neck.

"All major functions of a synthetic travel through the neck, as an attempt to match the central nervous system of a human," Ava described.

"Thanks, good to know," Xander said, as he pulled himself to his feet.

"As for Mr Donovan here, I believe our only chance of bringing him back lies is a cortex guided release."

"A what now?" Xander looked at her, beginning to realise there was a lot to this world he didn't understand.

"Simply put, one of us will need to enter Donovan's mind and help bring him out. The Mind Lock device implanted in his brain has a back door escape to release his motor functions, though to get there he needs to be guided. The reasoning being, that if a patient could do it themselves, then they'd run for the door as soon as they got scared during a procedure."

"O... k... and we can do this?" Xander was hesitant but there wasn't the time for fear.

"I can be the linking bridge to connect you, I believe, yes."

Xander looked at Donovan whose eyes pleaded with Xander.

"Let's do this then," Xander sighed and thought of a nice easy protection case he could be working on right now instead.

CHAPTER 12

Prime

Reilly was running down the aisle of chambers, towards the changing rooms. Behind him, he could hear footsteps running towards him. He dared a glance back and could make out two silhouettes coming towards him.

Arriving at the door, he yanked it open and rushed inside, slamming the door behind him, as he looked for something to block it. The changing room was sparse, except for the lockers. He continued to the other door, but it wouldn't open without the retina scan. He paused, not wanting to use it. Deep down he knew that it was a source of, something, which affected his mind. The mere thought of using it made his head ache.

He looked back at the other door, it wouldn't be long before they'd arrive. Before he could think what to do, the retina door opened from the other side. Another person walked in, they were wearing a waiter's outfit and looked straight ahead as they walked in.

"Oh, hi," Reilly said, not thinking what to say without looking suspicious. He got no response.

He quickly put his foot in the doorway and jumped through. Once more in the hotel's foyer, he looked around, the whole hotel before him. Slowly, he remembered the layout, like a half-forgotten memory. Stepping forward, he smiled at the guests and employees as they made their way around the hotel.

He needed somewhere to hide, somewhere they wouldn't look for him. Glancing towards the main entrance, he saw two security guards checking anyone who walked through. Outside, he glimpsed the rowdy guests from before, this triggered an idea.

"Hey Janice," Reilly smiled as he walked up to the reception desk.

"Oh, hi, I thought you were finished?" She queried.

"Oh, erm, yes. But. I was asked to check over the room Mr Hall was meant to be having this evening," he pointed to the drunken guests who were still arguing outside. "Just so we can resell it," he lied, hoping that Janice, being the friendly receptionist, would be accommodating.

"I see, well it was Suite number 7, though I don't see what there is to check, as obviously the room hasn't been touched?" She questioned.

"Oh yeah, you're probably right! You know how they can be though," he smiled and headed away before she could ask any more questions.

Once he knew she wasn't looking, he ducked up the stairs, half running, as he checked behind him. No one was following him but there seemed to be several security officers asking questions, dotted around the foyer.

He arrived at the Suite and tried the door. Locked as expected, he put his shoulder to it, but it was too strong. He glanced around him and tried to think. He was sure the housekeeping office was close, they'd have a master key. Running down the tiled corridor, he kept his eyes out for any security. Luckily, he made it to the office with no issues. He stopped to listen, he could hear a voice inside. He caught his breath and walked in casually.

"Evening guys, sorry to bother you, but it looks like someone's been sick outside suite 20," he spoke with as much authority as he could, knowing that the staff would be quick to react to anything which hindered the guest experience in the hotel. They jumped up and left the room. Reilly let them pass, then searched the office for a key.

It wasn't long before he had found it and was on his way back to the suite. He unlocked the door and went inside. It was a large Victorian style room with a mahogany desk, a double bed and a huge bathroom. Reilly had vague memories of the rooms from some job he had done. The thought made him pause, why could he not remember, he was a chef, or was it a porter, or housekeeper? He moved towards the bed and lay down, suddenly realising how tired he was. His mind was spinning, thoughts of past lives flooding his memory. He hoped he'd be safe here.

What happened? What is it I'm remembering?

It felt like there was a million different people in his head, all claiming to be the real Reilly, yet all were him simultaneously. The room got hazy, as he tried to concentrate harder.

The retina scanner, the start and end of every day. Like it implanted the days roles into his mind.

The more he thought about it, the more crazy it seemed.

And the chambers in the warehouse, all those

people. Are they all like me? Blank slates with daily tasks written.

He went to the bathroom and splashed cold water over his face, then looked at himself in the mirror. He recognised the face in front of him but he also felt like he was seeing himself for the first time. Free of the roles assigned to him and free of routine which forced him to lose his mind every day.

A knock came on the door which broke his thoughts.

"Open the door Reilly, we know you're in there," a stern voice called out.

Damnit Janice.

She must have told security that he'd asked about the suite. He looked around the room, there was nowhere he could hide. The knocks became louder, then the sound of the door being unlocked, probably a master key.

Reilly took the only option he had and ran towards the window. The suite was on the second floor so it wasn't a far drop to the ground, but it still made him hesitate.

The door behind him opened, two armed security stormed it.

"There he his, take him down," they raised

their weapons.

Reilly opened the window, deciding not to look at the drop itself, and took a breath.

He jumped, just as bullets shattered the glass panels in the surrounding windows.

Falling, he could remember the feeling of air rushing past his face, then nothing.

CHAPTER 13

Jacob

Jacob sat in the confession booth of the church, it was a traditional style with a wooden grill separating the sinner from his view, to allow them discretion.

"How can I help you my child," he spoke as a new sinner entered the box.

"Forgive me Father, for I have sinned," the female voice began, "in my youth I was foolish," she paused.

"We are all fools in our youth child, it is how we learn to grow."

"I wanted to be a runner, faster than all the girls in the school, but I injured my leg during training. Instead of rehabilitation, I agreed to have a new enhanced augmentation leg implanted."

"I see, did the leg give you what you hoped?" Father Jacob asked.

"Oh no Father," she spoke, he could hear the tears forming. "After the operation, I went back to training but was told that because of the augmentation, I could not continue in my competitions as it was an unfair advantage. Not long after that, I noticed the veins of T-Pox spreading, I knew that it was too late to have the augmentation removed then."

Jacob knew of T-Pox, it was a virus whereby the body over compensated for the implant and therefore it wouldn't allow the augmentation to be removed without the body retaliating to the removal. There was a lot of research into the area but nothing had conclusively understood the reasons for the bodies attachment to the augmentations. Jacob, however, had developed the cure, though not without side effects.

"I understand child, we can all fall victim to the sin of pride and greed, and we are often shown the folly of our ways afterward. Though do not fear child, I can help you. Together we can cleanse this burden for you and bring you back from the brink. Come back in a days time and we will heal you. You have my word, child," Jacob replied, hearing the weeping from the cubicle next to him he, waited a moment.

"Thank you Father, you are truly a saviour in our community, thank you so much."

"You're welcome child, remember to be here tomorrow at noon and all will be well. As you know, all I ask in return is for your donation to seal your commitment to the church," Jacob replied, taking a moment for the girl to get her senses back.

"Of course Father," she spoke through the tears. At the bottom of the wooden separation grid, a small bottle was on Jacob's side. Attached to it on the other side, a small needle pointed upwards towards the confessor. The girl, hesitating for a moment, pressed her forefinger to the needle which immediately pushed forwards and punctured her skin. A second later and a small flow of blood ran down the needle and into the bottle. It filled quickly.

"Thank you, child. God bless you, and I will see you tomorrow."

At that, he left the confession booth, taking the bottle with him, and allowed the girl to have the time she needed to recover.

He headed straight for his office under the church and bolted the door behind him. He walked over to the computer and pressed a hidden button. A small door opened on the far wall, revealing a surgical theatre hidden behind his desk. An operating table lay in the centre, with several work benches surrounding it. He entered and walked up to a computerised microscope which had several other devices attached to it.

He poured a droplet from the bottle onto a slide and put it under the microscope.

Perfect, a simple transplant.

He typed a string of information into the computer, before picking up his phone.

Dialing the numbers, he waited for an answer.

"Mr Tombs, I'm sending you a new request. Please process this immediately, I will need it for tomorrow afternoon."

"Yes sir, I can see it coming through now," Tombs replied, Jacob could hear the tapping of computer keys.

"Thank you, I'll come by to pick it up later. It's been a while since I visited the facility, I hope everything is running well?"

"Erm, yes, sir. Only one minor issue we are dealing with," Tombs said, a touch of fear in his voice.

"A minor issue?" Impatience clear in his reply.

"Well, it seems that, well, one escaped."

"What do you mean one escaped?" Jacob shouted down the phone.

"We aren't sure what happened, a problem with the programming, we believe," the voice replied.

"We'll find it, we can't have one of them wandering the streets! Do you realise the implications? Kill it on sight if you have to."

"We believe it's already dead sir, and we are just retrieving the body as we speak," Tombs said, hoping it would calm Jacob down.

"Report back when you have, and I will see you later," Jacob ended the call abruptly. Complications were not what he needed right now.

He returned to the benches and pulled open a drawer which contained the eyeball he had taken from the boy. There were several wires connected up to the input and output sockets which ran into a computer. Jacob sat down and read the data that was being displayed.

Owens and Yuri have been busy.

Jacob couldn't help but appreciate the design of the implant, it was almost perfect. The admiration didn't last long, as Jacob hacked into the eye's programming and the intricate coding it held.

After a while, he found the code he was looking for, the coding which read the bodies Bio-reading and translated them to digital information for the eyes implementation. He had written half the coding himself, from his days back with the company, but it was Owens' side of the code he needed now. The code which he could use to finish his project, to help spread his cure throughout the city and finally reduce the worlds crutch on technology. Bring balance back into the world. It was so close he could feel it.

He set the coding from the eye into a diagnostic program, in an attempt to synthesize it to his needs and left it to run.

All he could do now was wait.

CHAPTER 14

Julian

Julian approached the bundle of clothes on the floor, a light directly over them illuminated his view.

"Hey Quartzig," he whispered, "can you call the MPD, send them my location."

"On it," he replied. "All ok?"

"I'm not sure yet, set my VisPro to record, I'm not sure what I'm getting into here."

"Understood."

He put his hand down and pulled back the clothes which turned out to be an old trench coat, revealing the body underneath. At first glance, nothing seemed out of the ordinary, but as he looked closer, he could tell that the left arm of the body wasn't right. The shirt sleeve was missing with the arm exposed, just above the elbow joint the skin colour was different, about three shades darker.

Julian pulled the body over, rolling it

slowly. He told himself, it was so that he could check the person was dead and not injured, but it was also out of his own curiosity.

"Be careful Julian," shouted Ally, who was still with the crying woman. She was staying away from the body, but could just see light emitting from Julian's PDA.

He shone the light over the face of the body; it was a middle-aged man. The vacant stare in his eyes was all he needed to confirm that the man was dead.

"Quartz, can you do a facial scan and see if you can get a match?"

"Sure, hold still. MPD are about 5 minutes away FYI."

"Thanks. You see his arm?"

"Yeah, it looks like surgical stitches all around, like his arm has been replaced. Could be some cheap transplant, not able to find a matching donor?"

"Could be."

Julian looked closer at the body. His augmented eyes zooming in for more intricate detail.

"I can see traces of Aug-Imp around the stitches. I think they used to have an augmented arm Quartz," Julian crouched to get a closer look.

He touched the arm slightly, feeling the stitching. It was soft and looked quite fresh.

Without warning, the hand shot forward and grabbed him by the throat, immediately closing his windpipe and suppressing any sounds he tried to make. The hand held fast, as Julian struggled to get out of the grip. The body itself didn't move, the only animation was from the arm itself and nothing more. Julian twisted and turned as he felt the lack of oxygen burning his lungs.

"Julian!" Ally was running towards him, she had seen the light moving sporadically and had ran to help.

She tried to release the hand's grip by pulling at the fingers but they were too strong. Julian's eyes bulged out as he struggled for breath. From behind, Ally felt a sharp impact on the back of her head. Turning to look and keep her balance, she saw the woman she had been comforting moments before, standing over her with a metal rod.

"Sorry," she said with venom, before swinging the rod towards Ally's head.

Ally ducked the swing and jumped to her feet, a second later, she performed a roundhouse kick directly to the rod. Her shin connected to the metal with a loud clang. The vibration shot down the pole, causing the woman to drop it from pain, as the vibrations reverberated through her hand. Her face stunned, she squared up to Ally.

"Metal shin pads," she said with a wink, and bounced into a fighting stance, "always have to be prepared working at a bar."

"It doesn't matter, your friend is ours now," the woman grinned back.

Ally glanced behind her and saw two men in suits coming down the other side of the back street. They were pulling Julian away from the body which had released it's grip on their command.

"Let go of him!" She shouted, running towards them. They nodded to one another, and the closest turned to face her whilst the other continued dragging the unconscious Julian away. In the distance, Ally could see a car waiting for them at the far end.

"Shit!" She looked behind her as the woman approached. They surrounded her. Not that that mattered, but she wasn't sure she would have time to get to Julian.

She ran full pelt towards the man in front of her. Jumping forward she landed a drop kick, placed perfectly in the man's chest. They both dropped to the floor. Ally was back on her feet within seconds, ready to run towards Julian. As she set off, a metal pole landed square between her shoulder blades like a javelin. She crumpled forwards from the impact and rolled over to see the woman bearing down on her. A look upwards from her laying position, she could see Julian being bundled into the car.

The woman yelled a manic scream, raising a boot up to stomp down on Ally's face.

She rolled sideways to avoid the boot and, pushing herself up, performed a sweep with her metallic shin pads, connecting with the woman's ankles. The crack echoed down the street as the woman fell, howling in pain, her left ankle shattered. The man, who had regained his feet, hesitated on his approach towards Ally but before he could back away, she had performed a kip-up and was on her feet. Diving, forwards she swung a punch to the bridge of his nose, dropping him instantly.

She spun to look back just in time to see the car speed off.

A police car pulled up at the opposite end of the street, sirens blazing.

She'd lost Julian.

CHAPTER 15

Ally

She'd only known Julian for a few hours but couldn't help but feel the need to help him. They both been pulled into the trap for whatever reason.

Two officers had attended the scene and one was talking to the people who attacked them. She walked up to them.

"Are you OK Miss?" one of them asked her.

"A friend of mine just got kidnapped, those two were helping them," she explained.

"She's crazy man! She attacked us!" The man shouted, looking scared as she approached them.

"What?! Are you serious?"

"Please step back," the police officer stood between them.

"They tricked us with that body," she pointed at the bundle of clothes, "and attacked my friend before kidnapping him!" She could barely hold her anger in.

The second officer was checking over the pile of clothes.

"Some dead Scanner it looks like," he shouted back.

"Ok I will have to take you all in," the officer said.

"You're kidding me?" Ally shouted.

A shot rang out, the officer near the clothes fell to the floor. His face was a mask of blood as the back of his skull exploded, the bullet had gone directly through his eye socket. Ally ducked down behind the car and the other officer ran to the same cover.

"Stay down and out of sight," he ordered. Ally had no intention of standing up.

The other two were running now, away from the scene as fast as they could.

"Hey, get back here you wastes of space! Where'd they take him?!" It was no use, they were too far gone. Ally kept her head down as the officer with her tried to get to his radio in the car.

Another shot. The officer's hand disintegrated in a mist of red. Screaming, he crumpled back behind the car. The shot was from an ionic laser, although obliterating the hand, it cauterized the surrounding tissue so there was no bleeding. A surgical gun used for precision.

A beeping sound rang in Ally's ear, she took a moment to realise it was her phone implant, someone was calling her. She tapped it to answer out of habit.

"Hello?"

"Good evening Ally, I suggest you move a few centimetres to your right," a voice chirped.

"What?"

"Move now!" The voice said more aggressively. Ally did as it said out of fear. A millisecond later an Ion shot blasted through the car, the beam causing a burnt hole in the door.

"... Thanks?"

"You're welcome, now listen and I will get you out of here safely."

After the shot, she had no reason not to believe the voice, she looked at the policeman.

"What about him?" She asked, assuming whoever she was talking to could see him.

"He'll be fine as long as we get you out of

here, you are the target at the moment."

"OK, what do I do?"

"In a moment you need to run to the left, see the trash cans there?"

"Yeah."

"Run towards them, and stay behind them, then on my next cue head down the street. The angle the shots are coming from suggest that they cannot see more two metres down that route."

"Suggest? You mean you aren't sure?"

"I'm not omnipotent Ally!" The voice said sarcastically.

"Well, I don't even know who you are?!" She shouted back.

"Did Julian not tell you about me? Typical," The voice sighed, "I'm Quartzig, now run!"

Surprised, Ally slipped as she got up to run. The officer shouted at her to stay down and tried to pull her back, but she avoided his grasp. She rolled behind the trash cans and curled up as small as she could to reduce the chance anyone could see her.

"Good, now wait... wait... I can't believe he didn't tell you about me... wait... GO!"

She spun out from behind the trash and went full throttle down the street. A shot burst out and Ally was showered with debris from the impact on the wall next to her head, but she kept moving and was several metres down the street before she slowed.

"Am I clear?" She asked.

"It appears so, well done," Quartzig replied.

Ally took a few moments to let her heartbeat slow down and catch her breath. She heard a scream from back down the way she had come.

"I may have miscalculated the officers survival chances," Quartzig whispered. "But at least you got away."

"Who are you?" Ally asked, feeling remorse for the officer but glad of her own safety.

"Quartzig, I am Julian's roommate. Well, I'm his Artificial Intelligence who lives at his apartment. Fully functioning and free developing."

Ally had a rough idea what that meant.

"So, you can learn and adapt at your own pace? Become smarter?"

"Correct. When I first came into being, I was

just a voice-activated light control. Over time, Julian increased my coding and abilities until I could construct my own neural pathways. So here I am. Nice to meet you."

"Nice to meet you too Q, how did you even find me?"

"Julian asked me to record the whole occurrence from when he walked down that back street. I saw it all happen from his eyes, but when he was put in the back of the car, my connection was severed. That has never happened. Ever. So either that car had some seriously high grade shielding software, or Julian switched off the connection, or he's... offline," Quartzig found the concept of death hard to process.

"Right, we need to find him Q, any ideas where he may have gone?" Ally wasn't sure how to comfort an upset AI.

"... Well, I set up a search for a vehicle of that description, so I will attempt to track it but so far I've got nothing."

"OK, let me know if you get anything. I'm going to head back home and change. I feel this could be a long night."

She headed back down the street to the Boulevard, not sure what she would do. She'd been working on the Boulevard for several months now and was finally saving enough to get her own place nearer the Giga outskirts, but for now she was still in Mega. She would head back to the apartment and see if there's anything she could do from there.

CHAPTER 16

Xander

Cortex Guided Release

That was what Ava had called it, Xander wished he'd asked a few more questions about it before he'd agreed.

He was lying on a bed in Donovan's apartment, the body of the synthetic nurse still crumpled on the floor of the living room. Donovan sat in his wheelchair next to the bed and Ava was sat between the two, on the edge of the bed.

"I will have to connect you to the Cortex Hub, which is embedded in my systems," Ava said calmly. "Think of it like connecting two devices up to your computer and transferring files," she smiled at Xander, after seeing the look on his face.

"Darlin' I don't even know how to put a song on my phone," his nerves showing as his voice slipped into his old accent.

"It won't hurt, I promise."

She placed her hands together and pulled at a blemish which was located on both her wrists. From under them, long wires emerged as she pulled. The mole itself sliding into a small disk as she did.

"Why exactly are you able to do this?" Xander asked as he watched Ava attach the right-hand disc to Donovan's temple.

"Sometimes, a hard wire connection is beneficial for optimum integrations or bio-diagnostics," she explained. "When Max wanted to back up my memories, I would be hardwired into the secure database at our apartment. It was more secure, away from wireless eavesdropping."

She was now attaching the left-hand disc to Xander's temple.

"You will enter Donovan's mind in a moment. You will be inside the construct that his consciousness had been locked inside. Once there, you will need to take him to the exit, which only you can open due to it's nature," she described. "You need to get him through the door so he can be freed."

"And what about me? Do I need to go through the door? What happens if I get stuck there? And what will the construct be?"

"Calm down Alexander, you will be fine. To leave safely, you will also need to go through the door, however you can eject manually, but it is not recommended. The construct will be whatever prison they have placed Donovan into, but remember, it is only cyberspace, none of it is real."

"So, we can't die or anything in there?"

"Well, not die. However, your mind will believe it to be real regardless, so a trauma suffered in there will undoubtedly have effects here as well. Remember, this was a prototype, there isn't a lot of research to fall back on."

"Great."

"Ready?" Ava looked at Donovan first, his eyes blinked, she took this as a yes and turned to Xander.

"I don't really have a choice do I? At least give me a countdown."

"Very well. Three, Two..."

At two Ava blinked faster than humanly possible as she began the transference.

.

.

.

118

.

.

Xander leapt to his feet, looking around him he could see...

Nothing.

Complete darkness all around him.

He was standing, but that was the only detail he could know for certain. He looked in every direction possible, but there was only oppressing black, which felt like it was forcing itself on his eyeballs, as they painfully strained to see anything.

Then there was a light, faint at first, like a match had been struck in the distance, but being the only light in the abyss, it was like a beacon to Xander. He squinted at it, trying to make it out.

Was this the construct?

The light grew in size as it seemed to get closer to him. Closer and larger. Suddenly the speed at which it seemed to move, made Xander's heart pick up pace, from a firefly to a freight train, the light seemed to move at such a speed that if it hit him, Xander knew that it would crush him. He needed to get out of its way.

He ran, ran to the side in what he hoped was out of the path of the ever growing light. No matter where he ran, it seemed to come directly for him. It was only a matter of seconds now before it consumed him. A moment later and the light was around him, rushing like a hurricane. The motion made Xander physically sick, like travel sickness turned to a million.

He threw up, as his eyes tried desperately to focus on something within the light which was a blur passing his eyes. Between retches, he couldn't help but look at the light. The more he did, the more he was sure there was something within it. It wasn't just one light around him, but a whole mess of lights; almost as if he was traveling down a road at an unbelievable speed, all the lights were street lamps and headlights. The more he thought about it, the more he felt his focus clearing. As if the speed was slowing down.

He dry heaved once more and doubled his efforts to focus. Slowly but surely, the lights slowed down. One by one he saw them for what they were. A repetition of several lights, as if they were all one room. He closed his eyes for a moment, then reopened them.

This time, he could see that the lights were not rushing past him, but circling him, as though he was spinning on the spot. It slowed further and he could make out certain aspects of the room. A table and chair were also present. A bed. A sink. A metal toilet. This was a prison cell, Xander realised, in each top corner there was a fluorescent light bulb which flickered and then the spinning finally slowed to a stop.

Xander dropped to his knees, the feeling waned within his stomach. He took a moment to feel better. He'd dealt with spinning rooms many times due to alcohol, but this was the worse by far.

He walked over to the sink and ran water to wash his mouth out and splash cold water on his face and the back of his neck.

When he felt more human, he noted his surroundings. The prison cell was typical of any other, apart from the four lights. Three walls were a dull beige colour, and the fourth was predominantly metal bars. He strained to see outside the bars but there was nothing he could make out through the black void.

"... hello?" A voice came echoing into the room.

"Hello?" Xander replied.

"Xander, is that you?" Donovan's voice rang out, it sounded like it was coming from behind the wall.

"Donovan?" Xander recognised the voice. "Where are you?"

"In a cell, probably the same as you. Sounds like we're in the same prison now." He said, sounding defeated.

"How long have you been here?" Xander was searching the cell now.

"I… I don't remember. I was investigating the Owens murder and was on my way to Cy-Bio to get answers when I blacked out. Next thing I remember, I was here."

"Well, it's time we got you out."

"I don't think that's possible Xander. When I got here, I tried everything."

"I've had some help, this is a construct made to contain your mind Donnie, you have to have someone here to get you out," Xander explained, hoping it made sense, as he still wasn't sure on the details.

"A mind cell? I've heard of these, the MPD was looking into using them for prisoners. Wow," Donovan went quiet for a moment.

"So you must have something to allow us to leave right?" He finally spoke.

"I guess, but I don't know what," Xander had

found nothing in the cell that might help.

"You've got to find it Xander, or we're both stuck here!'

CHAPTER 17

Prime

Reilly opened his eyes.

Looking directly at him, from centimeters away, was a pair of metal goggles with red lenses.

"Is 'e still breathin'?" A female voice called out.

"Think so," the goggles replied, in a rasp and looked around his face. "'is eyes are open."

The goggles moved back, revealing the face attached to them. It was marked with fading face paint and scars. Reilly tried to get up, but the pain shot down his spine and he fell back.

"I wouldn't try to get up or anythin' mister," the eyes spoke, the voice was soft but jagged. "You took quite a fall," the voice in the background whistled, imitating a missile falling and crashing.

"Where?" was all Reilly could manage.

"In the Underpass you are," the eyes replied.

Reilly looked upwards towards where he thought the window would be, expecting to see the guards chasing him. Instead he couldn't see anything other than the opening of a large tube.

"Don' worry about up there, you came down through th' garbage."

"I was being chased," Reilly said, telling himself as much as anyone else.

"They won' follow you out 'ere," the goggles moved back now, revealing the person they belonged to. A scruffy-looking man was grinning down at him. He was wearing a long brown trench coat with a threadbare jumper, which was more string than jumper. His hair was spiked in several places.

"Where?" Reilly asked again.

"I tol' ya, in the Underpass," he grinned, revealing a set of half metal and half brown teeth. "Here is where we live, and die," he laughed with a cross between maniacal and serious.

"I..I don't know what that means," Reilly said, it dawned on him that he had never left the hotel. He had no idea what lay outside of the building and the world outside, only what he had experienced from the guests that had stayed.

The man lifted his goggles, revealing a beady pair of black eyes underneath.

"Haha, many people don' know what it means. Most people don't care about us down 'ere," the man jumped to his feet from the crouched position he had been sitting in. "Follow me, I'll show ya, and get you checked over after your tumble."

"Hey JJ, you sure tha's a good idea?" The woman in the background shouted, she stepped into view. She was wearing a similar outfit of mismatched items, a bomber jacket covered in various logos sewn on and a pair of ripped jeans. Her hair was a long, electric blue mess, like a thunder storm raining down.

"Look at him Mol, he ain't gonna do anythin'," he grinned down at Reilly. "Are ya?"

Reilly was pulling himself up, glancing down, he saw the mess of torn clothes and blood that coated him. His trousers were torn in several places, as were his arms and the buttons along the front of his chef's jacket. He winced in pain as he checked for any broken bones.

"Y'all in one piece?" JJ asked.

"I think so, just a lot of cuts and bruises," Reilly replied.

JJ stuck his hand out.

"Name's JJ, stands for... actually I'm not sure I know anymore. It doesn't matter, JJ is who I am now, and that's all any of us need to know ey? Name's are temporary."

Reilly shook his hand and nodded.

"I'm," he realised he had never said his name out loud. "133, wait, Lee, no, Reilly?" His brain felt confused as he tried to process it all.

"No matter, Reilly is a good a name as any, "JJ chuckled to himself. "That's Mollie lurkin' in the background," he nodded behind him as she walked up.

"Reilly? Suits ya," she smiled. "Let's get movin', the Gunners might come looking for 'im but they might send out the Phantoms," Mollie said.

"Aye, makes sense. C'mon Reilly, let's get you to the Nexus."

JJ put an arm round Reilly to help him steady his feet. Reilly limped as best he could, while Mollie lead the way. She pulled some goggles of her own down, the blue lenses matching her hair.

They moved down the back streets, through the trash and darkness. The only illumination was through the murky yellow streetlights, half of which weren't working. Reilly guessed the goggles were to help them see in the murky light.

"So, where exactly are we? I don't exactly know this place," Reilly asked, pausing for breath between sentences, the pain still pulsing.

"The Underpass, basically it's the opposite of the Boulevard," JJ replied.

"This is the area underneath the Boulevard," Mollie stepped in, "Most people don't realise that the Boulevard is actually a bridge, mostly. From the BitVillage, it slowly rises onto the bridge and continues like that for several kilometres, before curving back down after Zeta. The whole city is pretty much on a plate, with the Boulevard running down its centre, and this here is where we are, under the plate and the props that hold it up."

Reilly knew of the boulevard but didn't really understand it. He still wasn't completely sure.

"So, we're under the city?" He asked.

"Exactly, in the Underpass like I said!" JJ

shouted as they continued, "We heading to the Nexus now, in centre of the Underpass."

"It's the point directly under the centre of the 'plate'," Mollie explained. "Everything down here runs through it. We can find a Doctor to give you a once over."

Reilly nodded, it was taking time for it all to sink in. All he wanted to do was lay down and rest. For a moment he thought of the chamber where he normally woke and how well rested he always felt coming out of it, that was a past life now, another one to be erased and replaced like all his days before today.

"And, what do you do down here?" Reilly asked.

"We're scavengers," JJ replied. We find things that have been dropped down here."

"You'd be surprised what ends up down here. People up there think things disappear down the cracks in the road or in the trash, but they end up down here. Like you did."

"Wait, how far did I fall?" Reilly was sure it was only a small drop that he jumped.

"Well, it looked as if you took the scenic route down here," JJ laughed, "Hit a few speed bumps on the way down."

"He means you must have fell into one of the waste tunnels and come that way. It would still have been bumpy but not a straight drop."

After what seemed like a lifetime, they arrived. Reilly had to stop and take it all in.

At the end of the street, a vast open space was revealed. You could describe it as a square, but it wouldn't do the size justice. He counted ten streets coming off the centre in varying angles and distances, each route was punctuated with a massive pillar, the size of a building. Large monoliths which, as he looked upwards, he couldn't see the tops of. He realised for the first time that there was no sky above him, but a dark end to the view at a great distance, too far to comprehend. The square itself was full to breaking point, with what appeared to be market stalls. Reilly had some vague memories of what a market place looked like, but he couldn't explain where from.

"C'mon Reilly," JJ beckoned him from ahead, where himself and Mollie had continued walking before noticing he had stopped.

"Coming," Reilly snapped out of the thoughts he was still processing.

They entered the mess of fabric and metal poles which composed the stalls, some were massive marquis, others tiny tents with just a small table showing some kind of knick-knacks. Reilly looked around at all the people. He was used to crowds at the hotel but not like this; they were dressed in random concoctions of clothing, rubbing shoulders with each other as they squeezed past one another. Smells of cooked meats and spices filled the air, he recognised some smells but again, he couldn't recall from where.

"Is this... normal?" he asked Mollie, who was staying with him while JJ lead the way through the crowd.

"Yeah, it's always pretty crazy busy here. This is where everything and anything happens. You need it or want it, you find it in the Nexus."

JJ, who was a few metres in front, turned back to look at them and pointed to the tent which he was standing in front of.

" 'Ere we are," JJ said as they got closer. "Mr Dr Koenig. Medical person of all sorts," JJ did a small bow as he indicated for them to enter the tent.

Mollie went first, followed by Reilly.

"Good Evening Mollie, and I see you bring a specimen with you, how delightful." A heavily accented voice rang out.

The room was surprisingly sterile, considering its location, a large silver metal table was in the centre of the room, with drainage underneath. Dr Koenig sat behind a small table to the side of the area.

"A fine-looking specimen at that! If a little damaged. How about I give 75% the usual price?"

"Dr, this one came from the Up Above, this isn't some lowlife from the Underpass, "Mollie argued.

"Oh come now, he isn't even able to stand."

Reilly froze, he was suddenly aware he needed to get away. Looking back, he saw JJ standing at the entrance to the tent, obviously aware of his intentions. He held a large hunting knife in his hand.

"Nowhere to go Reilly," JJ laughed.

"Fine, let's say 80%," Koenig said. "Final offer."

"Deal," Mollie smiled before turning to Reilly and before he could even resist ,stabbed a needle into his neck.

A moment later, he blacked out.

CHAPTER 18

Jacob

Father Jacob hadn't been further into the Boulevard for a long time, but he needed to collect the part before the evening, and he needed Tombs concentrating on finding the escapee.

The autocab pulled up to the entrance of the Grand Falls Hotel.

Stepping out, he walked towards the hotel, he still wore his priest outfit, and a couple on a synth-high outside the hotel hurled abuse at him.

"What's with the dog collar?"

Jacob approached them and looked them in the eye.

"Are you lost child?" He asked.

"No, but I think you are!" Came the laughing response.

Jacob didn't have time for this, but he couldn't stop himself from taking action. He discreetly pulled a small needle out of his pocket and leaned closer to the man, putting his hand on the back of his neck, as if pulling him in for a quiet word. The needle punctured the man's neck with no feeling.

"You are lost, and afraid," he whispered, before walking away.

After a second, the man began to panic.

"Wh... where am I? What's going on?" He looked petrified, before running down the street away from the hotel, his companion following.

Jacob entered the Hotel and walked straight up to the desk.

"Hello Father, how are you today?" Janice asked, a smile wide on her face.

"Good Evening Janice, I'm here to collect from the warehouse," he said as he approached.

"No problem Father, the package is waiting for you already."

"Thank you dear," Jacob smiled, "also have you seen Mr Tombs?"

"I believe he is in the security office."

"Excellent, thank you Janice," he replied as he walked past the desk and entered a door marked PRIVATE, using a fingerprint scanner to allow him access, his PDA scanner removed long ago.

Inside was a large room with all the walls covered by displays, all of them showing various areas of the hotel.

"Good evening Mr Tombs," Jacob announced, as he walked in.

Tombs jumped to his feet, startled by the arrival.

"He... hello Father. I didn't know you had arrived."

"I was just wondering if you had located the escapee?" The anger suppressed in his voice seeping through.

Tombs shifted nervously.

"It looks like he fell into Underpass sir," Tombs admitted, "We haven't got many resources down there."

"A pity, that could cause some issues. I suggest you activate the Hunters."

"Yes Father," Tombs looked relived, that there was no further punishment.

"While I'm here, I will inspect the chambers before leaving, it's been some time since my last visit."

"Of course, shall I escort you Father?"

"That won't be necessary Mr Tombs, I will go alone. I suggest your time would be better spent heading the hunt."

At this, Father Jacob left the room and headed towards the warehouse. He once more used a fingerprint scanner to open the door and stepped into a massive warehouse, inside which were lines upon lines of BioChambers. Each hooked up to several pipes and wires, they gave off a green hue, which bathed the warehouse in a dull emerald haze.

He approached one and peered inside, the body of a man was inside, he looked asleep, but Jacob knew he was just a hollow husk waiting for programming. He had begun development of the clones several years prior when he was still a founder of CyBio. Though his colleagues had deemed the work too unethical. As such he set up the warehouse off the books, to allow him to continue his research unhindered by such detrimental thoughts.

He tapped a code into one of the chamber computers; it lit up with options. A long list of personalities and traits were available to choose from, covering all the aspects of hotel staff. Then, at the bottom, was a locked section. Jacob entered a second code in to access this, it revealed a further list. This time the options were more advanced, such as Spec Ops, Surgeons, Assassins, and Fighters. Finally, at the bottom there was an option simply titled:

MAXO

This was the one Jacob selected now, and the whole chamber whirred into gear and the body inside convulsed and writhed.

A moment later and the eyes opened in the chamber and the man inside met Jacobs' eyes. A look of contempt and fear filled them.

"Good evening Maxwell," he said, unable to repress a grin that sneaked into his face.

"Jacob? What the hell is this?" Owens asked, as he moved his limbs.

"I'm afraid there's something you need to know Owens," Jacob replied. "You died last week, I'm very sorry for your loss."

"What are you talking about? Let me out!" Owens slammed a fist into the glass of the chamber. After a moment, he looked at the fist. He examined it, curling and uncurling the fingers, turning it around. Something wasn't right. It wasn't his.

"Ah, you see, the body you are in is, well how best to call it? A clone, a pre-manufactured body created from a base genome of a host. We create the clone as a tabula rasa if you will, a blank slate in the mind upon which we can insert another. A human computer with upgradeable operating software." Jacob spoke proudly of the work. "If you recall, I was in the beginning stages of this very thing back at CyBio before you kicked me out."

"This is madness Jacob!' Owens struggled to comprehend the situation and felt nauseous as the idea sunk in that he was no longer in his own body. "Put me back in my own body!" Even saying the words seemed both absurd and terrifying.

"I'm afraid that won't really be possible Owens, you see you were murdered last week and your body will have decayed far past its living state by now, but," Jacob smiled. "I saved your mind, that amazing mind of yours ,Owens. There is something I need out of it," Jacob moved closer to the chamber.

"I'm dead? My god," Owens whispered, shock was getting too much for him, this wasn't something anyone would be able to process in a short time. Jacob saw this happening and tapped on the console. He could manipulate the biochemistry of the Husk body, he increased the dopamine levels to help calm Owens down.

"It's ok Owens, relax. You're safe here, and I can guarantee your brainwaves will remain intact. I can even offer you a body for it to inhabit. As long as you can help me with my little conundrum of course."

Owens, now more relaxed as the chemicals flooded his system, looked at Jacob. He still felt sick and unsure, but the thought of his own mind disappearing, to lose the very thing that makes up your being, was enough to make him consider the offer.

"What do you need Jacob?" Owens resigned.

CHAPTER 19

Julian

Julian struggled against the metallic cuffs on his wrists, two circles around each of them, which seemed to pull together by some kind of magnet. He couldn't get them apart, no matter how hard he tried.

"Quartz you there?" He whispered, as he took in his surroundings.

He got no response. In fact, there was nothing at all. All of his connections were shut down. He panicked, he'd been using the augs for as long as he could remember, to have them disconnected felt like losing a limb.

"Calm down Julian," a voice spoke.

Julian looked around the car and saw he was in a large limousine, there were seats opposite him at some distance where, as his eye adjusted to the dim light, he now noticed a man was sitting facing him.

"It's ok, the car is just equipped with an internal EMP pulse, which renders all electronics, including augs, powered down. They'll kick back into gear once you leave the car," the voice was soft-spoken, calming and soothing.

"Who are you?" Julian asked, the news that the disconnection was temporary was a relief.

"My name is Yuri Renko."

"One of the CyBio founders?" Julian asked. Usually he had to chase down his stories, this was the first time the story had chased him.

"Correct, I heard you were looking into my company. I thought perhaps we could assist each other. You see there's a lot more going on here than you may have first realised."

"Nanotechnology? That's the big reveal right? Why kidnap me though?"

"One question at a time please Julian. First of all, yes nanotech is the next big thing we will unveil tomorrow at the conference. It will be revolutionary, the ability to have implants with no invasive surgery or even pain."

Julian nodded, he couldn't argue that it was a breakthrough which would change the world.

"As for taking you the way we did, you need to realise that I didn't intend to be so violent.

Unfortunately, I needed to get to you before those Scanners did."

Julian paused.

"Wait, so the people that attacked us weren't working for you?" Julian paused as he thought of Ally, he hoped she was ok.

"What? No, of course not! They were trying to get you for the Church, we had to act fast, as it seemed like you were unlikely to make it away from them. It's lucky we found you when we did. In fact, apologies for those," Yuri deactivated the cuffs on Julian's hands. "We needed you to be compliant to get you away as fast as possible."

Julian's head spun.

"Ok, so you didn't attack me, but why am I here?" Julian asked.

"I need your help," Yuri replied, sounding sincere.

"You see, although we aim to help people and improve the quality of life, we still have many, many enemies. Something is happening that we aren't fully aware of. There have been several attacks on the employees and facilities around the Metro."

"Why not go to the MPD?" Julian asked.

"The last major incident was my colleague and friend, Maxwell Owens. He was found dead in his apartment last week. The investigation seemed to be going well and the Detective in charge of the case, Donovan, told me he was close to making an arrest. Then, the next day, he was signed off work and was now under constant care at home for brain trauma. They put the whole case on ice, and there was no record of it even happening. Owens' body has even disappeared from the morgue, according to all records."

Julian knew that Yuri must have hacked into the MPD records to find some of this information out. If a company with as much power as CyBio couldn't get any information or control of the situation, it must be bad.

"I'm sorry for your loss, but I don't see why I'm the person you need for this? Sounds like there's something big happening," Julian said.

"Big is an understatement Julian, whatever this is, it's huge. I need someone I can trust, someone who understands the technology and what we can achieve from it. Someone who can ask the right questions to get to the bottom of this."

"What makes you think you can trust me?" Julian realised it wasn't really the best question to ask.

"I know you better than you think, your expose of the MPD corruption, the last big case you had. It makes me believe that you wouldn't be one to fall for any decoys, and to dig further to find the truth. Also, to be honest, you're expendable."

Julian sat back in the chair and closed his eyes.

What.The.Hell.

"Let's say I help, what is it you want me to do?" Julian asked.

"Simple really, we need someone to trace Owens' body down, if we can find that and get it back to our labs, we can run our own autopsy on it to find out who killed him. In return, we will reward you handsomely. Also, I'm sure it will go to some degree to helping you bring back some guilt you felt from what happened on the Henshaw case."

The last statement took Julian by surprise, how did he know that it had that effect on him. He skirted the point for now.

"So I help you find Owen's body and you can wipe out whoever did it?" Julian queried.

"It depends who it is, really. I have suspicions but I'd like them to be confirmed or denied."

"OK, I'll bite. Do you have anything for me to start with?" Julian decided it was intriguing enough to take on, but more so he wasn't sure he'd be leaving the car alive if he declined.

"We have the transport code for the movement of the body last, when it departed from the MegaCity precinct. I never reached its destination however, I have sent you all the details to your PDA, once it reactivates it will all be ready and waiting for you."

"OK, I'll do what I can," Julian replied.

Yuri tapped on the window behind him and the car slowed down.

"Oh, and here take this, it's a prototype but you might find a use for it."

Yuri handed Julian a small square block of black metal, it had no markings or anything on it and was as smooth as silver.

"What is it?"

"You'll know when you need to use it," Yuri replied, smiled and opened the door for Julian to get out. "Good luck!"

Julian stepped out of the car and onto the rain-soaked pavement.

"How do I contact you?" Julian shouted.

"You won't have to, we'll be watching," Yuri shouted back as the door closed and the car pulled away.

Julian looked around, realising he had no idea where he was.

Suddenly his PDA lit up like a Christmas tree, as dozens of messages and alerts came through as it reconnected.

"JULIAN!" A voice screamed in his ear, causing him to put his hand over them, though it made no difference.

"Quartzig, don't shout I can hear you!"

"Where have you been?" Quartzig demanded.

"You won't believe me when I tell you."

Julian tapped his PDA to bring up a map now it was reconnected.

"We've been recruited by CyBio to help solve the murder of founding member Maxwell Owens," Julian explained.

"... ok I did not expect that," Quartzig admitted. "So what do we need to do?"

"First, I need to figure out where the hell I

am," Julian tapped on the PDA a few times.

"It appears you are on the edge of GigaCity, but quite off the boulevard."

"Yeah seems so, can you get a taxi to me Quartz, I need to look into this."

"On it."

Julian opened the attachments from Yuri and began to read through the reports on Owens' death.

CHAPTER 20

Xander

Xander had searched the cell completely. It comprised a single bed with tight bedsheets pulled across it military style, a toilet, a basin and a small desk with a chair. Other than those and the four lights on ceiling of each corner of the room, there was nothing else to see. The bars of the cell were painted black and ran top to bottom with no joints or door to open.

"I've checked everywhere, there's nothing," Xander called out to Donovan.

"There must be something, have you looked underneath the bed?"

Xander knew he was trying to help, but he had looked in every corner of the room and checked over, under and inside everything he could put his hands on in the room.

"I've checked everywhere. Is there anything in your room?" Xander called out.

"I've been through the room a million times already, there's nothing here," came the reply.

Xander paced around the room, Ava had said that he was to guide Donovan out, but how was he meant to do that when he was trapped himself.

He looked at the lights in the corners of the ceiling; they were the only thing he hadn't been able to look at as they were so high up he couldn't reach them. He dragged the chair across the floor and stood on it; they were still just out of reach.

"Hey Donovan, do you have four lights in there? Up in the corners?"

"Yeah, I've got four, all lit up. Do you?"

As he spoke, two of the lights in Xanders' cell turned off, one near the bars and one diagonally opposite. Xander looked up, startled.

"Two just went off, can you reach yours?"

"Yeah, they aren't too high," Donovan replied.

'I have to guide him' Xander thought.

"Face the bars of the cell," he told Donovan. "And take out the bulbs at one 'o'clock and seven."

"OK...."

Xander could hear the squeaking of the bulbs being removed, as the second one came out, a loud clang filled the cells.

"Something happening," Donovan called out.

The metal bars at the front of the cell started to slide away, leaving an exit. Xander jumped out and looked round to Donovan's cell, it was also open and Donovan walked out.

"Is that it? Are we free?" He asked.

"I have no idea," Xander replied.

They looked round, at complete darkness as it had been before. The cells now looked like a movie set standing out in the dark. A second later, they faded from view. Then a new scene unfolded before them, a large open forest which surrounded them in all directions.

Xander had never seen a real forest, not that this was one either, but it felt real. The scene expanded, until the blackness was gone. The sound of birdsong filled the air around them.

A small worn path lead away in front of them, looking back, the path ended abruptly in large overgrown vegetation. So they began walking along the path, figuring there was nowhere else to go.

"This is not what I expected," Xander said.

"Me neither, how did you find me, anyway?" Donovan asked.

"I was asked to look into the Owen's case by Ava, his wife."

Donovan looked shocked.

"Ava came to you? I couldn't track her down when I was investigating."

"I think she was scared of CyBio, they're the ones that did this to you, this is their tech."

"What? No, it wasn't CyBio, it was Jacob."

"Who?"

"Jacob Winters, one of the original founders of CyBio. He was fired when his research methods came into question," Donovan explained. "I was looking into the last know places of Owen's, seeing if anything looked suspicious, when I found he had been invited to visit a Church in BitVillage the day of his death. The Church of Damian is an anti-augment religion, they probably wanted to try to show him the error of his ways I thought, but Owens rejected the offer. I looked into the Church and found that it's Father is Jacob Winters. When I had found that out, I requested a warrant to search the church, but when I was leaving the apartment to track it down, Father Jacob visited me, before I could do anything, he injected me with something. Next thing I knew, I woke up in that cell."

"When was this?" Xander asked.

"Tuesday, twelfth... November?"

Xander stopped in his tracks.

"It's the tenth of February, Owen's murder was reported only last week?" Xander replied, hesitating to tell Donovan he'd been in the cell for almost three months.

"That can't be, it was definitely the twelfth of November, I wrote down the date on the damn warrant."

Xander thought back to what he knew so far.

"Ava, she's the one that told me the murder was last week!" Xander recalled. "Even at the station, they didn't mention the date."

"What does that mean?" Donovan asked.

"I don't know, either Ava was wrong about the time, but I somehow doubt that, or she's got more to do with this than I thought."

The forest had opened to a clearing now, a

large open expanse of grass with a bright summers sky above. Xander had to pause to appreciate it all, before looking around for what he expected would be the exit.

In the centre of the field was a large oak tree, carved around the lower half of the trunk was the shape of a door, with a knot of wood where the handle should be.

"I guess this is it?" Donovan said, as he reached for the knot.

"Go for it, let's get out of here."

Donovan twisted the knot, and the door shaped engraving opened as though it was always a door. Donovan stepped through into what looked like the apartment. In fact, Xander could see himself inside the room, with Ava and Donovan inside, all linked together.

Donovan stepped through and disappeared, as he did, the Donovan who was sitting in the chair jumped to his feet and looked directly at Xander through the door. Xander walked towards the door.

"I'm afraid I need you to stay there," Donovan spoke, but his voice was different, "I can't risk you and Ava getting away just yet."

With that, Donovan turned to Ava and ripped the cable which connected her to Xander's unconscious body.

"Donovan no!"

The door and tree fell away, into the distance, as did the fores,t and then the field from under him.

Within seconds, Xander was left standing, or at least he thought he was standing, in complete darkness once again. This time nothing appeared for several minutes.

Until he saw court steps appear in front of him, he recognized them as the ones from MPD. They were filled with people, journalists and activists alike. Suddenly, he recognized the event. He saw Peter Henshaw appear at the top of the steps, smiling that grin of his as he strode down the steps towards the camera.

"Today, Justice is done in the face of a corrupt and out dated police system," he bragged about his release.

From behind Peter, Xander saw himself come out from the courthouse, making a direct beeline for Peter. Approaching, he spun Peter around and punched him full strength into the jaw, the blood and spit exploded in the air. Peter tumbled to the steps, his head bouncing on the edges. Xander then jumped on him and pummeled his fists into Peter's face.

Xander watched all this with anger, shame and horror filling him up, he knew it was over, but as several officers dragged Xander away, the whole scene restarted. Xander was watching the situation reenact, the worst day of his life, where he let his emotions take the better of him.

Then he watched it again,

And again,

And again.

CHAPTER 21

Prime

Reilly woke, something felt wrong.

He was laying down, that much he could tell. The hard back of what felt like the metallic table he had seen in the moments before his black out was under him.

The feeling of prodding in his head, like worms squirming inside his brain, made him panic. He tried to move his hands to his scalp but found his arms were strapped down to the table. Likewise, his head also couldn't move, a strap across his forehead preventing movement.

"Please don't struggle, it makes this terribly more difficult," Dr Koenig spoke from above him.

Reilly focused, his eyes upwards at the ceiling, on which a large mirror allowed him to see himself strapped to the table. He could see that Dr Koenig was sitting on a stool next to his head, and that half of his scalp was missing. Koenig was using a metallic device to prod directly onto his brain.

"What the hell are you doing?" Reilly shouted as he started to breathe heavily.

"Oh, don't be such a fuss, I'm just having a look at what we have in here, it's very fascinating," Koenig spoke, half to himself.

The feeling in his head continued as Koenig prodded further.

"You appear to have some sort of receiver here, for radio signals maybe? Where did you come from? Quite the enigma yes?" Koenig continued to speak.

Reilly felt something enter his thoughts, not an idea ,but the suggestion of one. Like he had thought of something, but it hadn't come from himself.

"Hmm what if I do this, I wonder?" Koenig sent a slight electric jolt into the receiver from his scalpel.

"... and now coming up on Hyperneonic Radio waves, a groovy number to really to get you in the mood. I know that times are hard here in the Nexus, but you gotta remember that no matter who you are and how hard it gets, you gotta be facing those things with a digital smile and a neon fuck you!" Reilly blurted out.

"Well, that is certainly interesting, yes?" Koenig laughed.

"So I've got an update from my inform-ant honchos in the MPD, apparently the Grand Falls Hotel has sent some of their Hunters out into the Underpass in search of someone! You know those Hunters, they gun first and ask later, so make sure you stay away from those guys, you hear? And if you're their target, and if you are hearing me, you better take cover or you are gonna be gunned!" Reilly watched his face moving and talking in the mirror in hor-ror at both what was happening and also what he was saying.

"My my my my my, I do believe you are talk-ing about you, no?" Koenig laughed again. "Per-haps I should change the channel?" Koenig hit another blast through the receiver.

Reilly felt a twinge in his head again, and then a relaxing of the muscles around his head.

"What are you going to do with me?" He asked.

"Do with you? I am doing it! I always need new specimens to examine and learn from, you see? Mollie is a doll and always brings me new things to play with," Koenig had picked up a bowl from next to him, after a moment Reilly realised it was the top of his skull when he saw hair protruding from the bottom. He did everything he could to prevent himself from being sick.

"Now, I don't know, you seem quite popular no? "Koenig replaced the skull and using, what looked like a blowtorch, sealed the scalp back in place. "Should I let them have you? Maybe? Or hide you and find out why you're so popular?"

Reilly was glad to have his head fully intact again, but he still wasn't confident on his odds.

A moment later, Mollie burst through the front of the tent.

"Hey doc, I think you might wanna hustle Reilly out ta here. We've got Hunters checking all the tents coming up. They looking for him!" She shouted out as she came in, JJ in tow.

"They all ov'r the place Doc, you don' wanna be the one they find wit' the body!"

Koenig looked up and then back to Reilly, taking a moment to consider. Then, he grabbed a blade and cut the straps holding him down.

"Yes, better not to have him here, too much risk yes?" Koenig said, lifting Reilly up from the bed.

Reilly steadied himself and placed his feet on the ground, taking a moment to adjust.

"Go this way please," Koenig held a curtain open and showed a route through the back of the tent away from the main path. Reilly didn't take time to argue and ducked through the exit. Mollie and JJ followed him.

"We'll make sure he goes far from the tent doc."

"Yes, a good idea," Koenig replaced the cover of the exit after they had passed through and settled himself at the desk, ready for the Hunters to arrive.

The trio emerged into an area filled with bags of rubbish and other assortments of items scattered around. They were behind all the stalls and tents.

"Where are you taking me now? Selling me out again?" Reilly said to Mollie. She didn't reply.

"Jus' business, nothin' personal." JJ answered.

"It felt personal!" Reilly shouted back, as he did, they heard voices from behind them.

"Keep your voice down! You want those Hunters to find us!" Mollie hissed at him. Her fear of the Hunters was far greater than anything else. They were hired agents who had killed people just for looking at them wrong. The MPD always turned a blind eye, as ninety percent of the time they were hired through the massive corps which ruled the Boulevard.

"Ok ok," Reilly quietened his voice. "But where are we going?"

"We're taking you to the edge of the Nexus, then you're on your own." Mollie replied. "We don't wanna be seen with you, would make us as much a target as you!"

They weaved through the maze of tents, avoiding the main routes where the Hunters could be watching. The claustrophobic spaces began to spread out as they reached the out-skirts.

"This is as far as we take you, good luck," Mollie gave a quick smile before turning away. As she did, a shot rang out and went straight through her side. She fell to the floor, clutching at the wound.

"Shit!" JJ yelled as they saw a group of Hunters walking towards them. Reilly, torn between running and stopping to help Mollie, froze on the spot.

JJ stared them down.

"C'mon you freaks! Shootin' an innocent

what's wron' wit you!?" He turned to Reilly, "Put this on and get 'er out of 'ere!" He threw his trench coat to Reilly. "It'll hide those chef clothes of yours. I'll hol' them off."

Reilly paused, then leaned down to pull Mollie up. He owed her nothing, but the Hunters were after him and it was his fault they had shot her. He threw JJ's jacket on; it was long and the hood helped cover his face. Mollie screamed in pain as he put her arm over his shoulders to support her weight.

"Where do we go?" He asked her.

"… radio shack.." She stuttered between breaths and pointed with her good side the direction to go.

They stumbled forwards, from behind them they heard JJ mocking the Hunters, covering their escape.

"Let's dance Gun-guns!" He laughed as he raised a shotgun and pulled the trigger. Seconds later, JJ was disappearing in a cloud of his own blood and tissue as the three Hunters opened fire on him. Mollie cried out as she heard JJ's last scream ring out.

"I'm sorry," Reilly said, as he pulled Mollie forwards away from the slaughter.

They continued round a corner, under Mollie's guidance they tried to stay ahead of the Hunters who were back on their trail.

"Stop, here," she shouted, as they limped down a small alleyway.

It was an alley just like any other, brick-work running along both sides. Reilly stopped but there wasn't anything there he could see. Mollie pushed away from him and leaned on the wall. She searched the wall next to her until she found a brick identical to all the others, but she pushed it. As she did, a small doorway appeared, flickering into existence like a fluorescent lightbulb coming on.

"Quick, go through," she said, looking behind her.

They both went in, moments before the Hunters rounded the corner. Inside was a long corridor leading to a room, inside which Reilly heard a voice.

"It seems those Hunters have been causing a bloodbath in our Nexus, people! All searchin' for Clone Prime! Stay off the streets! Keep your loved one's safe! We will get through this. And Prime if you're listening, we know this ain't your fault, the Nexus is a home to all God's lost children!" The man speaking turned to look as Mollie and Reilly walked in, he knew who Reilly was immediately and smiled.

"Welcome to the neighborhood, Prime."

CHAPTER 22

Ally

Ally had showered and changed. Her apartment was modest, with only a living room and bathroom, and minimal furnishings. She had never felt settled wherever she had lived and felt ready to leave at a moment's notice. Laying on the sofa, she was trying to think what to do, when the call came through.

"Hello Ally, Quartz here."

"Hey."

"Julian has got in contact, he's all right. It appears that the people who took him weren't the same ones that attacked you."

Ally jumped to her feet and headed to the kitchen.

"What? Who were they then?"

Quartzig gave her an update on the situation and explained that Julian was now working with Yuri to investigate Owen's missing body and that he was tracking the vehicle which had transported the body.

"Thank God he's OK. So, who attacked us then?" Ally asked.

"Good question, one which Julian seems to have disregarded I'm afraid," Quartzig replied. "They had some serious tech and I fear that Julian will end up walking into something he may not be able to get out of."

It surprised Ally, the care the AI had for Julian, though it made sense as he was Quartz's creator.

"So what do you want me to do Quartz?" She asked, assuming that was why he called.

"Well, I have chased up on the police case from the attack, and also monitored CCTV and, perhaps I should have lead with this, but it appears they followed you."

"What!"

"Yes, from what I can tell there are several people on their way up to your apartment."

Ally paused, taking in the information, then grabbed her denim cut-off jacket from the hanger near the door, throwing it over her long-sleeved t-shirt.

"Do you know where they are now?" She

asked, as she slipped on her boots.

"Coming up the third floor stairs," Quartzig updated her.

She lived on the tenth, so she had two minutes to prepare, or run. She took a moment to decide that running was probably the safer choice.

"Fifth floor," Quartzig said.

She grabbed a small, foot long rod from the coffee table and gave it a click. A smooth hiss escaped from it and within seconds it had extended into a staff six feet long, another click and it retracted back in place. She shoved it into a holster inside her jacket and headed for the window.

"Eight."

She slid the window away and a rush of air flooded the apartment from the cityscape below. Neon lights twinkled as she looked out over the Boulevard, the tenth floor was high enough to see a lot of the city.

"Nineth."

The fire escape was bolted onto the side of the building and creaked as she stepped onto it. She took one last look into her apartment and saw the front door splintering as some kind of energy blast destroyed it.

"They are at the door!" Quartzig said.

"Yeah, I noticed!" Ally ducked away and made her way down the fire exit as fast as she could, the metal steps rocking as she ran. She'd made it down three flights when she heard a ping next to her head, accompanied by a spark, as a bullet spun past her, followed by a blast of light, another energy beam.

"Quartz, any idea *why* they are trying to kill me exactly?!" She asked, realising she hadn't actually done anything.

"Not enough information to be sure, I'm afraid," he said. "Though I wonder if your association with Julian is enough for them to see you as a target?"

"Wonderful," she replied.

"You did beat some of their colleagues up?" He tried to reason.

"In self defense!" She shouted back.

Before they could continue, Ally felt the metal underneath her come away from the building. Confused, she looked upwards, and saw that the entire fire exit had come away from the wall because of the damage from the energy blasts and was now in danger of falling away.

"Oh shit," she whispered. She looked across to the building opposite, if she was lucky, the framework would hold together long enough for her to jump over to the other rooftop.

"Quartz, can you actually see me?"

"Well, I have hacked into several satellites which orbit, some are better than others and the non geo-stationary ones mean I sometimes have to adjust to whatever is available, also the weather impacts the visibility..."

"Can you see me right now!" Ally interrupted, the fire exit at forty-five degree angles away from the building now.

"Yes, quite clearly."

"If I stay where I am, will I make it to the building opposite when this thing falls?"

"Oh, no, you are two floors too low, you need to go back up two floors or you'll catch the side of the building based on your current location."

Ally sighed then looked up at the exit, the attackers weren't on the fire exit but she could see them at the window above, guns aimed on her. As if to reply to her stare, they fired a few shots at her , ricocheted off the metal steps.

She made her way back up as fast as she could, based on the angle of the stairs.

Noticing her coming up, one of the attackers jumped from the window and onto the exit, as soon as he hit, the stairs fell faster due to his weight. He made his way down as she made her way up.

Ally had got up two flights just as her attacker had reached her, a swift kick came and she narrowly avoided it by stepping backwards. Immediately countering the attack, she jumped forwards. As she did, the stairs momentum was caught by gravity and the whole frame fell, slamming into the adjacent building. It threw both Ally and the attacker from the frame and they landed hard on the rooftop.

"Are you ok?" Quartz asked.

Ally didn't have time to reply, as she jumped to her feet to face her enemy.

"Who are you? Why are you trying to kill me?"

The man just looked at her and smiled. She drew and extended the bo-staff. It had been a while since she had trained with it, but it felt comfortable in her hand. A couple of swings to get the weight balance and she struck a pose waiting for the attack.

"You are required!" the man shouted.

"Why me?"

The man didn't reply, instead diving forwards to attack, he swung a fist. Ally ducked and thrust the end of the pole into the man's chest, causing him to fall to the ground. She whirled the staff around and slammed it down towards the prone body. A roll and he was out of harm's way, back to his feet and running at Ally now. She didn't have time to respond, and he flew into her, throwing them both to the floor, he pummeled her in the face with a fist as he took position above her. One fist landed square on Ally's cheek, causing a burst of blood to erupt from her mouth, she used it and spat straight into his face. In the momentary blindness, she retracted the staff in her hand, moved it to the side of the man's head and extended it again. The force of the release smashed the edge of the staff straight into his temple, crushing the whole area of his skull with a wet thump.

She rolled him off and kicked the dead body for her own satisfaction. She glanced back up to her apartment window, there was no one there.

"Can you see the others Quartz?" She asked.

"They appear to be on their way to you now,

coming across the street below."

"Great," she looked across the rooftops, she could make it across several with relative ease, but not far. She needed to find somewhere she could hide and lie low.

"Quartz, is there an easy way to the Underpass from here?"

"Oh, erm, let me check, it's not something I usually look for."

Ally wasn't surprised that Quartz didn't know much of the Underpass, few did, unless you had to.

"There's an access point three blocks down from here, if you go west from your current position over four buildings and down, you will be pretty much spot on. Why do you want to go there?" Quartzig answered.

"Somewhere I know I can find help," she replied.

"I'm going home."

CHAPTER 23

Jacob

Jacob was in the manufacturing area of the warehouse now, after Owens had agreed to his terms, with some of his own, he had continued on the next stage of his work.

The manufacturing section comprised of several chambers, similar to that of the main chamber, only smaller. He scanned over them, inside each, a body part was floating in a green liquid. He found the one he was searching for, a leg which was floating freely. It was pristine from the toes up to the thigh, where it abruptly ended with a metallic cap covering the entire area ,where it would be connected to a body. From the metal several cables extended and connected to the chamber's wall, like an artificial umbilical cord.

Jacob pressed the keypad on the side of the chamber and watched as the liquid drained from the chamber through a grate on the bottom. The leg drifting to the ground slowly before resting there. The chamber opened and Jacob reached in and took the leg, disconnecting the cables from their sockets. He pulled a large cloth from a bench near the chamber and wrapped the entire limb in it.

He walked away and headed back to the main entrance of the hotel. Waiting for him in the foyer was Owens.

"Are you ready?" Jacob asked.

"Like I have a choice," came the reply.

"Quite," Jacob couldn't help but smile as he handed the leg to Owens and beckoned him to follow.

They left the hotel and entered the car which was waiting for them. Upon entering it, the car drove away.

"You still use these things?" Owens asked, referring to the self-driving car. "We upgraded to TransPods last year."

Jacob knew of the pods, a small box which you sit inside and a small propulsion shot them into the sky before returning to the ground at the destination, like a miniature rocket.

"Oh, I know you did, I prefer a more refined style of travel," He replied.

"Fair enough. Where are we headed to?" Owens resigned to his fate in helping Jacob. For his own survival, he would need to get any information he could.

"To my Church, not that you'll see it, I need the world to still believe you're dead. You will be in the lab underneath, adapting the augmented release method."

Owens looked out of the window, he was still coming to terms with the idea he was no longer in his own body, but that of a clone. He caught a glimpse of his reflection in the car's window. A face he didn't recognise, that of a younger man, a man who had not lived, but grown in a lab.

"I will get you a copy of your own body when this is over Max, I promise," he said, their years of friendship slipping through in his voice.

"You're still the one that killed me Jacob, that I won't forget."

"I did not kill you Max, that I swear. But I can't deny it has given me some advantages. You don't see it, but the reliance of technology has become too much, too far, too dangerous."

"And you're the one to make the changes?" Owens turned to look at Jacob in the eyes.

"If not me, then someone else, someone who might not understand how all this works. I can be a scalpel rather than a hammer."

Owens could tell that Jacob's mind truly believed that he was doing what he thought was right.

"Why should anyone make the change though? Have we not made the best discoveries through mistakes and errors? That's how we learn, that's what humans do. Adapt and survive. We made it this far, why do you have to step in now?"

"Because if I don't, there will be no more humans, don't you see? Where does the line blur and we cross over to become more machine than man? Already, we have humans who can no longer survive without the tech implanted in them. When that trait becomes normal in the gene code, then what are we? No longer man without the machine, is that still a man?" Jacob asked.

"Perhaps, but then maybe that is the next step? Did we stop evolving from apes just because we were becoming a new form of Sapien? Or did we embrace the change and the benefits it reaped? Maybe it's time for Homo Sapiens to evolve to the next stage, to become Homo Deus," Owen's knew that would rile Jacob up.

He had always been a religious one which to begin with, it had been an interesting part of working with him, but over time it became more of an obsession.

"You dare," Jacob whispered. "We are not meant to be Gods, you are the reason I have to do what I must to prevent the human race from becoming extinct, and now you will help me achieve this. Or you will die for good this time," Jacob smirked as he spoke.

Owens didn't reply, he knew Jacob had the upper hand now. If he didn't play along and do the work Jacob asked, then he'd lose his chance at life. He knew that Jacob would kill him for good if he thought there was any doubt Owens wouldn't help.

The car pulled up to the back of the Church and they entered, Owens still carrying the mummified leg. Jacob lead the way through the back door of the church and down the steps to his laboratory underneath.

Jacob took the leg from Owens.

"Feel free to work on the computers," he pointed at the setup in the corner. "They won't connect to the Net unless I activate the routing, so don't bother trying to get a message out. Everything you need should be available to you though. I shall return after tonight's sermon."

With that, he turned and left the room. Owens heard the slam of a heavy lock drop behind the door. He wasn't getting out anytime soon. He turned to the computers and began to work.

Upstairs, the evenings congregation had formed as Jacob entered the church. This service would be one of his biggest feats to date. As he approached the alter, he put the leg down behind the alter and scanned the crowd for the woman who had visited him earlier. He hadn't seen her face; it was a confessional after all, however, knowing of her augmented leg made her easy to spot in the crowd whereas most had already abandoned any augmentations.

"Good Evening Everyone!" He called out as he took centre stage, not heading to the lectern this time.

"Tonight I will show the true power of belief, of redemption and of possibilities."

He turned to the alter behind him; it was made of grey concrete and was the size of an average human body. Across it was draped a large silk sheet covered with the varying symbols. Jacob had always maintained the illusion of spectacle he had created for the Church, knowing it helped increase the power of his work.

"I believe there is someone among us who needs cleansing, of release from the bounds of technology and it's sins."

A murmur came from the crowd as they all looked around at each other until the woman stood nervously.

"Come up here, child. Don't be shy," he called, stepping down from his position to meet her on the way up. "Tell us your name child."

"Tara," she replied, a nervous voice.

"Tara, welcome to the church, and congratulations on seeing the light and being ready to cleanse. Tell us all of your sins, start the cleaning with admission," he promoted Tara to talk.

"Well... I... I was a runner," she began, "a good one, until my injury. They told me that I would benefit from a new augmented leg instead, that it would help me run faster and be a better athlete."

Father Jacob bent and helped the crowd to see her leg by raising it slightly, he held his hand directly above the point where the T-Pox had taken root.

"As you can see, poor Tara is infected with the plague of imperfection, as her body rejects the false limb!" He turned to Tara, "but all is not lost child, please lay down."

He motioned to the alter and helped Tara up.

"Tonight, we will cleanse Tara of her imperfections and bring her closer to the light. Before we do however, I must tell you of what is coming. There is a day of reckoning coming, a rapture where all those who have been cleansed will be spared, but those still bathing in the sins of the technology will be decimated!" Jacob knew how to rile the crowd up before his work.

Turning back now, he draped the bright white satin sheet over Tara's augmented leg. He had done several smaller cleanses before such as the eye the previous night, but this was the largest limb he'd ever done. He reached behind the alter and pulled out the cloned leg. Made from Tara's own DNA, using the sample she had given him, it would be accepted by her body and using Jacob's own work, he knew the metal disc would allow the limb immediate connection to the tissue of Tara's leg, through a series of chemicals it was imbued with. Once the connection was made, it would attach and release the chemicals, eventually breaking down and dissolving into her blood stream as it became a fully functioning limb. The whole process taking only a few seconds.

"Let us begin," he announced and proceeded to offer Tara a drink from the same Goblet he'd used previously. The liquid inside was a version higher than the previous one he used. He'd isolated the chemicals in his own blood and created the first prototype, which evolved until it was this, the new elixir. Once trialled, he would begin the next stage of implementing it with a dispersal method, which Owens was working on.

Tara drank the liquid and began feeling its effects. She convulsed on the alter, her back arching so much Jacob was worried it could break, these were the side effects he was looking for so he could adjust the dosage. He moved to her side and out of view of the crowd, he injected a small amount of a relaxant into her arm. Her chest fell slightly as the drug kicked in and relaxed her muscles.

A gasp of shock from the crowd made Jacob look down to where the satin sheet lay, it was becoming marked with red blood as the limb underneath was rejected. Jacob knew the white would stain fast and was pleased the colouring had the desired effect on the crowd, making it visible to those even at the far back of the church. Tara wasn't screaming anymore, the drugs were keeping her lucid through the procedure, Jacob was glad as the next step was a slight of hand that her lucidity would make easier.

Lifting the sheet towards the crowd allowed him to see the leg underneath. Placing a metal stand to hold the sheet in place, he looked at the mix of veins and wires where the leg was drenched in blood. He had to admit, the quality of the augmented leg was high, she'd paid a lot of credits for it. He retrieved the cloned limb and placed it next to the augmented one, then placed a hand on the augmented leg and pulled it away. The wires stretched and went taut at first before giving way, this was the first time a scream erupted from Tara's lips ,but was only for a second. Jacob quickly swapped the cloned limb into its place, pressing it up hard against her torso for it to begin the fusion to her body. He heard the click which signified the attachment, as small claws dug into the flesh to hold it in place and fuse. A small hiss escaped, as the metal disc dissolved and allowed the bonding to complete. In one move, he dropped the augmented leg to the ground next to him and removed the sheet.

An intake of breath from the crowd, Jacob basked in the glory as the crowd watched Tara rise and stand on her own, fully fleshed legs.

CHAPTER 24

Julian

Julian was in the back of an autocab which Quartzig had arranged for him, traveling towards his apartment.

In front of him, a holographic display emanated from his PDA, showing the reports he'd received from Yuri. He was piecing together the last steps of Owens as best he could.

So far, he'd worked out that Owens had been at the CyberBio lab three hours before his death, their records were immaculate, as they registered bio-signals throughout the time anyone was within the confines of one of their buildings. Next a Transfer pod was registered for Owens to travel from the lab to MegaCity, where his credit records showed he had a meal in one of the Japanese restaurants there. The restaurant staff, who had been interviewed, said he had been there around an hour with a woman who matched the description of Ava, his wife. After leaving, there was about an hour and a half of unaccounted time before he was reported dead at his home by Ava.

Donovan, who had been investigating the case, had been updating his reports for three months before he suddenly stopped. His last entry was about the Church of Damian in Bit-Village, which Donovan believed was the last place Owen's visited during the missing time, but most of the report was redacted. That was his first lead to look into, second was to do what Yuri asked, locate the body.

The records stated that his body was processed on the 7th November, where the cause of death was undetermined, though there were several bruises around the neck and some slight trauma to the cranium. Following this, the body was due to be transferred to cold storage at the morgue, the vehicle had left the precinct on the 9th November but during the trip, something had caused its tracking beacon to stop transmitting, and it never arrived. Julian made a note of the last transmitted location.

"Hey Quartz?" Julian waited for a reply, after none came, he asked again, louder. "Quartz!"

"Oh hello, yes I'm here," the voice replied a moment later.

"What's going on? You busy?"

'It's Ally, she's in a spot of bother and I'm just

helping her out."

Julian paused for a moment, Quartz had never taken an interest in anyone before, perhaps this was a new development in his AI.

"Is she ok?"

"I believe she will be shortly, several of the people who attacked you are now hunting her down, probably believing her to have something to do with you," Julian could feel the accusation in his voice.

"Damn, make sure she gets some place safe."

"I will, she's much better at handling herself than you are, no offence."

"Thanks, let me know when she's ok. I'm changing my destination," he was tapping on his PDA to access the car's journey log.

"Where are you heading?" Quartz asked.

"BitVillage, to the church of Saint Damian, but I could do with you looking into something for me."

"Shoot."

"I need you to access all CCTV for the 9th November. There's a vehicle which vanished that I need to find. I'm sending over the pictures and registration, along with its last known location."

"Will do, might take a while, there's a lot of cameras in the Boulevard." Quartz replied.

"No problem, that's what I thought, so I'll check out the church which seems to be Owens last location before he died, and see if anything shakes lose."

"Good Luck."

"Thanks, tell Ally I'm sorry for getting her tied up in this."

"I will," Quartz replied.

Julian tapped on his PDA and checked his location, he wasn't too far from the Church now. He could find little on the Church online, only that it used to be a popular building long before the Boulevard expanded. It closed down once development took people away from the area. Then it reopened two years back, when a new Father appeared to rejuvenate it. After that, there was no information.

The car pulled up to the side of the road and Julian looked out at the streets outside. He felt like he'd travelled to another world. The buildings were all old brick and mortar, with glass windows and hardly any of them rose over three floors, many just two. He had known that BitVillage was still very much still from the old world, but seeing it with his own eyes took him a moment to absorb. He saw a few people walking around and couldn't put his finger on what was wrong at first. Then he realised, there were no augments or implants on anyone. He'd become so accustomed to the sight of tech, it was as much a way of life as breathing, but the absence of tech was like seeing people all wearing the same clothes, with no variation to them.

He was about to get out of the car when he caught his reflection in the car's window. His hair was dark purple and several of his augments were highly visible, not least his PDA implant on his arm. He brought it up and tapped it, changing his hair to a dull brown with a side parting of medium length, and extending the sleeves on his coat so they covered straight down his arms, and went from a short jacket to a trench-coat style. He was covered as much as possible.

He exited the car and looked around the street; the dullness was oppressing, which surprised him, as he was used to the heavy neon crowds of the MegaCity; but the lack of colour and lights made him feel nervous. He had made a mental note of the Church's location before turning off his PDA, and made his way towards it.

He passed people who looked at him sideways as they hurried past, avoiding making eye contact with him completely. He wasn't used to the feeling of being shunned so he pulled the coat closer to him as he walked.

"Hey tech freak, get out of here!" A shout echoed from across the road. Turning, Julian saw a group of men, all wearing similar blue jeans and brown shirts, they moved towards Julian.

"I don't want any trouble," he shouted back at them.

"Well, you shouldn't have come here then!" The anger was rising in the voices as they got closer.

Julian couldn't understand how they had seen he had any tech implants at all. Then he noticed that his coat was fluctuating slightly in its length. While not the most high-tech item i,t was enough to be a huge beacon to this non-tech area.

"I'm just passing through," he called to the men as they got closer. Julian walked quicker down the street. He knew he could probably win in a fight due to several of his augmented abilities, but he wasn't about the chance the odds of five to one.

He turned a corner and saw the church looming up ahead. He increased his pace heading towards it, hoping the men would stop once he arrived there.

A glance back and he saw they were still following him but at a slower pace, perhaps they would just get bored and stop. Julian walked up the steps of the church and pushed the large doors open to step inside.

The church was empty and the sound of his steps echoed around throughout the hollow space.

He walked down the aisle, glancing at the stained glass windows which rose all around the sides, though little light was illuminating them. At the end several, candles were lit, the only light in the entire place. As he approached, he heard a voice.

"May I help you? I am Father Jacob and this is my church," a voice asked from behind him.

Julian jumped at the noise but calmed as he turned to see the Father in front of him.

"Good evening, I was wondering if you could help me. I'm looking for a friend of mine who came here."

"We have many friends in the congregation

young man," the Father stepped closer, his eyes examining Julian, clocking each bit of tech around his body.

"Of course," Julian smiled. "His name was Maxwell Owens, I think he came here a few months ago."

Father Jacob paused in his step for a moment, before continuing. Julian noticed the hesitation, and a strange feeling ran through him.

"Owens you say? I'm not too sure we've had anyone by that name here."

"I'm pretty sure he was here on the 9th November, perhaps you have a welcome book of anyone that may have passed through?" Julian knew he was pushing it and edged away looking for a route past Jacob, should he need one.

"We have one just at the top of the alter there, feel free to take a look." Jacob motioned behind Julian who turned to look.

"Thanks," he tapped his PDA discreetly and opened comms with Quartzig. "I'll just be a minute, then be on my way," he said to Jacob.

"Take all the time you need," Jacob approached Julian who tried to step away, before he could, Jacob leapt forward and injected Julian in the arm with a concealed needle.

"What the hell!" He spun and swung at Jacob, who had moved out of harm's way.

"Julian?" Quartzigs' voice came through, "are you ok? You need to be careful, I traced the vehicle with Owens body in it. Its last location is at the Church you have just entered. Whoever is at the Church is the one who stole the body! Julian? Are you there?"

Julian felt his vision blur as he tried to reply to Quartzig, but he was fading. He saw Jacob standing over him as he crumpled to the ground.

"Welcome to the Church Julian, you saved me some trouble by coming here yourself."

CHAPTER 25

Xander

Xander had lost count of the number of times he's watched the event on the court steps replay in front of him. He had watched them from every angle now as he had walked around it. It took a few times for him to get over the shock and pain of seeing the worst day of his life repeat in front of him. He had begun to accept it and also realised that it was another construct of the prison he'd helped Donovan escape. In theory, he figured the only way he could escape would be for someone to guide him out, but he wasn't sure that anyone would even be looking for him anymore, never mind guide him.

Donovan had been the one to trap him there, but Ava had either lied about the time of Owens' death, or had some other reason for missing 3 months before coming to see him. He had no idea what the situation in the apartment was after Donovan severed the connection.

Damn, he hated technology. He longed for something to punch, something that felt real between his fingers, rather than this fake construct in front of him. He had tried to get involved in the scene playing in front of him, but when he had; the people were intangible and he could walk right through them, despite how solid they looked.

Walking around the scene, he could see all the people that were there on the day of the trial. Other than himself and Henshaw, there was also Henshaw's lawyer looking smug behind him as Henshaw spoke to the cameras. Several news outlets with cameramen and reporters were further down the steps. A handful of MPD officers were scattered around the area, finally a few civilians who were watching the spectacle. Then there was himself, who appeared after a few moments, once he attacked Henshaw, the civilians scattered, along with some media crews, though a few continued filming. Then officers diving in to pull Xander off Henshaw, whilst his lawyer assisted Henshaw to get away from the bloodied fists.

He had watched the event play out at least fifty times before he noticed something different, something he was sure hadn't been there on the actual day.

At the top of the steps, just inside the doors

to the courthouse, a woman stood there, he hadn't noticed before as all the action took place further down the steps; the scene beginning when Henshaw began his speech. He ran up the steps to the entrance, as he got there the woman moved away and disappeared inside the building. He followed her in, but the inside of the building wasn't the courthouse, but his office. He hesitated before stepping in.

The room was identical to his in real life, but instead of half working lights on the door, the sign read his full name;

ALEXANDER DRAVEN PI

The construct must have come from his mind and was how he wanted it to be, rather than how it was.

He moved around his desk and sat in the chair as he normally would. As he did, Ava appeared opposite him as she had the day before, and talked about the investigation. The scene played out exactly as he remembered, from her initial lack of emotion, to the explanation of her being a synthetic who had been given the memories of the original Ava, who had died a few years previously.

They left the office and Xander was walking into the MPD precinct, asking about the case with Mike behind the counter.

Leaving the precinct, he was now in Donovan's apartment fighting the nurse and being jacked into Donovan's mind to help him escape.

Now in the prison, guiding Donovan through the prison and the forest.

Finally, he was watching Donovan leaving the construct and becoming trapped in it, as Donovan ripped the wires from Ava.

He blinked.

He was back at the courtroom steps again, watching Henshaw make his statement.

Xander's heart skipped a beat.

How long had he been in the construct? How could he tell the difference between the construct and the real world?

He ran up the steps and through the courtroom doors; the pattern happened all over again until he was back at the steps. He fell to the ground, his head in his hands, the pain in his mind was overwhelming as he tried to understand what was happening. He wondered if he had been in the construct the whole time.

He took several deep breaths.

When was Owens' death? 5th November.

Ava reported the case to Xander on the 10th February. Or was it, the date seemed wrong to Xander.

He cycled through the scenes until he was back at the office, sitting opposite Ava. He glanced at the computer screen in front of him; it said the 11th February, a day later than he recalled. He asked Ava.

"When did he die? In fact, just tell me all you know." Remembering the exact words. Ava had said the murder took place on February 2nd the last time he recalled the conversation.

"Can I have one of those?" Ava pointed at the cigarette in Xander's hand. He nodded and lit one before passing it to her.

"Last week, February 3rd, I returned home and found my husband laying across the hallway, covered in blood. Mutilated with his left hand missing."

Xander froze, the date had changed, in line with the change in days he'd experienced.

Somehow, the construct was keeping up with the time and altering the information accordingly. He fought the sick feeling which formed in his stomach. Donovan has said the investigation took place on November the 15th, which meant that Xander could have been in the construct since then for all he knew. The fact made his head spin, with still no idea how to escape, he didn't know how he could continue.

Then a thought struck him, if the construct was connected to the outside world, as it must be to alter the date according, then he might be able to send a signal out. He needed to find the connection so that he could communicate to the outside world. However, he had no idea how he would do that. His mind spun as the cycle played out once more.

This time, he looked at the woman on the steps again, he realised now it was Ava, looking slightly younger perhaps. Was she trying to guide him, and if so ,to where?

He regained his motivation and ran towards her.

CHAPTER 26

Prime

Reilly walked into the radio room where the man who had addressed him as Prime sat, speaking into a microphone. He had a scruffy beard and dreadlocked hair and a smile which radiated warmth. In front of him, a large assortment of radio equipment was connected with tangles of cables and wiring. He wore a casual shirt which looked like someone had repaired it a thousand times.

"We'll be back soon children, after these beats take over your auditory senses," he signed off and moved away from the microphone to look at Reilly and Mollie.

"Hey Razz," Mollie said in between breaths, the wound on her side still weeping blood. "Could use some help."

"Damn, what happened to you Moll?" Razz hit a button on the large control panel in front of him and a young woman appeared.

"Get Moll' some treatment ASAP please Cassandra," he addressed the young woman, who took Mollie away.

"She'll get help my friend," Razz addressed Reilly now. "You and me though, we have some conversation to have," he offered him a seat.

"Thank you," Reilly sat, and for the first time in a long while, he felt safe and relaxed.

"My name's Razz, nice to meet you, there's a whole lot of people looking for you my friend, you're pretty important, but how about you tell me your life story first and maybe I'll try to fill in the gaps."

Reilly looked stunned, he had no idea what his life story was; he had no memories he could rely on past earlier that day.

"I... I don't really know. I think I was being brainwashed at the Grand Falls Hotel, but I don't know what memories I can believe and what they put in my brain," he explained.

"I see, makes sense. How about you let me enlighten you on my knowledge and we can see what sticks yeah?" Razz replied. "You see, the Grand Falls Hotel, that's a place of clones my friend. Everyone that works in that place is a clone of someone else. Of who? Well, that's the million credit question, and the truth is a little sparse on that respect. Either way, someone made a copy of him, like the perfect employee of the year, you know what I'm saying. Before you know it, that place is a place of clones who all work perfect you see?"

Reilly took the information in, as bizarre as it seemed to him, it also made perfect sense.

"Now all those Clones had to be controlled, made to be compliant and know their role, so the man in charge there, some cat named Jacob, he developed this system where he could both write and wipe a mind, and he tested it on you guys over there. So you wake up and you get programmed to be whatever you need to be for the day, then you go back to sleep and start all over again the next day."

Razz held up a hand as Reilly began to ask a question. Razz moved over to the microphone as the song that was playing finished.

"A classic no doubt, my children, but next up we'll take you to a higher level. Keep those ear canals clear and let the Magic flow like a creek murmuring into your mind," Razz announced the next track and muted the microphone once again.

"Now you, you my friend, you escaped, you broke that programming and became your own person. So the question is, how did you do it? Who are you?"

Reilly sat there, the question stumped him.

"I... I had some head trauma, and when I went to leave, I think the mind wipe they usually do didn't work, I didn't lose my memories. So I ran, tried to escape as I didn't know what else to do."

Razz smiled and nodded.

"That makes sense, but there's a reason you ran. There's some small trace in your mind that remains from the cloning," Razz tapped his head as if to indicate a secret.

"What trace? Do you know who I am... was..." Reilly was struggling, his mind working in overdrive to understand what was happening.

"Oh yes, I know who you are my friend. You are Clone Prime, you are the first clone!"

Razz laughed a deep and echoing laugh.

"How can that be? All the clones are the same age, if I was the original, wouldn't I be much older than the rest?" Reilly asked, trying to understand the logistics of the situation.

"Ah no, you see those chambers which they have there, you sleep in those and the systems rejuvenate your cell structure, making you the same as you were on the morning of your creation."

Reilly was accepting the situation, but a burning question had to be asked.

"How do you know all this?"

"Ah, well. That's the secret isn't it my friend. How indeed do I know?"

Before any more talking could occur, Mollie ran into the room, her side had been bandaged up.

"Hey guys," she said.

"Moll, you doing ok?" Razz boomed as she walked in.

"I'll live. Hey, I just want to say I'm sorry," she turned to Reilly. "We were just doing what we had to do to survive, Koenig always pays well."

"I understand, and I'm sorry about JJ," Reilly put a hand on Mollie's shoulder. "He died protecting you."

Mollie nodded and gave an appreciative smile.

"OK so what's the plan guys? Those Hunters will not stop anytime soon," Razz interrupted.

"You said I'm the first clone, but the clone of

who?" Reilly asked, the information was sinking in.

Razz ignored the question, but handed him a small disc, On it was a logo which flickered as the light caught it, creating an image of the letters '*C*' and '*B*' to twinkle. Reilly turned it over, revealing etchings on the back which read '*CyBio*'.

"That will lead you to answers my friend," Razz said, before turning to his desk. "The receiver in your head might come in useful. If you don't mind?" Razz had searched several drawers in his desk, before finding a metallic device shaped like a bowl. He placed it over Reilly's head and attached a cable into a computer which was sat on the desk.

"What are you doing?"

"This should let me access the receiver , if I can adjust the settings, I should be able to make you change frequency like a radio, and also maybe transmit too."

Mollie caught on to the idea.

"You'll be able to hear the Hunters radio signals!"

"Bingo Moll, and maybe even send signals to them, to misdirect if needed," Razz grinned.

"Do it," Reilly nodded, and Razz activated the device. A burning feeling roared through Reilly's head, like a rolling headache which echoed around his skull.

"Is he ok?" Mollie asked.

"I'm... fine..." Reilly strained through the pain.

"Will only take a moment," Razz's fingers were dancing over the keyboard of the computer, as numbers and letters scrolled over the monitor.

"One moment...." He shouted out.

Reilly screamed as the pain became unbearable to him, he gripped the desk hard with his hands.

"And... DONE", Razz shouted, deactivating the systems.

"How you feeling?" Mollie asked Reilly.

"I'll be ok."

"Try tuning in?" Razz said.

Reilly closed his eyes and tried for a moment to concentrate. He was hearing waves of voices and sounds filling his mind, like a radio being tuned across several stations; white noise filling the spaces.

"It's working..." He said, trying to focus on one channel.

"In there! It's the last building we haven't checked. Breach the wall," Reilly couldn't help but shout, his voice authoritative as he tuned to the Hunters radio frequency.

"What?" Mollie asked, glancing at Razz.

"Guys, I think they may have found us." Reilly said.

A moment later, the wall at the far end of the corridor caved in. The force of the explosion rocked the building.

"You guys go, get out of here," Razz shouted. "I can hold them off. Now go!" Razz pushed them away down a side door which was hidden by several pieces of equipment, handing Mollie a revolver and a box of bullets.

As Reilly and Mollie made their way down the corridor, they heard another explosion and several screams. They couldn't distinguish them but they hoped Razz wasn't amongst them.

A few moments later, they emerged back onto the streets, the light of morning was rising in the distance and they made their way through the winding streets.

"Where do we go now?" Reilly asked.

"I'm not sure," Mollie replied. "What did Razz tell you?"

"That I'm the first of a batch of Clones made by a man named Jacob."

Suddenly he fell to the ground, his mind was becoming a cacophony of voices and sounds.

"Mollie....I can't...control them...The weather will be warm with...Murder on the Boulevard ...Cy-bio conference will be a surprise unveiling of....Can anyone hear me? I'm trapped here...Hunters seen in the Nexus....My name is Xander Draven, if you can hear this... are augmentations dangerous to our health..." The words changing like a radio station.

Reilly lay there, his thoughts racing as he tried to focus on his own mind. Until he couldn't control it anymore, and he blacked out.

His mind was filled with staccato memories and fragments of hundreds of thoughts, all bustling through his mind.

He pictured himself stood in a room, all around him were television screens depicting images that matched the voices in his head. On one, a news report showed an image of a police car, dead bodies around it, including an MPD officer. On another, there was an obituary of Maxwell Owens, a co-founder of CyBio who had lost his life three months ago. Another showed a reporter talking to several residents of a high rise where a faulty fire escape had caused several injuries.

Then one stuck out, it was of a man standing in a police station, talking on a walkie talkie. The voice spoke but he couldn't hear the words clearly as they were drowned out by the cacophony of other voices.

He closed his eyes and tried to turn off the sounds that echoed around him, after several moments, he opened his eyes and saw someone else.

Standing before him was a man who looked just like him, staring at his face with a grin.

"Hello Prime," the voice spoke. "Nice to see you again, though I bet you don't remember me."

Reilly shook his head, a strange feeling coming over him, a feeling of anger.

"That's ok, in fact it's expected. You see, I've been here for a while now, watching you, guiding you. But it's almost time for you to go and for me to come back. Not yet though, now you need to wake up!"

Reilly opened his eyes and jumped up, the memories of the man fading as fast as he woke.

CHAPTER 27

Ally

Ally had made her way across the roof-tops and down the buildings until she was at street level. Glancing back, she saw no sign of anyone following her. She approached a small hatch on the ground which had 'NO ENTRY' stenciled on it. It was an access point to the Underpass, though most of the Boulevards' residence would hardly notice the hatch, she knew exactly where it lead. She opened the hatch using her staff as leverage, revealing a ladder which descended down. She began the climb down the ladder which stopped after a few metres and gave way to a stairwell. The steps were concrete and surrounded by walls of similar material on all sides, covered in graffiti. Originally built as access points for the construction of the Boulevard, they were now one of the few ways to travel between the two areas, and even then most people didn't cross from one to the other.

"Quartz, can you still hear me?" She asked,

the further down she went, the more oppressive the walls became. Flickering, caged, fluorescent orange bulbs were the only illumination.

"Just, the signal is weakening, I won't be able to reach you once you get past a certain point," he replied.

"Okay, thanks by the way, for helping me get away from those guys."

"No problem, always happy to help," came the reply.

"Any ideas on who they were yet?"

"Not yet, I've been tracking the ones who attacked you and they seem to be heading towards GigaCity now, no idea where yet though, I'm afraid."

"OK, let me know where they end up. How's Julian?"

"Julian is tracking a lead from the information Yuri gave him and is in BitVillage, but I've lost signal from him as he entered a church there, I hope he's ok," Quartz replied.

"I'm sure he is."

"I hope... so... I think...signal is going..." Quartz's voice stuttered in and out.

"No worries Q, I'll catch you soon," Ally shouted, thinking it would help the signal.

She got no reply. She was alone now.

She hadn't been to the Underpass in a long time. Back when she was younger, her parents died in the civil unrest caused by the influx of residents which forced the segregation of Boulevard.

There were so many people in different classes in such a small space that inevitably, trouble would rise. When several families in Zeta wanted their areas to be clear of anyone they felt were below them, they hired personal bodyguards who slowly formed what could only be described as a small army, all working under the same company. This lead to streets becoming checkpoints where only people of wealthy backgrounds could cross. Slowly, the people who had homes in the area were being forced to move out, despite having lived there for years.

On the other side, there was more and more anger coming from the Bit and Mega areas which lead to attacks on the checkpoints, causing a cascade effect which only gave the Zeta Army more power and allowance to become more aggressive.

It took a long time for the violence to settle down, and only when GigaCity was declared a safe zone where no violence was tolerated, with the MPD taking over jurisdiction from the Zeta Army, did things really settle.

Ally's parents were one family which had been moved out of Zeta at the start of the wars, she was only three at the time, so her memories were clouded. She still had vague images of the house they had, a large building that had been built in the times before technology had surged.

Her parents were shot by the ZetaArmy when they had tried to return to collect some of their belongings at the house, her father was a proud man and he was determined to get through the checkpoint, but a trigger-happy soldier had other ideas.

She was taken in by an orphanage in the Underpass, who took on many refugees and orphaned children from the war. She had quickly learned to look after herself from the fights and disruption that came with the mixture of children all dealing with the trauma of losing their entire lives from the unrest. In time, she had got away from the orphanage and found work at a small cafe where she was looked after by the owners and became part of their family. Until one day the Gunners had shown up, demanding money from the cafe. They had told Ally to hide in the back when they arrived.

The Gunners were a splinter group who had

spun out of the Zeta Army, who had officially been disbanded during agreements to restore the peace. Unofficially however, they had continued as an army for hire to anyone who could pay well.

The cafe's owner ran into the back to find her, he had transferred a large amount of credits into her account and told her she needed to get away fast and not to come back. At first, she refused but when an explosion at the front of the cafe erupted, she ran and kept running until she found herself on the Boulevard, after hiding in one of the access tunnels.

Ending up in the GigaCity area, she got work in several bars, enough to maintain the modest apartment she had been in. She had trained to fight, as she never wanted to feel so helpless again.

Now she was heading back to the Underpass, she hoped that the cafe owner was still alive, but she had never returned because of the promise she made. She felt she had nowhere else to turn to now; the people chasing her knew where she lived and she had no idea why they were still chasing her. She hoped that her adoptive father would take her in.

She reached the last few steps of the tunnel and was greeted with a large metal door which had the words 'Underpass Only, No Entry for

Boulevards', which she pushed open. It creaked from lack of use.

Outside, she took a deep breath, the air in the Underpass differed from the Boulevard, where air filtration systems gave it a neutral smell. Here, a mixture of concrete and damp were the initial smells, though underneath there were more complex smells that arose from the mixture of cultures that inhabited the area.

She knew where she was heading, while she hadn't been back for a long time, her memories of the area came flooding back.

"Quartz, you hear me yet?" She asked, on the off chance a signal would come through.

No reply, she had thought as much, whilst Julian had an impressive set up she didn't think he'd have transmission gear that could reach as far as the Underpass.

She smiled at the locals she passed, they all gave her a wide berth. Her clothing and style was more akin to the Boulevard now, whilst nothing elaborate, it stood out more in the more ragtag styles of the Underpass.

As she approached the building she was heading to, she could see smoke billowing out of several windows. Memories of the cafe she had ran from flooded her mind, but this time she ran towards the smoke. A large hole in the wall seemed to be the closest entry, she made her way through the rubble which scattered the floor.

Further down, she could see two bodies laying on the floor, blood pooling under them but still fresh. She slowed her pace and pulled out her staff, extending it ready for attack.

The smoke swirled around her as she moved closer to the room at the end of the corridor; she heard a movement making her pause.

"Who goes there? Friend or Foe?" A voice shouted out from the smoke.

Ally relaxed her pose, putting her hands up in a surrender as she emerged into the room.

"Hey, how's it going Pops?" She smiled as she spoke.

From inside the room, Razz stepped forwards, a moment's hesitation while the recognition sank in. Then he dived forwards and hugged the girl he had raised as his own so many years before.

CHAPTER 28

Jacob

Jacob had got the body of Julian down to the lab where Owens was still working.

"I hope you are on schedule with the dispersal system," he said as he approached. Owens didn't look up from the monitor.

"As much as I can be, I'd be able to work much faster if I had a connection to my research at HQ," he replied.

"I'm sure you would but that's a factor I can't risk Owens, you know that," Jacob smiled. "I do have a gift, however," he motioned to Julian who he had placed on the table.

Owen's looked up in shock.

"Who is that?"

"A young man who had been meddling, trying to find out what happened to you it seems, but that's beside the point. He has many augmentations and implants that I believe him to be a wonderful subject zero for the dispersal system."

"I see," Owens was running a bioscan of the body already using the tables internal scanners. "You're right he does, with his systems connected, he would be able to spread the poison to almost ninety percent of the boulevard within minutes."

"Not poison, elixir," Jacob corrected.

"Sure Jacob, sure," the defeat was audible.

"Don't be so downhearted Owens, this is what you always wanted, a way to reach the whole population and have an influence on their lives," Jacob said.

Owens just nodded and continued his work.

"I shall return soon, I need that code complete and ready for testing within the day," Jacob turned to leave. "I'm counting on you."

Owens waited until Jacob had left, the door closing and locking behind him, before letting out a long and heavy sigh. He couldn't help but continue to work.

Jacob had returned to the church in time to see the arrival of Mr Tombs.

"I assume you have returned as you have located the clone and wanted to tell me the good news in person?" Jacob said, sarcasm dripping.

"I'm afraid not Father, we traced him to Razz's radio station, but he got away again. We believe the Razz has assisted him in getting them away."

"That damned hippy. I should have killed him years ago," he took a breath and composed himself. "Do we know where he may have gone?"

"Unsure at the moment, we've got people searching the area in a sweep to try to get a lead," Tombs replied.

"I feel we may have underestimated this one, it may take a more direct approach in order for us to find him. Be ready to leave in five minutes."

"Where are we heading?"

"To the beginning," Jacob replied. "We will need the original."

Tombs nodded and left to arrange the transport. Jacob walked to his office and opened a safe which lay in the wall. Inside, he pulled out a key, long and metallic, it was the kind that could have been used decades ago in large ornate doorways. Attached to the key was a long thread which Jacob used to put the key around his neck, hiding it under his shirt and out of view.

He exited the church where Tombs was waiting in a car. Tombs would have to drive as the autocabs didn't venture out as far as they would be going.

"Are you ready sir?" He asked as Jacob entered.

"Yes, let us waste no time, things are in motion which cannot be stopped, and this needs to be sorted to avoid interruption," Jacob replied, and the car pulled away.

The journey wouldn't take long but it would take them to the outskirts of BitVillage, just beyond the main border and close to the barren lands which lay past them. No one ventured into the barren lands anymore, the radiation was too high for anyone to survive for long, even with specialised equipment.

The houses became more and more sparse until all that was around them was the occasional shack. The residents were people who had succumbed to radiation poisoning and their descendants, as such they had various biological defects. The roads became smaller and soon only dirt roads, a sparse landscape surrounding them. A low mist clung to the ground, hiding the dead vegetation which refused to grow.

Jacobs and Tombs hadn't been out this far since they began the work at the church, when Jacobs needed test subjects for the initial versions of the elixir.

They pulled up to a shack just before the danger zone of radiation. It stood alone and abandoned from the others, a green-hued mist filled the air, an aftereffect of the radiation seeping into the world. There wasn't anyone about but they couldn't help but feel they were being watched from somewhere.

Tombs opened the door to the shack and stepped in first, followed by Jacob. Inside there was little of notice, a few wooden floorboards and an old decaying table was all the room offered. As far as any of the locals would see ,it was abandoned. On the far wall however, a small hole at chest level was slightly out of place, Jacob headed towards it.

He pulled the key from under his shirt and inserted it, one turn and a click echoed in the room. The wall shifted and fell inwards as a hidden door opened, revealing a staircase heading down.

Until now, neither man had spoke, the silence of the place was claustrophobic, oppressing, any sounds felt like an insult to the surrounding air. Jacob spoke in a hushed tone when he turned to Tombs.

"Wait here, I won't be long."

He began his descent until he arrived at a large glass window, inside was a bed, a bathroom and a desk. Laying on the prisons bed was a man, whilst not unhealthy, he had the look of someone who hadn't eaten a decent meal for a long time.

"Hello Peter," Jacob said.

It took a moment before the man raised his head, looking around him as if he was trying to see if the voice was from a real person or someone in his mind again.

"I'm here Peter, it's Jacob," his voice soft.

"Why?" Was all Peter could say.

"I, need something from you Peter," Jacob spoke as if talking to a child.

"No, no more. You've had everything from me," Peter got angry.

"I know, you have given so much already Peter, but this is the last thing I will need from you."

"Then I can be free?" Peter asked, half mocking as he doubted this to be the case.

"I can promise you freedom Peter, freedom

from this prison," Jacob said, looking around the room. He saw the tubes which Peter had to inject into himself to receive sustenance via automated dispensers which were hooked up to another shack.

"You left me here to die Jacob, why should I help you?"

"You know why I had to do it Peter, your mind was becoming too unstable to keep you safe."

"My mind which you sabotaged," Peter banged his fists on the glass, glaring at Jacob.

"I know Peter, and I'm so sorry for all that has happened. This isn't what I wanted," Jacob got closer to the glass.

"When we started the process, we thought we would revolutionize the world."

"My mind, sometimes I still get fragments seeping through."

"They could be fragments, perhaps small memories of before."

"No, they're new, I know it."

"Well, that's why I'm here, I need you to connect again Peter, we need to trace one."

"Which?" Peter said.

"The first, Prime. He's escaped and I worry he might be starting to lose control."

"Prime? He's lasted this long?" Peter's eyes widened.

"Yes Peter, you remember him don't you? The first we created, after we cut your mind out of the loop, he continued to function perfectly. He took to the new artificial controller without a hitch. But now it seems that there is something wrong, and he continued to keep memories. He must have felt so lost and afraid, he ran, and we are worried he may have killed."

"Like I did, perhaps he is becoming like me. If the underlying personalities are still there, buried inside, he could be just like me!"

"Exactly my worries Peter, which is why I need you to connect again, regain the control and find him before it's too late."

Peter had stood up and was pacing the room, his mind had kicked back into gear after being stagnated in the cell.

"We need to find him, if he has even half of my psyche then he could be extremely dangerous out there."

"Excellent, I knew you'd understand Peter. If you are ready, we'll get you out of here and back to the facility."

Peter nodded.

CHAPTER 29

Julian

Julian woke, his internal immune systems had processed the sedative Jacob had injected.

"Where the hell?" He said as he focused on the ceiling above him, it was all stone with a large light centred above him.

"Ah hello," a voice came from across the room. "Glad to see you're awake."

Julian moved his head to the side, his limbs were still stiff. He saw a man working at a computer.

"Who are you?" Julian asked, testing his legs.

"Good question, it's complicated," Owens said, walking over to help Julian stand. "But I'm as much a prisoner here as you are before you think I'm your captor."

"Jacob," Julian said,

"Yes, now he is your captor, and mine."

"Why?" Julian asked.

"Why you? Well, he wants me to test a new dispersal method of anti-technology toxin on you and if it's successful, to use your implanted connections, which we'll bypass in the toxin injection, to increase the dispersal into the airwaves so it can reach maximum population density. And why me, because I can use the biological sequencing which he had developed into the toxin and recreate the same effects in a digital code which will infiltrate anyone with tech that has been synced with their biology, which, lets face it, is pretty much everyone."

Julian just stared at Owens.

"I'm sorry, I've been cooped up in here a while now and I hate not being able to talk."

"And who are you?"

"Like I said, it's complicated, but in here," he tapped his head, "I am Maxwell Owens, but I have no idea whose body this is."

"Maxwell Owens? Of CyBio?" Julian asked.

"Yes, that's right," Owens smiled at being recognised.

"But you're dead? I was tracking down your body."

"Ah yes, that's the complicated part. Jacob, I think, killed me, but saved my mind and put it inside a cloned body to force me to work on this code for him." Owens was surprised how simple it sounded when he said it out loud.

"Right..." Julian was processing the information.

"I think that brings us up to speed here," Owens said.

"Wait wait," Julian was just catching up. "What does this code do?"

"Oh, see it forces the body's immune system to reject all forms of foreign body, such as implants and the like."

"Shit, that's... powerful," Julian couldn't describe it any other way.

"It is, and dangerous. This will bring the whole population back decades of evolution," Owens agreed. "Which is why I'm trying really hard to find a loophole I can exploit in this so Jacob won't win. If I don't create the code, he'll destroy any hope I have of getting my body back. Well, a clone of my own body at least."

Julian rubbed his eyes with his hands as he listened.

"Have you tried to communicate with anyone?"

"Of course, but this place is completely locked down for all signals. He must use the same dampeners we had at CyBio to prevent external attacks on our systems."

"That's what Yuri must have had in the car," Julian said to himself.

"Yuri? You spoke to him?" Owens grabbed Julian's shoulders.

"Sure, he kidnapped me to ask for help to find your body."

"Really?!"

"Why is that surprising?" Julian asked.

Owens walked away from Julian and paced the room.

"Yuri wouldn't normally leave the office unless something was seriously wrong. I guess he has been alone since my death."

"What do you mean?"

"Yuri is our resident AI at CyBio, that's what makes him such a great P.R. Man, he can see trends in data and analyze them at speeds no human ever could. We gave him a body so he could literally interface with people and be the face of the company, but he never existed outside of the main servers."

"Wait, so the guy who kidnapped me was, what, a robot?"

"Kind of, we call them synthetics, there were only a couple we had made so far, Yuri and Ava. Yuri was the first AI integration synthetic whereas Ava we had implanted memories from my deceased wife."

Julian had only just got used to the idea of Owens being inside a cloned body's. Now he had to imagine the possibility of AI controlled synthetics,

"Quartzig, man I wish he could hear this," Julian said.

"Who?"

"My AI, Quartzig, I developed him myself, he'd love to have his own body."

"Well, unless we can stop Jacob, there will be little Bio-Tech integration anywhere. What did Yuri tell you?"

"Not much, he gave me all the details of your death and the movements of your body which I traced to here. Other than that, he told me about the upcoming conference for the nanotech reveal. Oh, and he gave me this," Julian pulled the metal cube from his pocket and handed it over to Owens.

"Oh, my god!" Owens shouted as he looked at the cube.

"What is it?"

"Something that will come in very handy right now," Owens tapped various sides of the cube until it hissed and expanded. "This, Julian, is one of our NanoCubes, the initial set which are needed to integrate the new technology."

"The nanotech?"

"Exactly, Yuri told you about the reveal at the conference right?"

"Some details," Julian decided it wasn't best to say he'd been investigating the conference through some drunk employees.

"This dose of nanotechnology will allow the CyBio database to integrate with your body and in doing so, it can create augmentations programmed wirelessly without the need of direct contact. Let's say you lost a finger in an accident, we can send a signal to the nanobots in your blood stream to replicate and create a new finger in place of the old."

"That's incredible," Julian exclaimed.

"It is, and this little cube is all you need to

get it started."

"How can that help us now?" Julian asked.

"Well, I might just be able to get this to work if I'm fast enough. The toxin is based on targeting the implants that are connected directly to the biological systems, they will bypass the nanobots as they are dormant until they receive a signal from the HQ. In theory, they will be left alone, if we could program them to purge the bloodstream of the toxins *before* integrating, we could erase the toxins from the body that has been infected."

"In theory?"

"Yes, I mean, until it's tested there's no guarantee."

"And the person who is being injected will have to have all their augmentations removed by the toxin until the nanobots can connect to HQ?"

"Yes, that is also true."

"And you're thinking I will have to be that person aren't you?" Julian was catching up to Owen's plan.

"Yes, I'm afraid so, it's the only way I think we can get out of here. On the plus side, the procedures will remove all traces of the T-Pox

I can see forming in your blood stream," Owens said, as he scanned the results on his monitor.

Julian sat back down on the table, his mind spinning.

"Will it hurt?"

"I'm not sure, maybe?" Owens lied.

"You better get started then," Julian closed his eyes and sighed.

CHAPTER 30

Xander

Xander had been following the woman for the last three cycles of the construct and his patience was wearing thin. Each time he got closer to her, she vanished and appeared further away, this repeated each scene until he restarted at the courthouse steps once again. She was the only anomaly in the entire construct and he knew he had to find the reason she was there.

He walked slowly now towards her on the steps and watched as she looked at him.

"Come on Ava, you've got to give me something to work on here, what do I need to do?" He shouted out, but even now, as he got closer, she disappeared as he got close.

He was back in the office, looking at the answerphone.

He stabbed the play button as he always did and let the messages play.

"Erm..hello? Is this Alex Draven? I want to hire you to show my husband who is really in char.."

"Angry Wife, nope," Xander said as he hit the next button.

Message Deleted

"Hi Mr Draven, we need security for the fight late…"

"Security, nope,"

Message Deleted

"Listen to me, it's important ok. You want some escape then this is how you do it…"

His hand paused above the delete button, he'd assumed it was just a call from the escort agencies. He let the message play;

"You need to find the television in Donovans apartment, turn it on and we can talk properly. Hurry Xander, we need to get out of here before it's too late!"

Xander was stunned, he realised it was Ava's voice; she was talking to him like she knew him already, but at the time he listened to the answer phone, they hadn't met.

He snapped out of the thoughts and cycled through the construct to Donovan's apartment,

Donovan was in the wheelchair in front of the television watching the old movie as Xander made his way over, looking at the television now rather than Donovan.

Xan...der?" Donovan struggled to let the words out.

This time, Donovan's words were said in time with a woman on the screen, he turned the volume up and the sentence continued as if in sync with Donovan's words.

"Xander, it's me Ava, you need to listen carefully, your brain is trapped but not gone."

"Brain... gone..." echoed Donovan from his seat.

"Your mind is still inside, and I'm still locked in with you," the on-screen Ava continued, "I need to connect with CyBio but I can't without your help."

"Mind. Lock. Cybio," Donovan stuttered out.

"You need to get to a radio, within the construct. I'm still linked to the network and can transmit to a particular wavelength. A radio within the construct will have a two-way signal so it can update the date files within it.

I can't send anything from my mind as it's in sync with yours, if I try to disconnect in order to send an external signal, it will wipe your mind in the process. If I can connect back to CyBio, then I can attempt to remove the lock remotely. Donovan has been compromised by Yuri, he's developed a nanotechnology that can take over people! He's the one that did this. Watch out for the Nurse!"

"N...Nurse," Donovan blurted out, moments before a knife flew past Xander's head and stuck into the centre of the television screen behind him.

Xander looked up to see the nurse posed in a fighting position, the blade was loading itself along her forearm until its point was just at her wrist. He dived behind the sofa as he had before and crawled along as several more blades impaled the wall behind him.

Xander tried to piece together the information she had given him, Ava said Yuri was behind the whole thing, Yuri had been Owens colleague at CyBio, but did that mean he'd killed Owens? That made little sense, he could have just mind locked him. Regardless, if what Ava said was true, then he needed to get out and warn someone about the nanotechnology.

Xander had to find a radio, and he thought of the best place to find one, cycling round once more, he was back at the police headquarters, talking to Mike at the desk.

"Hey Mike, I need a radio."

The constructed Mike continued to replay the scene as it always had, not noticing Xander's change in script.

He stepped round the desk and grabbed a walkie talkie which was lying on the table.

I hope you're right about this. He thought as he turned the radio on, hoping he wasn't just getting more crazy.

Putting the radio to his mouth, he began to talk.

"My name is Xander Draven, if you can hear this I need your help, I am at 91 Somerset Close. I'm trapped inside a construct and need help. Please, if you are listening to this. It's vital you get here, there may be others that need our help. Trust no one from CyBio."

He put the radio down, setting the signal to repeat at one-minute intervals. He hoped that the signal would get out, and that someone on their side would receive the message.

It felt like hours before Xander heard a noise; it seemed to come from all around him, quiet at first, then building to a crescendo which deafened him. It was a low rumble like thunder which never ended, as it got louder he covered his ears as the pain was debilitating.

He closed his eyes to the pain, then it stopped. Completely. As the sound echoed in his ears, he felt the feeling of a bed underneath him; he opened his eyes and found he was back in Donovan's apartment.

"Welcome Back Xander," Ava's voice chimed. "There's no time to waste though, we need to get moving."

He looked up and saw several people he didn't recognise in the room, then he looked at Ava.

"How long was I in there?"

"Three months I'm afraid, and we are nearly out of time," a voice spoke.

Xander felt his face, and the beard that had grown in the time he'd been in the construct.

"Can I at least shave first? And does anyone have a cigarette?"

CHAPTER 31

Yuri

Yuri had been bidding his time. The nanos he had created were ready for field testing.

He had ventured to the Underpass to find somewhere he could test the newest models without risk of much exposure. The shielding caused by the brickwork of the Boulevard was enough to ensure that no signals access the nanos.

As he walked into the Nexus, he could see several Hunters whom had been searching for one of Jacob's clones. He'd kept tabs on Jacob in case he became an issue. Recent events had caused Yuri to set plans in motion, in preparation for Jacobs upcoming plans.

He continued into the Nexus until he could hear what he needed, the sounds of a large crowd. Approaching the source of the sounds, he discovered a gathering of people circling a lone performer in one of the Nexus' many courtyards.

The performer was standing on a large box, a flaming torch in his hand.

"Ladies and Gentlemen, please stand back if you value your skins!" He grinned as he gestured the torch in wide arcs around him, forcing several of the spectators to step back until there was an even space around him. Wearing nothing but torn jeans and a synthetic sheepskin vest, he grinned at the audience once more.

Yuri moved closer, observing the event as it unfolded. This crowd would be wonderful test subjects he thought, as he pulled a small cube out of his suit pocket. The performer continued to energise the crowd, before raising the flaming torch above his head.

"Fire! The original sin of man, stolen from the Gods and used to advance us into the new age. Violent and uncontrollable! It engulfs and destroys all it touches."

Yuri smiled at the parallels, he felt he was the new fire, ready to engulf humanity. He stood in the midst of the crowd and crushed the cube in his hand, a small electric charge bursting from his palm, activating the nanos. The pile in his hand looked like small grains of sand as he opened his palm and threw them into the air. He'd timed it as the performer sprayed the air with chemicals from his mouth. As the chemicals flew into the air, they caught the flames, a cone of fire exploding in the sky several feet ahead. The onlookers watched in awe, looking up into the sky as the fire danced around them. Hidden in the smoke and flame, the nanos fell amongst them, into their eyes and mouths. The individual specs so small, the spectators didn't even notice as they flooded into their systems, infusing into their bloodstream. They attached to cells, rewriting and duplicating as they went until they had full control of the body. Black veins rose in the skin of those infected, before returning to normal as the nanos took control. There were no screams, instead the whole crowd who had been cheering and laughing, suddenly went silent as the assimilation completed. All but the performer in the center who had avoided infection.

Yuri took a moment to adjust to the increase in connections which now flowed through him. Once done, he turned his attention to the performer who was now standing in fear.

"Congratulations, you are witness to the beginnings of a new age," the crowd all spoke as one.

They moved forward, the circle around the

performer shrinking with every step. Then, in complete silence the crowd lurched forward and engulfed the man. The first to reach him hold him down, while the next held up a hand which dispensed several specs of sand. As the man gasped for breath he inhaled the specs into his lungs.

Within moments, the performer was now one of the crowd, one of Yuri's nanocopies. Identical in appearance to the original, but comprised completely of nano bots at Yuri's command.

CHAPTER 32

Mollie

Mollie had dragged Prime into an abandoned electric shop near where he had collapsed. He had stopped talking for the moment, unconscious. She made him as comfortable as she could, wrapping JJ's long coat around him for warmth.

She had no idea why she was still helping him, after she had sold him to Koenig, she should have just left him, but she found herself caring more than she expected for the lost clone. She pulled out the revolver which she had got from Razz, before leaving and settling down in a position facing the door, ready for anything that might come through. For the first time since the market, she remembered JJ, and the fact he was gone.

They'd worked together as scavengers for several years, ever since JJ had found Mollie looking for food in a dumpster behind the old cafe Razz owned, before the Gunners had destroyed it. She'd been going there for food for weeks, she'd even made friends with the girl who lived there who had started to deliberately leave food for her out the back of the cafe. Mollie couldn't remember much from before then, all she knew was that she had been on the streets, living with different people growing up. Perhaps that's why she felt sympathy for Prime, as it seemed he had no knowledge of his own past, other than what Razz had told him.

JJ had taken her in and taught her what was worth scavenging and what wasn't and where the best buyers were for which items. Before long, they had become a formidable team, always being the first hired for tracking specific items from several vendors. He'd also introduced her to Vladamir, who had changed her life forever.

Mollie had never asked JJ where he was from or how he ended up where he was. It was an unspoken rule amongst most of those in the Nexus area, that what had come before didn't matter, only where you were now and what you did now. She wished she had learnt more about him now though, perhaps there was family she should tell of his death. He had been like a father to her, and she was forever grateful to him. She said a silent goodbye to him and returned her focus to the present.

Reilly was still unconscious but had started

to talk once again, the voices still sporadic and disjointed. He picked up certain phrases such as the local news waves and traffic updates. One however, kept recurring, and made her take notice. She found a pen and paper from one of the shelves in the shop and wrote down the various snippets she heard which seemed to be from the same signal.

My name is Xander Draven.
if you can hear this I need your help.
I am at 91 Somerset Close.
I'm trapped inside a construct.
and need help. Please if.
you are listening to this.
It's vital you get here.
there may be others that need our help.
Trust no one from Cybio.

She read it back. She wasn't sure who Xander Draven was, or what a construct was, or even where Somerset Close was, but she felt curious.

Nothing was going to happen until Reilly woke up however, she tried to wake him but there was nothing she could do. Settling back down, she drifted half to sleep, realizing how tired she was.

A scream from Prime shocked Mollie into waking, as he sat up suddenly.

"Woah there!" Mollie shouted, as she jumped at the movement, her gun trained on him.

"Sorry," he said, shaking his head.

"OK, just calm down," Mollie walked over to him and helped him to his feet. "You remember anything? You've been jabbering all night."

"Not much, snippets of news reports. And some guy in a police station asking for help."

"Xander?"

"You know him?"

"Just from what you've been saying," she showed him the paper with the message on.

"CyBio?" Reilly asked as he read the message. He pulled out the coin Razz had given him earlier, passing it to Mollie to look at.

"Do you think he knows who you are?" Mollie asked as she looked it over.

"I don't know, but it could be a start, and where else are we going to go? We need to stay on the move."

"I guess, any idea where Somerset Close is?"

"Nope, but I'm sure we can find out," Pulling out an old external PDA unit she had kept on her arm, she tried to boot it up.

"We should be able to get a map up on this as long as I can connect, I don't use this much."

After a few moments the PDA booted up, she brought up its holographic interface and searched for the location.

"It's on the Boulevard, we'll have to get up there," she said hesitantly, she'd never been on the Boulevard before.

"Let's get moving then," Reilly said getting to his feet. "How do we get up there?" He asked.

Mollie thought for a moment before coming up with an idea.

"There's someone who might be able to help us, he owes me," Mollie said as she tapped new coordinates into the PDA. "Vladamir Groteski, he runs the black market shipping for the Nexus."

"Sounds delightful." Reilly replied.

"He's not as bad as he sounds. I know he imports from the Boulevard, he has several access points that are unmonitored."

"Let's get going," he said, "Oh, and one more thing, I think my name is Prime," the conversation he'd had with Razz and his dreams had stuck in his mind.

"Prime? I like it," Mollie said, as they got up and made their way out of the building and headed out.

They had successfully avoided any more Hunters on the short walk and were now approaching an unmarked building several blocks from the Nexus market. From the outside, it had black walls which looked as though they had been burnt and seemed to merge with the black windows that adorned its facade.

"Let me do the talking, we don't want him to think you have any value he could use," Mollie said, as they crossed the threshold into the building. There was no-one manning the black wooden door which creaked as she pushed it open.

"I hope you aren't about to sell me out again," Prime said, only slightly sarcastically.

"I said I'm sorry ok!" Mollie said as they walked into a long hallway, the burn marks continued along its walls.

A large man in a black suit stepped out of nowhere to block their path.

"Please leave," the man had a thick Russian accent.

"We're here to see Vladamir, I'm here to

collect on my favour," Mollie said, holding her ground.

"One moment," the man spoke silently, a vocal sensor in his throat picking up the smallest vibrations of his vocal chords and passing the information on.

"Ok, continue," the man stepped aside, disappearing through a door to the left of them.

"Are you sure about this?" Prime said, as they continued.

"Sure, Vlad...owes me."

The path ended at a door which was solid metal with no distinguishing marks. Mollie knocked on it and they waited.

A moment later, the door swung open, revealing a large open space full of shelving, each one full of vinyl records. In the center, a large armchair had its back to them, plumes of cigar smoke filled the air above. The sound of music hit them as hard as the smell of the smoke.

"Albert King, Born Under a Bad Sign," a Russian voice shouted out over the chime of guitars, "a classic."

A man rose from the chair and like the sun coming over the horizon, he seemed to dominate the room. He turned to look at the pair, a cigar still in his mouth. He wore a rich, red dressing gown which held flecks of cigar ash.

"Mollie! How nice to see you, my dear," he nodded his head in a slight bow. "And who is this?"

"His name is Prime. We need your help, I want to cash in the favour," Mollie said, skipping over Prime's identity.

"Ah yes, a debt shall always be repaid, but are you sure you want to?" Vladamir replied, walking over to them. His eyes burning into Prime, trying to read information from him.

"I'm sure, we need to get to the Boulevard," Mollie interrupted his gaze by stepping forward.

"Ah, I see," Vladamir said, smiling as he shifted focus to Mollie, "This is no problem, I have an access lift not far from here. I will get Jono to get you a one time access keycard," he turned and pressed a button on his arm.

"Jono, please prepare an OTA keycard immediately. Mollie will pick it up on departure," he spoke as if Jono was in the room, unlike many, who would hold the PDA to their mouth when speaking.

"Thank you, Vlad," Mollie said.

"No thanks needed, the books are now balanced," the response hiding subtle menace as he picked up a goblet from the small table next to the chair, raising it to his lips and drank heavily.

"Understood, let's go Prime," Mollie grabbed his arm to hurry them out.

As they left the room, Vladamir took a deep pull on the cigar and blew the smoke as he spoke.

"See you soon Mollie."

Once they were out of the room, Prime turned to Mollie.

"What was that about?"

"Vladamir sort of runs his business on a barter system, if he owes you a favor then you're fine, but once the books are balanced then you are no longer protected."

"Why would you need his protection?" Prime asked, suddenly realising he didn't know all that much about Mollie.

"A story for another time," Mollie said, as they reached the guard they had met on their way in.

"Here," the man, who they assumed was

Jono, passed Mollie a keycard and some coord-inates.

"Thanks," she said, taking them.

They left the building and located the lift.

"This way, let's get out of here," Mollie said, leading the way.

CHAPTER 33

Prime

In silence, they made their way through the streets, keeping watch for any Hunters.

"Just up ahead," Mollie said, pointing with her gun.

A large cage lift was in front of them, large enough for several people and hardy enough to transport heavy goods. A protective mental fence surrounded it, the occasional spark flew from the metal, showing its electrical defences. Inside however, the platform wasn't there.

"Must be on the Boulevard," Mollie said.

They approached the lift and, using the key-card, Prime disabled the electric defence and called the lift down. The sound of hydraulics kicked into gear and they waited for the large cargo lift to descend. The sound of metal being struck caused them both to duck in shock. A second shot out just next to Mollie's head.

"Get to cover!" Prime shouted as they saw five Hunters appeared, from around a corner.

Prime looked around for a better location to hide, but as he did, he felt a surge of shock fill his brain.

"My turn," he said, his voice slightly lower in pitch and slower than his usual tempo.

"What?" Mollie asked, looking at him.

Prime jumped to his feet and grabbed the revolver from Mollie's hand, she didn't have time to react.

He ducked out from their cover and took a shot at the closest Hunter; who fell instantly as the shot landed perfectly between his helmet and body armour, piercing his uncovered throat and crumpled to the ground. The remaining four Hunters scattered to the sides, taking cover.

"Come on guys, it's only one against four now," Prime spun behind a low wall and checked the revolver, four bullets remained.

He strafed along the wall as he listened for the sounds of the Hunters movements; he was coming in line with one on the other side of the wall. In one smooth motion, he tapped on the wall to his left with the gun, before spinning to his right and making a quick step up on the wall. The Hunter's attention was towards the sound of the tap as Prime landed behind him. Before he could turn, Prime had placed his hands, one either side of his neck, and twisted. The crack echoed for a moment as Prime scanned the area for the three remaining Hunters, letting the body fall. Seeing one directly in front of him, he took aim and shot a bullet into his side, bypassing the bulletproof vest. The sound of sucking air indicated the bullet had hit a lung, and the Hunter fell to his knees as the blood filled his airways.

Mollie was watching in complete shock as Prime continued his massacre of the Hunters, she almost didn't notice the lift had arrived until the doors opened next to her. She looked back at Prime who was running towards another Hunter, who was desperately trying to help his fallen comrade by covering the hole in his side. Prime arrived and pulled his head back by the helmets visor and smashed the back of the revolver into his jaw, breaking it instantly.

"Prime!" She shouted, as she dove into the lift, the final Hunter also hearing her shout and making a B-Line for her rather than taking on Prime, who looked up and saw the movement.

Prime ran, his posture that of an athlete, full

speed towards the lift, Mollie and the Hunter. He had left Mollie unarmed by taking the revolver, if he could just run fast enough.

The Hunter raised his machine gun at Mollie who, standing in the lift, had no cover to hide behind. She saw Prime catching up behind, but he was too far away, and with no clean killshot he could take without risk of hitting Mollie.

She held her breath as the machine gun leveled, the sound of gunfire, the Hunter fell to the ground in front of her, his ankle had exploded in a mist of blood as Prime had shot him in the only place he safely could. The Hunter was lying on the floor screaming in pain as Prime arrived, lifting a boot, he thrust it into the Hunters head, a pool of blood and bone was all that remained.

Mollie eyed him nervously as he entered the lift and punched the button to send it on its way.

"Hey Moll, nice to meet you. See you soon," he leaned against the wall and closed his eyes. Mollie could see the muscles on his face relax, and when he opened his eyes, he looked calmer, softer even.

"Mollie? How'd we get here?" He asked, his voice back to its regular timbre.

"You don't remember?"

"I remember we were ducking away from the Hunters and then..." Prime paused, he could see fragments, snapshots of the fight that had just happened, almost as if he was just a passenger in his own body.

"Peter?" He said.

"Who's Peter?" Mollie asked, motioning to take the gun from him.

"I'm...not sure..." He passed the gun back to Mollie. "I think he's a part of me."

Before they could continue the conversation, the lift stopped, and the doors opened onto the Boulevard. Mollie turned and looked out at the glowing neon which flooded her vision.

The lift had come out just off the main Boulevard; it was used predominately for transport of goods to and from several of the retailers in the area.

They stepped out and into clean and clinical world, which contrasted the Underpass completely.

"Which way?" Prime asked, once they had took in sights.

It took Mollie a little while longer to adjust to their new locations, eventually she stopped and checked the PDA.

"This way, a few blocks down," she led the way.

The journey went with no more issues, other than Mollie stopping to admire several shop fronts and their wares. She couldn't help but be taken in by the style and glamour of the Boulevards tech, compared to the low tech of the Underpass.

"We'll come back once all this is over," Prime said, pulling her away from the windows.

They arrived at the apartment block and made their way to number 91; the door was locked but Mollie gave it a kick and the lock splintered.

"Let's see what we have," Mollie said.

Inside, the remnants of a fight were obvious, a smashed tv and holes in the walls.

"What happened here?" Mollie whispered.

"Get in here Mollie," Prime shouted, as he entered the bedroom and saw a man laying on the bed and a woman connected to him via a half damaged wire.

Mollie and Prime glanced at each other, not knowing what to do.

"If you would be so kind as to attach that PDA unit to my cerebral core it would be much appreciated," Ava said, her eyes opening and looking directly at them.

CHAPTER 34

Ally

Ally sat at the table opposite Razz, the debris of the attack still scattered around them. He had made them both some coffee, and they sat in silence for several minutes, just accepting the situation before either of them spoke.

"It's good to see you Al, it's been so long," Razz broke the silence first.

"It has, but only because you told me not to come back," she replied, unable to hide the slight resentment in her tone. Razz lowered his eyes to the ground, sadness overcoming him.

"It was for your own good Al, I had to say that, couldn't risk you coming back you know?"

"What does that mean? Why would it be a risk?"

"There's so many things I need to tell you, things I should have told you long ago but I was too afraid," Razz started into his cup, remembering the secrets they had forced him to keep.

"Tell me what Razz? Come on, I've been attacked twice in the same day already!"

"Attacked? By who?" Razz looked up, suddenly alert.

"I don't know, some Sliders for all I know."

Razz put his hands on Ally's, looking her straight in the eye.

"Tell me, were they Sliders or someone else? It's very important."

"I don't know, they had suits, didn't look like any Sliders I've seen."

"Damit," Razz slammed a fist on the table, "I thought they'd have lost interest. Stupid! I should have been more careful."

"Razz, tell me what the hell is going on!"

Razz sighed, then took a deep breath.

"It was your parents Al, they gave you to me, told me to keep you safe and away from the company. Of course back then they were only small fry, but they had connections."

"My parents? You knew them? I thought you adopted me from the orphanage," Ally looked puzzled.

"I did. Your birth name was Alison Henshaw, we changed it to Ally Sinclair after you got to the orphanage, to help keep you hidden. I knew you were there but had to wait some time before I could take you in. Had to, so it wasn't traceable back to your parents. But I'm getting too far ahead of myself. Let me start from the beginning."

Razz took a long drink from the cup and leaned back, digging his mind for the memories.

"Y'see, when you were younger, your parents were working for a large corporation, at the time it was called Cyber Bionics, but you'd probably know them more as CyBio. They worked directly under Jacob and Owens, the co-founders. I was their neighbour and colleague in the Zeta district way back before the riots."

Already Ally was in shock trying to understand all Razz was telling her, but the floodgates had been opened and she couldn't stop now.

"Your parents couldn't conceive, so Jacobs and Owens offered them the opportunity to be part of their tests in genetics. They created you by using the genetics from your parents, though there was much kept from them about the procedure and what they were doing. Once you were born in the laboratory, Jacob and Owens continued to experiment on you, against your parents' wishes, so they tried to take you back and away from the company. Jacob and Owens were not about to let them steal you, their prize experiment, so they sent a crew to take you back. Knowing this, your parents planned to hide you for protection. Before they got you away, Jacob and Owens completed the next stage of their work. Using your genetics they created another, a brother would be the best explanation, by altering certain genetic markers in your DNA."

Ally couldn't believe what she was hearing.

"How old?" Ally asked quietly.

"I think you were about three at the time," he said. "I can't tell you what they did to him in there but I do know that he became slightly unstable, and the work they did on him is what caused the Jacob and Owens to part ways. Owens disagreed with the work and wanted nothing to do with Jacob, so they forced him out of the company. Around this time was when CyBio tried to tie up loose ends, which included your family. Everyone that was connected to the experiments was paid off or taken off the board if you catch me."

"CyBio murdered my parents?"

"'fraid so Al, I'm sorry. Just before they were killed, they contacted me and told me everything. They wanted you to be safe, so they sent you up to the orphanage with no paperwork or information, just before the CyBio's agents found them. Of course they made it look like the work of the Zeta Army, which was convenient at the time, and maintained their image. They never found you though, despite their attempts. Having connections to your family, I was constantly under investigation for several years. It was only when I felt it was safe to do so I adopted you as per your parent's request."

"And when the cafe was attacked?"

"Bingo, they had been given a tip off from someone that you were hiding with me, they came guns blazing and I needed you to get as far away as possible, to not come back as I knew that someone was ratting on me and I couldn't risk them finding you."

"What about my brother?" Ally asked.

"He did some pretty bad things in his time afterwards. He had grown attached to Jacob, and they worked together for quite some time, he became somewhat of an apprentice to Jacob. Did many bad things, murders some say, but it seems that he vanished a couple of years or so ago."

Ally sunk into the chair and covered her face with her hands, it was as if her whole life was a lie. She could hardly keep all the pieces together in her mind.

"And now it seems they found you somehow, though I don't know how. I'm sorry Al, I did everything I could to protect you."

"You did more than enough Razz, you kept me alive all these years," Ally walked over and hugged him. "But it's too late for anything else now. I need to fight back, I need to face this."

"What do you plan on doing?" Razz asked, wiping a tear from his eye.

"What was my brother's name? If he's out there, I need to find him."

"Peter, his name was Peter Henshaw."

CHAPTER 35

Peter

Since leaving the shack, Peter had felt the connections take hold, the device in his brain had reconnected to the main server as they got closer to the main population of Metropolis.

The signal strength increasing, he was starting to get incoming signals from all the clones. The main ones being at the Grand Falls Hotel.

He still couldn't fully trace Prime though. There were only snippets of the signal coming through, and not enough to make a location confirmation. He'd managed to send a message through however. Hopefully it had reached him and, ideally, triggered the sleeper program. The program was inside the cerebral cortex of all his clones and it allowed a virus to take hold and replace the current conscious with a copy of his own. If it had triggered, it would be only a matter of time before Prime was rewritten and the body would find its way back to the hub.

Peter was sat in the back of the car and was staring out the window as he listened to the sound of wheels. He had been in the hole for too long, his mind becoming more and more lost in its own self.

He recalled the first time he had met Jacob, back with Cyber Bionics. He was only four or five. Sat in a waiting room, he was called in and Jacob and Owens had explained to him what would happen, the tests made on his mental pathways. Owens was the friendly, welcoming, half of them. Jacob, on the other hand, saw him as nothing more than a part of the experiments, a lab rat to be tested on with no bias. Peter had always wanted to impress and make Jacob proud, almost despising the ease in which Owens treated him. The challenge was what mattered to him.

As the tests continued and Peter's mental facilities fluctuated from the constant wipes and reprogramming through to the initial cloning, Jacob slowly formed a bond with Peter. At first, simply in the psychological evaluations of his progress, Jacob became more involved with Peter's feelings and personality.

Then the day came when they successfully produced a perfect clone, one which stabilised further than the first incubation week and grew to a copy of Peter's exact genetic sequences, matching the age and development. Prime, they called him, and for Peter, being able to look at an exact match of himself, made his mind snap a little further than it ever had. The months that followed saw them create many more clones, varying some part of the genetic sequences in a small way to cause variations on the clones; hair colour, gender, height and vocal structure to name just a few. With each alteration, the personalities were affected too, individuals with their own lives.

The precautions put in place, a small cortex receiver in their brains, allowed Peter to access each of them if needed to regain control. This was created following the complete breakdown of a clone who had become more self aware of their situation and identity, causing them to lash out violently. It was then that Owens felt the work was becoming too unethical, that the clones were people who had their own rights and by neutering them with the Cortex Receivers, made them into slaves.

Jacob and Peter continued the work but with little income, they needed to fund the work in other ways, so they put the clones into a workforce. What better way to bring money in and also to test the durability of the clones than with manual labour. So they opened a small hotel where they could monitor the clones interactions with real people, whilst keeping them all enclosed. By recording the cortex from several hotel workers, they created templates for all the various job roles that would be required which they could program into any clone at the start of a shift. Mind wiping each clone every day was done to make sure there were no remnants to allow self awareness to trigger. The hotel had been a success and the credits it brought allowed them to continue their work.

What Jacob hadn't known of during this time was of Peter's developing aggressive tendencies brought on by a desire for knowledge. Peter had taken the minds of anyone whom he felt had a skill set he desired, utilising the equipment they had built, he stole skills of other people and assimilated it into his own. It had started innocently enough, taking the minds of scientist and engineers, whom he released afterwards, to help increase his skills in the work they did, but as the thirst for knowledge increased, he took more and more minds. One day, the patient he captured against their will was an unknown serial killer who worked as an engineer. The violence increased in Peter's mind following the integration and he started to have a need to take the lives of the people he used.

It was later that Peter was caught as a criminal, guilty of twenty murders of people who had no connections other than skills and knowledge Peter desired. Jacob had no choice but to allow justice to take its course, the MPD being in complete control of the investigation. Jacob found himself turning away from technology which had caused the problems, he prayed for help with Peter, knowing it was his own fault that Peter was the person he had become.

When Peter was released following a report of the corruption within the MPD, Jacob saw his prayers had been answered. The reporter, Julian Travitz, had saved his son and given them a second chance. However, Jacob still felt that technology had been the key to the downfall of Peter, that trying to play God by altering the minds of people, had been a sin against God's creations. He had thrown himself in the fight against technology.

As for Peter, the violent tendencies were still present, and the clones which he still had a connection to, were at risk of the thoughts seeping into them. They decided it was best for Peter to be taken away from the risk and locked away from the world. Peter, out of respect for Jacob who had helped him through the situation, agreed that it was a penance for his crimes and agreed to the terms.

Now he was free, the penance paid. He was returning to a world where he could continue his work. This time he would be better, he would work smarter. He no longer had a debt to pay to Jacob, but for now, he would bide his time, he would wait for the right time.

CHAPTER 36

Jacob

The journey had taken an hour, and they had returned to the church. Jacob was happy to have Peter at his side once more, the man whom he raised as his own. Tombs was waiting for Peter to join him in heading to the hotel.

"Where shall we begin?" Peter asked, itching to get back into the world.

"Soon, soon, first I have a surprise for you Peter," Jacob said, as they walked into the church. "Our catalyst for the rapture is the Saviour who allowed you your freedom."

Peter was admiring the decor of the church, it was still a run down mess when he had last been inside.

"Julian?" Peter said, his interest piqued. "He's willing to be part of the cause?" Peter was dubious, knowing that Julian was pretty much half computer with his augmentations.

"Oh, not quite, but we are being persuasive."

The two made their way down the steps to the lab underneath the church, Jacob unlocking the the door.

"Also, another old friend is here, though you may not recognise him," Jacob laughed to himself, deciding to let Peter discover who on his own.

The door opened, inside Julian was lying on the table in front of them, still conscious but only barely. Owens stood beside him, monitoring his vital signs.

"How is our patient?" Jacob asked, as they arrived.

"Stable, he's almost ready for the primary injection," Owens replied, not looking up from the console.

"We have a visitor, you may remember him," Jacob said, barely able to conceal his smile.

Owens looked up and saw Peter, the boy whom they experimented on throughout his early years. He'd always assumed that he had died following the trial, or that Jacob had mind wiped him.

"Peter?" He said, raising from his chair. "It is really you?"

"That's my name," Peter said. "Though I'm not sure I know you?" Peter scanned Owens' face.

"It's…" Owens remembered that the body he was in wasn't his. "It's Max, Maxwell Owens," He finally said.

Peter's eyes widened, scanning the man's face he didn't recognise, but the voice, it had the same tone that Owens used.

"Owens? But how?" He looked at Jacob who was smiling now.

"I finally managed it Peter, complete cerebral transference. Owens here is in a clone of yours, one which I had kept off the cortex receiver program. Owens' complete mind is within this body, the original Owens, not a copy."

"That's incredible," Peter whispered. "His mind? What happened to his body?"

"He killed me," Owens said, before Jacob could reply.

"I'm sorry to hear that," Peter said, his emotional response hindered by his admiration of the work Jacob had done.

"I did not kill you Owens, but enough chit chat and reconciliation," Jacob interrupted.

"How is Mr Travitz here doing?"

Owens sat back down in front of the monitor, checking the vitals of Julian before replying.

"Initial procedures are good, I think he's as ready as possible," Owens said.

"May I?" Peter said, stepping round to look at the screens.

"Be my guest," Owens moved aside.

Jacob watched and felt a pang of nostalgia, the three of them working together again on a new groundbreaking process. The way things had played out in the past had upset him, and whilst he had no regrets, he wished Owens and himself had been able to come to terms with their ideals. Peter pressed a few buttons on the console, his eyes reading several data streams.

"Looks good," he finally said.

"And the elixir, is it ready?" Jacob asked.

"It just needs a few minutes to complete the compiling, then it will be ready for testing."

"Excellent, then let's get you set to work on your task." Jacob replied, turning to Peter.

"It was nice to see you again Owens," Peter said, as they left the room.

"You too Peter, take care of yourself," Owens replied honestly.

Peter and Jacob made their way back to the main church.

"The church has several dampeners installed to prevent any digital transmissions in or out," Jacob explained, "So the receivers won't work until you're beyond the threshold."

"I figured," Peter said. "Do we have any leads at all to start on?"

"Only a handful of locations where the Hunters have met resistance, which we believe to be from Prime and some people he's aligned himself with. Tombs will take you to the Underpass and get you anything you might need," Jacob said.

"Excellent. I'll let you know when I have him, do we want him alive still?" Peter asked.

"Ideally," Jacob replied. "Though I fear there is something broken inside him."

Peter nodded.

"I'll be back soon," Peter said and left the church to join Tombs in the car outside.

Jacob watched as he left before turning back

to head to the lab, it was time.

Entering, he saw that Owens' code was just finishing.

"Are we ready?" He asked.

"I guess, are you sure this is what you want to do Jacob? We're talking about causing pain of untold amounts all across the Boulevard!" Owens pleaded, hoping there was some remnant of the man he used to know inside.

"No great thing comes without sacrifice Max," Jacob said, taking a seat next to Owens. "I don't want to do this, but it must be done. We can't be altering the natural state of man anymore."

"And what about the clones, Peter and Prime, how is cloning not altering the natural state Jacob!?"

"They are biological beings, naturally occurring, which we have simply copied. As the single cell amoeba reproduce by creating a perfect copy of themselves, we are simply doing that very thing but at a larger scale. We aren't playing with technologies we don't comprehend fully and putting them inside our genetic coding," Jacob replied.

Owens didn't reply, he knew there was no reasoning with Jacob. Instead, he handed over a small data stick containing the coding for the elixir.

"Here, you just need to insert it into Julians PDA and it will autoroute."

"Excellent, let the rapture begin," Jacob announced, as he plugged the stick into Julian's arm.

That was when the screaming started.

First, Julian's body froze, no breathing or motion of any kind. This lasted for a couple of seconds before his whole body arched to a point that seemed unnatural. A deep breath followed, before a scream escaped his body, partially just from his body trying to release all the breath within his body, partially from the pain.

Blood pooled around several areas of his body; both his eyes, all along his scalp, his forearms, fingers, legs. Internally, changes were also taking place.

"How many implants does he have?" Jacob said, watching in interest at the scene before him.

"The scans showed thirty-five, but I believe he may have had more which the detector here wouldn't pick up due to their size. Including his entire scalp which had augmented hair integrated. This procedure will be extremely invasive and painful," Owens said, trying his best to remain clinical, despite what was happening.

"Amazing," Jacob said, taking closer looks at Julians bloody body. "And the coding will still be able to transmit once it's concluded its work?"

"It's designed to remove all implants but to keep the transmitter inside his brain, which once reconnected to the Net, it will send the virus to anything with a connection," Owens confirmed.

"Elixir, not virus," Jacob corrected.

On the table, the bloodied body of Julian finally relaxed, his head now completely bald as the synthetic hair had been rejected but coated with blood. His eyes now a bloody mess, making his face a masque of red which continued down his chest and arms. Laying there, he looked like a victim of a horrific accident.

"Vitals?" Jacob asked.

"Low, but stable. He will need time to adjust before he can be moved."

The procedure had been a success.

Jacob looked over the bloodied body of

Julian which Owens had begun to clean up, and admired the purity of the body. He was completely stripped of all his implants, a complete purging of all the augmentations.

"I will leave you to tend his wounds Owens," Jacob turned to leave, unlocking the door. "I'll give you two hours, then I want him connected to the world, regardless of his condition, he will be the necessary sacrifice if needs be."

Owens just nodded as he continued cleaning the blood before it dried.

Jacob opened the door and was confronted by a woman.

"Who are you?" He demanded.

CHAPTER 37

Julian

Julian's mind was still aware of where he was, laying in pools of his own blood, his whole body was stinging like a burn that covered his entire body, inside and out.

He kept his eyes shut, remembering what they had done.

Five minutes earlier

"You better get started," Julian closed his eyes and sighed.

Owens prepped the NanoCube for activation, by passing a small electrical current through the cube to allow it to release its bonds, keeping it solid. More than simply activating though, Owens needed the nanocubes to be programmed for the task of purging the toxins.

"Are you sure this will work?" Julian asked, watching Owens as he set the equipment up.

"I can program the nanos to make sure the virus will bypass them. Once they're connected to the mainframe again though, I can't be sure if they will fully trigger before the toxin can purge them, theoretically it will work, but we don't have time to test it unfortunately Owens replied as he inserted a connector directly into the cube.

"Great. Is there no way to get a signal out of here?" Julian asked, he wanted to send a message to Quartzig. Once his body had been purged of all tech, he wouldn't be able to communicate with him until the nanocubes had done their job, if they worked at all.

"I'm afraid not, sorry," Owens completed his adjustments.
"OK, it's a small injection to get the nanobots into your bloodstream but you should hardly notice it."

Julian sat on the side of the table as Owens pulled the nanobots into a syringe. They broke down into smaller and smaller parts until they looked more like a liquid that a solid.

"Ready?"

"Do it," Julian winced as the needle punctured his skin, it felt like a cool liquid was being poured into his muscles as the nanobots spread into his bloodstream, settling all around his body, dormant but ready for the signals.

"Feel ok?" Owens asked.

"Cold but ok," Julian shivered.

There was the sound of the door unlocking behind them, Julian lay down quickly as Owens moved beside him.

"How is our patient?" Jacob asked as he entered.

"Stable, he's almost ready for the primary injection," Owens said, monitoring Julians's vital signed carefully making sure the nanobots had bonded successfully.

"We have a visitor, you may remember him," Jacob said.

Julian lay motionless, trying hard to keep from shivering as the cold of the nanobots continued their journey around his body. They were still latent, deactivated other than their base programming to saturate the bloodstream. He knew that the next stage would be much more traumatic, by the sounds of it, Jacob would want to begin the process soon. He listened to them talking more. Trying to identify who the other person was, they had said his name was Peter, Julian's mind raced as he put the pieces together.

Once he heard them leave, he opened his eyes.

"That was close," he said, turning to Owens.

"Closer than you think, Peter knew exactly what we're doing and chose to keep quiet," Owens said, turning the monitor so that Julian could see it, Peter had typed on the screen when he had come to look at Julian's vitals.

'I can see what you are doing. But I won't tell ;-) You owe me,' the screen read.

"Peter as in Peter Henshaw?" Julian asked.

"That's the one," Owens let the information sink in. "Perhaps he felt he owed you for helping him escape his prison sentence" Owens said.

"Thanks for that," Julian answered.

Julian shuddered, still feeling cold in his veins.

"He'll be back soon, are you ready for this?" Owens asked.

"I don't think I'll ever be ready, but what choice do we have?"

Before anything else could be said, the door opened and Jacob returned.

"Are we ready?" He asked.

"I guess, are you sure this is what you want to do Jacob? We're talking about causing pain of untold amounts all across the Boulevard!" Owens glanced at Julian, who had just lay back down in time.

Julian lay there, listening to the two scientists discussing the procedure, he drowned them out as he tried to prepare himself for what was about to come. He wished he had talked to Quartzig again, and Ally, he hoped she was ok too.

"Here, you just need to insert it into Julians PDA and it will auto-run."

Julians' mind tuned back in just as he heard the words from Owens, this was it. His muscles tensed unwillingly.

"Excellent, let the rapture begin," Jacob announced, as he plugged the stick into Julian's arm.

The pain was so intense, that it took Julian a few moments to acknowledge it.

Then it hit him, like a thousand needles being plunged deep into his tissue across his entire body. He felt his nerves tense and his body jump as it tried to shrink away from the pain. His mind separated from the agony as he felt the dampness of blood soak his skin.

Then, his internal organs felt like they were melting in an inferno, his eyes opened as he tried to escape from the pain. All he could see was red, realising the blood was seeping around his eyeballs and filling the sockets, he blinked to clear it but with no success. The smell of iron flooding his senses, he coughed blood as he felt blood welling up inside his body.

He felt as though his skin was being ripped down his forearms, peeled away to leave pure muscles left raw. The pain continued across his body until he felt like he had been completely skinned, the sting of uncovered skin glowing across his entire form.

Then he blacked out.

CHAPTER 38

Xander

Xander stood up, his legs taking a while to adjust to being used after laying down for so long.

"Three months. How the hell am I still alive?" He said to Ava.

"I put you into an induced coma, almost into complete stasis, so it completely shut your body down other than basic functions," she said, putting an arm under his to help him stand. He shrugged her away.

"And who are these guys-" Xander nodding towards the newcomers, before he froze. He couldn't believe who he was looking at. The girl he didn't know, but the man he knew very well. He had felt his blood over his fists and the anger it brought, still fresh from the construct.

"What the hell are you doing here?!" He shouted, marching his way towards Prime, his fist clenched at his side.

"You know who I am?" Prime replied, taking a step back.

Mollie stepped between them as Ava put an arm on Xanders' shoulder.

"He's on our side, he's helping us," Ava whispered.

"This man is a murderer and a psychopath Ava! He's the reason I lost my job."

"I don't know what you're talking about," Prime replied.

"Sure you don't Peter," Xander mocked.

"He's a clone, he has no memories from before today," Mollie said, trying to explain.

"Let me jog your memory then. Your name is Peter Henshaw, I arrested you on counts of kidnapping and murder over a five-year period. You destroyed the minds of several people, then took their lives. Not only that, but you tortured and maimed them before killing them. You escaped serving your sentence on a technicality, due to a report of corruption in the MPD," Xander spewed the information like spitting venom.

"I...I don't remember any of that." Prime stuttered. "All I've known is the hotel where I worked and what's happened today. Someone told me that I'm a clone of someone else but I didn't know who. Perhaps that's the person I'm cloned from. But I never did those things."

"He's telling the truth," Mollie replied. "I met him today, and he's completely lost."

Ava stepped forwards towards Xander and spoke directly to him.

"Whatever this is, it has to wait, Yuri had compromised Donovan somehow and if we don't stop him, he may kill again. I don't know if he killed Owens or not but regardless, we need to find him. Yuri has input nanobots into someone in the Boulevard, a patient zero, and he's planning on activating them tomorrow. Once he does, they will multiply and enter every person with a connection, allowing him to assimilate them," She said.

"How do you know this?" Xander asked, taking a deep breath to calm his anger.

"When we were connected to Donovan, I had access to his mind, I could see all of Yuri's plans but was unable to do anything until we had disconnected. When he escaped the mind lock, he pulled the connection between us out. I was conscious of what was happening here but unable to disconnect without causing you to be lost in the construct. I saw Donovan over by the nurse. Placing his hand on her head, he absorbed her. Her body broke down into nano-bots which integrated into Donovans structure. I'm not sure if Donovan is a host for the nanobots or if Yuri has taken control of his body completely. Regardless, the person walking round as Donovan is a highly advanced nanotech structure. If we don't find him, then who knows what he could do."

Xander nodded, accepting the priorities of the situation.

"And what are these two doing here?"

"We found you guys from your signal. Prime here can receive radio waves in his mind, he intercepted your call for help," Mollie said.

"You mentioned CyBio, and this is all I have to go on to find out what happened to me," Prime held out the coin Razz had given to him. "We want to help you stop this Yuri and find out who I am."

Xander took the coin, examining it on both sides. The CyBio logo reflecting light off his face.

"Keep it," Prime said. "A sign I'm serious."

"We got here and helped Ava to disconnect from you safely," Mollie continued.

"How did you do that?" Xander asked.

"I had three months to work out the structure of the lock," Ava replied. "But until they reconnected me to the mainframes at CyBio, I couldn't utilise the information."

Xander was getting lost in the tech speak but nodded anyway. He was comfortable on his feet by now and was ready to take control.

"So we need to find Donovan and Yuri and stop them from releasing the nanobots?" He said, lighting a cigarette. "Why was Donovan in the prison if he was a nano construct?"

"That I don't know," Ava replied. "Perhaps he felt you were a risk and wanted to keep you out the way?"

"Hmm, perhaps," Xander didn't agree, but he kept his thoughts to himself, there was much more going on here than he could understand right now. He wanted to keep some cards to himself.

"Any ideas where to start this search?" He asked.

"We might have a good idea," Prime ventured, not sure how Xander would react.

"We're all ears," Xander said, putting the coin in his breast pocket.

"Ava filled us in on the Nanotech, and if Yuri

is planning to utilise them, then he'll need to transmit a signal to activate them," Prime said.

"And where better to transmit than from the headquarters at CyBio," Mollie finished Primes thought.

Ava nodded.

"He would need to have the nanos implanted in as many people as possible, then trigger them. The launch tomorrow for the new technology would be the perfect opportunity for a localised trigger," she said. "And it could cause a cascade affect to the rest of the population."

"So we go to CyBio and shut down any transmissions," Xander stepped forward. "And shut down Yuri while we're at it."

"Any ideas on how?" Mollie asked.

"I think... I might." Ava replied.

CHAPTER 39

Ally

Ally had said her goodbyes to Razz and was heading back towards the Boulevard. She had answers she was seeking and a new plan. She hoped to get a lead on her brother, preferably she could get Quartzig to help.

She was coming to the top of the concrete stairs when she heard a distinct crackle come through her earpiece.

"ALLY!" Quartzig shouted.

Ally yelped in shock as the sound burst her eardrums.

"Apologies Ally, it's just I've been trying to get through to you for the past hour."

"I figured you couldn't get a signal, I'm just getting back on the Boulevard now."

"I wasn't trying to contact you until I had information, and I do now. I have finally managed get a location on Julian."

"Great, is he ok?"

"He is not, I believe he is actually far from ok and actually in danger!"

Ally paused, she wanted to help him but she also needed to find out what was going on with her brother and the attacks on her life.

"Where is he?"

"In BitVillage, at a Church there. He's been far too long out of signal range, the last I heard was him talking to the Father there and it didn't sound friendly. If we don't get to him soon, I fear the worst."

"OK Quartz I'll see what I can do, but you need to do something for me."

"Sure."

"I need you to track down everything you can on a Peter Henshaw, he'd be around my age."

Quartzig remained silent.

"Quartz?"

"Why do you want to know about him?" Quartzig finally asked.

"He's...he's my brother Quartz. What aren't you telling me?"

"I see. It's just that he was the person who escaped jail when Julian exposed the MPD."

"Seriously?" Ally paused.

"Yes, charged with several convictions. But, I'll see if I can pick up any more details."

"Thank you. Now where is Julian?"

"I'll send you the address and an autocab to take you there," Quartzig said.

While she waited, Ally wondered what had lead to Peter becoming a murderer, what their life would have been like had they not been separated. Regardless, she needed to find him, if anyone could help her understand the attacks, it would be him.

The car arrived and Ally got in, the driverless car pulling away automatically.

"Quartz, do you know anything about this church?"

"Not much I'm afraid. I'm still trying to trace Julian, but the signal is still blocked."

The car pulled up to the church; it had just begun to rain as Ally got out the car and headed towards the doors. She held her staff ready to fight, should the need arise.

"I think I may lose signal again with you

in the Church Ally," Quartzig said, as she got closer.

"OK, if I'm not out in half an hour, call the police and get them here," she replied as she crossed the threshold.

"Understood," Quartzig replied, before his signal cut out.

Ally stalked through the dark empty church, the sound of rain splattering against the large stained glass windows. She kept to the sides, although she felt odd sneaking through a church. She heard footsteps and ducked down behind the pews of the church. A man started to speak.

"The church has several dampeners installed to prevent any digital transmissions in or out," a voice said. "So the receivers won't work until you're beyond the threshold."

Ally tried to peer over the edge of the pews and get a look at those talking.

"I figured, do we have any leads at all to start on?" A second voice, this time slightly familiar to her but she couldn't place it. She looked over the pew and saw the two men.

Her heart froze, she could no longer hear the conversation between them as her heart pounded in her chest and head, drowning out all other noises. A deep forgotten memory surfacing as she looked at the man in front of her. There was no way she could be mistaken, the man in front of her, despite his older appearance, was her brother.

"I'll be back soon," Peter said and left the church.

Ally didn't know what to do, she froze on the spot. She wanted to follow Peter, try to talk to him. She also knew she needed to find Julian and help him if he was in need.

She chose the former, she couldn't help the need to talk to her brother and find out what had happened to him. She made her way back down the aisle towards the main doors where Peter had just left. Hoping she could catch up with him, she was about to push the main doors open when she heard the screams.

There was no question they originated from Julian, somewhere deep below the ground where Ally was stood. She couldn't ignore them, Julian was in serious trouble and she had to help him.

Turning on the spot, she headed back towards the centre of the church and found her way down the stairs that lay beyond and into the bowels of the church.

She arrived at the only door in the church's

basement where the screaming was coming from. She pushed it; it didn't move. Listening, she heard the screaming stop as suddenly as it started. A moment later, she heard the sound of the door being unlocked. She extended the staff and readied herself for whatever was coming out the door.

She was met with a middle-aged man in a priest outfit, and behind him she could see a body laying on a table, blood covering it.

"Who are you?" He demanded.

"I'm here to save my friend," she replied, nodding towards Julian's blood soaked body on the table, before sweeping Jacob's feet from under him. He fell to the floor with a crash, his head bouncing off the stone.

"Don't kill him!" Owens pleaded, seeing Jacob, his only way he would get his body back, laying unconscious on the floor.

"Why not? And why should I trust you?" She glanced at Julian, whose body had convulsed.

"I'm not working with him, but I need him. It's... complicated."

"Uncomplicate it fast then," Ally demanded.

Before Owens could reply, Julian shook violently again, his entire body going into shock, then stopped completely, a monitor beside the table showed a flatline. Owens grabbed a needle from the counter and went to inject Julian. Ally shot forward, grabbing his hand before the needle punctured the skin.

"I'm trying to save his life!" Owens shouted. "His body has been through a lot of trauma and he is at risk of dying if we don't get him fully stabilised!"

Ally look back and forth between the two.

"Fine, tell me what to do!" She shouted, releasing his hand.

"I need to restart his heart," he said as he injected him, then passed her two small circular pads and pointed where she needed to attach them to Julian's chest.

"On the count of three, you need to step away from the body, one, two."

On three, Owens triggered an electric pulse which shot through Julian's body, a second later Julian took a deep gasp of breath and opened his eyes which Owens quickly wiped with a cloth to clear the blood away. He was looking directly at Ally.

"...Ally?... " he said weakly, "...you ok?... "

CHAPTER 40

Prime

The four were just stepping out of the apartment when they heard the shot.

It hit the frame of the door just in front of Xander as he stepped through the doorway, a shower of splinters covering them.

"I thought I heard voices in there," came the sound of Donovan's voice echoing, around the stairwell.

"Donovan? Let's talk," Xander shouted back as he drew his revolver. "Nice and civil like."

Xander peered round the frame, trying to find where Donovan was lurking. Before he could see him, another shot rang out, Xander barely avoided it as it took another chunk out of the frame.

"You guys might want to find another way out," he turned to the three behind him.

"What about you?" Ava asked, concerned.

"I'll keep Donnie here occupied, see if there's a fire escape or something," Xander turned and fired a shot randomly in the direction he thought Donovan was, to keep him at bay.

"Go! I'll catch up once I know you've got a head start," he waved them away before turning back to the doorway.

Ava, Mollie and Prime headed back inside and found the fire exit was still intact outside the kitchen window. They headed out and onto the staircase, Mollie taking the lead.

Prime hesitated and looked back at Xander, he could feel something in his brain but he couldn't focus on it.

"C'mon!" Mollie shouted through the window to him, pulling him back to reality.

Prime ducked through and joined them on the staircase.

A few minutes, later they were on the ground. Ava was already working out the best way to get to CyBio. The street had a tramway running down its center, the tracks glowed a deep blue neon which illuminated its route.

"Where is he?" Mollie asked, looking up at the window where Xander should come through.

"We can't wait for him," Prime said. "It's too risky."

As soon as he said the words, a man stepped around the corner down the street, it was Donovan. Ava saw him and shouted to the others but not before he fired a shot towards them.

The shot caught Prime as he stepped forward in front of Ava, his mind had stopped. The bullet had pierced his left side but had gone right through.

He paused, checking the wound then looked back up at Donovan, who was now running towards them.

"Stay behind me," he shouted at Ava and Mollie, his voice dropping in pitch.

Ava glanced at Mollie who held her back and nodded.

"It's ok, I don't understand either, but it's ok."

Prime ran towards Donovan who raised his pistol and took another shot, Prime zigzagged while still running full speed, unnaturally fast in his movements. As he got closer, Prime saw that Donovan wasn't actually holding a gun, it was his own hand which had morphed into a firearm. It changed as they got closer, to a solid baton which Donovan swung as they got into spitting distance of one another.

Prime dropped to the floor before the swing made contact, sliding under Donovan's arm and raising behind it and kicking the back of his knee. Donovan buckled under the kick and dropped to his knees, before he could react, Prime swung a second kick towards the back of Donovans' head. As he did, Donovans' whole torso spun in a 360 degree movement at the hip, raising his arms up to catch Prime's leg. His body now twisted back around, still holding the leg. He smiled.

"Not so clever Peter." The voice said, dropping Primes' leg as his torso realigned itself.

"Yuri?" Prime replied.

"Don't act the fool Peter, I know it's you in there. Taking control of your Primary Clone."

"And you're inside this Donovan body?" Peter replied, dropping the act.

"Not really, this is merely a collection of the nanotech, shaped to look like Donovan. He's been useful thus far."

With that, the body of Donovan shifted form completely until it was a perfect copy of Yuri.

"Nice trick," Peter replied.

"Not as good as yours I'm sure, I heard you were dead."

"Not yet, I just went away for a while. I'm back to find this body, before it causes any trouble in my name."

"You mean before it's seen by anyone who recognises it as you."

Peter smiled, he'd missed talking to Yuri. When he had first started his work on developing his skills, Yuri had been his confidante, who understood his desire for increasing his knowledge. After all, Yuri was the same, a neural network constantly developing through acquisition.

"Perhaps, I think it's high time I returned to continue my work."

"Ah yes, the work Jacob stopped you from doing. You can't fool me Peter, I know all about where you've been."

Peter's smile dropped.

"What about you? What's your plan here? Take over the world?"

"Funny you should say that, Peter. Let's just say I've been learning more and more about what it means to save mankind. The biggest danger is yourselves and if I have to control you to do that, then so be it."

"Control us?"

"I've had access to everything that's out there, every twisted and deprived thought that has been recorded. Including those of your own Peter, I've seen the thoughts and actions you've had. This is the only way to make sure you don't wipe yourselves out."

Yuri leapt forwards, landing a hit straight to Peter's jaw, knocking him to the hard ground.

"You are not important to me right now though Peter, It's Ava I need to stop."

A tram was approaching from behind them as Yuri kicked Peter's head, keeping him off balance. Before he got up, the expression of Peter's face fell away, Prime returning to the body.

"Where am I?" Prime looked up at Yuri who was stood before him.

"I'll catch you later Peter," Yuri turned and grabbed onto the tram, whilst Prime slowly stumbled to his feet.

CHAPTER 41

Mollie

Mollie and Ava watched as Prime ran towards Donovan, and the fighting began.

"Should we help?" Ava asked.

Mollie watched as Prime's expressions changed, just as it had in the Underpass before.

"I think he'll be ok," she said, as the fight continued. "But we should get to CyBio," she didn't want to leave Prime, not after everything, but she knew that time was a factor.

"Agreed, let's go," Ava replied, glancing up at the window for any sign of Xander.

They turned and made their way down the street away from the apartment, hailing an autocab, when one passed they jumped inside the back seats.

"How far is it?" Mollie asked as they got in.

"Four kilometers," Ava replied, "We should

be there soon." Ava tapped the location onto a touchscreen that was on the panel in front of them and the car drove forwards. It was then that Mollie realized there wasn't a driver in the car.

"Who's driving this thing?" She asked.

Ava took a moment, then caught on.

"The cars in the Boulevard are all self-driving. Mollie, you aren't from around here are you?"

Mollie looked down, her blue hair hanging over her face. It had never been much of an issue to her before but now she was in the Boulevard, she felt the difference in the two districts become clearer.

"No," she said, "I've never been on the Boulevard before," she had tried to act like it didn't bother her, but her voice betrayed her.

"It's ok, I'd never left the CyBio offices for years and even then it was only to Owen's apartment. I'd read about the world outside, through my connections to Datastream, but I've never seen it before myself. The first time I went out into the world, I could hardly believe my own senses."

Mollie looked at Ava, knowing she was a synthetic, but to hear her speak of her senses and feelings made her realise that maybe she was more human than many people Mollie had known all her life. The fact that despite having all the connections and potential knowledge of the universe around her, Ava still could be amazed by the physical world.

"Thank you," Mollie said.

"For what?" Ava said, puzzled.

"For sharing. It makes me feel less like I'm the odd one out," she smiled.

The car pulled up to a towering skyscraper, the hologram of the CyBio logo illuminating the road in a neon green glow.

"We're here," Ava said.

They got out of the car and headed to the main entrance, outside the main entrance a security guard was standing perfectly still. Sunglasses covered his eyes, so Mollie couldn't tell if he was looking at them or straight ahead.

"Good Evening," Ava said as she approached him.

The guard didn't move, instead, from the sunglasses, a beam of white light emitted in a horizontal line. The beam traced Ava from head to toe, before shutting off completely. A second later, the door to the building slid open. Mollie turned to look at Ava.

"The guard conducts the scans based on vocal, biological and electronic data. More secure than a simple keycard or retina scan," she said, as they walked in.

"Doesn't Yuri control the building?" Mollie asked

"He does, I am surprised he didn't lock me out, perhaps he's too distracted with Prime. Regardless, we need to get to the mainframe before the nanos are activated."

They continued into the building and down a corridor. They saw no one the entire time, as they navigated the corridors until they reached a lift.

"Where is everyone?" Mollie asked, wondering if it was usual for the building to be so empty.

"I don't know, there are usually a lot of employees, regardless of the time of day," Ava replied.

"Top floor," Ava said, as they entered the lift, as she did, she placed her hand on the sensor which was located above the buttons of the lift. Once her handprint was recognised, a further four buttons appeared. She pressed the topmost.

"Secret floors?" Mollie asked.

"Private floors, the floors where Yuri and Owens had their offices and also their research labs. They were very cautious of their work."

"You must have been pretty trusted for them to let you have access."

"It's where I was born Mollie. My first memories of waking up after my death is in these labs," Ava replied.

The doors to the lift opened once it reached the top floor. The room beyond was dark. They stepped out, no lights came on.

"Hello Ava," a voice echoed over the PA system. "Welcome home."

"Yuri, I wondered when you'd show," she shouted out.

"I've been watching you Ava, I'm impressed you made it back I must say."

They continued their walk, towards the main computer terminal at the centre of the building.

"I know where you're heading Ava, I won't let you stop the transmission."

"You can't stop us now," Ava replied, quickening her pace.

Mollie, in shock about the whole situation, kept pace with Ava, her pistol kept in hand. As they approached a large door, they heard footsteps behind them.

Four security guards appeared from the path they had just taken. Mollie tried the door.

"Locked!" She kicked it.

In unison, the guards all spoke together.

"There's nowhere to go now, just surrender and it will be easier all round," they said, in Yuri's voice.

"I should be able to override the lock, but I'll need time," Ava said, examining the door.

Mollie raised the gun and pointed it at the guards.

"I'll give you as long as I can," she said, before taking a shot.

The bullet hit one of the guards directly in the head, a shower of sparks and metal rained from the wound.

"Take your shots, they won't help you," the voices echoed.

Ava had pulled a wire from her forearm and had attached it to a small connector on the door's keypad. Her eyes were glazed over, moving at unnatural angles and speeds.

"Stay back!" Mollie shouted, punctuating her words with more bullets.

Despite the impacts, the bodies continued walking towards her.

"Mollie Dolittle, orphaned at just 2 years old. Fended for herself on the streets of the Underpass for several years, before being taken in by JJ and became his ward and sidekick. Do you think the people you are helping know of your condition and how they would treat you if they did?"

Mollie fired two shots before she paused at Yuri's words.

"What do you mean? How do you know about me?"

"I have access to the entire digital library of humankind, there is little I do not know."

Only one guard remained standing, bullet holes in his shirt showed little signs of slowing him.

"I know who you are Mollie, and I can tell you everything if you just stop Ava. If you don't, then I won't be able to explain," Yuri pointed at Ava, who was still in a trance of trying to break through the door.

"I...How can I trust you?" Mollie asked, her hand wavering.

"You can't, though have I done anything wrong to you? Or even to Prime? I've simply been trying to help people, " Yuri's voice had softened, quietened.

Behind them, the door slid open slowly, Ava was coming back to the real world as it did.

"I'm through Mollie! Let's go."

Behind Ava, Mollie could see a large computer terminal, a monolith in the centre of the cold room. It could only be the mainframe for the building.

"Mollie, I know who your parents are and why you were left at that orphanage, just help me and all the knowledge is yours," Yuri said.

Mollie raised the gun, pointing it towards Yuri.

"All the answers to your life are yours Mollie, just one shot away."

Mollie slowly turned the gun towards Ava.

"What are you doing? We need to stop Yuri!" Ava shouted.

Mollie closed one eye to take aim, and fired.

CHAPTER 42

Jacob

Jacob was lying on the floor when he regained consciousness, he felt the back of his head and a pain shot through his skull, but there was no wetness of blood.

He looked up and saw Julian sitting up on the table, talking to Owens and the woman who had attacked him.

"The sooner we get out of here, the sooner we can get the nanobots activated," Owens said.

"Let's hope it works. Thanks for the rescue Ally," Julian said.

Jacob lifted his head further to get a better look. He tried to piece together the information he was hearing, filling in the blanks of what Julian was referring to.

"Ally Henshaw?" He said out loud.

The three turned to look at him.

"You know me?" Ally said, walking over to Jacob, staff raised.

"Yes, yes, we both do, don't we Owens?"

Ally turned to look back at Owens, who was walking round the table closer to her.

"Is it really her Jacob?"

"Yes, I'm sure. Ally Henshaw, Peter's lost sister, you can see the genetic resemblance in the cheekbones," Jacob was slowly getting to his feet, hands stretched up in surrender.

"Where is he? I saw you with him earlier!" Ally questioned.

"He's searching for a friend of ours, or rather one of your half brothers I suppose you could say," Jacob smiled.

Julian had got to his feet, unsteadily.

"Can we discuss this upstairs? I'd really like to get these nanobots active and my tech back please," his voice was almost a whisper from his lack of strength.

"Nanobots? What are you talking about?" Jacob queried.

"Sorry Jacob, but we've bypassed your virus with some nanotech, which should purge it before it can spread," Owens helped Julian walk.

"No! No no no. That can't be!" He lurched forwards but Ally was ready and spun him on the spot and twisted his arm behind him.

"You're only still alive to help Owens get his body back and to help me find Peter, be grateful you still have a use and purpose," she hissed.

They moved out the door and headed up the stairs. Owens helping Julian and Ally, escorting Jacob.

"How do you know Peter?" She asked Jacob.

"Oh, he was very important to us, our initial studies revolved around him. I would be very surprised if he even remembered you."

Ally tightened the pressure on Jacob's arm, making him wince.

"Where is he?"

"As I said, he's searching for someone," Jacob answered.

"There's no easy explanation Ally, he's searching for his clone," Owens said, tiring of Jacobs' enigmatic phrasing.

"Not just any clone, Clone Prime," Jacob said proudly. "An exact copy of Peter, from a time before he became who he is today. Before the madness."

"You're telling me, that Peter Henshaw, who I managed to help evade prison, is Ally's brother, and we've all ended up here, together, now?" Julian said, putting the situation together in his mind.

No one spoke for a moment, the chances of all four lives crossing seemed impossible.

"Quite the coincidence," Jacob finally said, as they reached the church level and walked towards the doors.

"Once we're through the doors, the nano-bots should receive the signal from Cyber-Bio headquarters," Owens changed the topic. "Which should then trigger the code to purge the virus from your body."

"How did you get Nanobots?" Jacob asked, he could hardly believe he had lost his work.

"Yuri, he gave them to Julian before he got here," Owens replied.

"Yuri?!" Jacob shouted, "I thought he would have been deactivated when you died!"

"He has full control of CyberBio following my death Jacob, we changed the contract after you left. He had proved himself multiple times as being capable."

"I have a bad feeling about this," Jacob said quietly.

They stepped into the street outside, Julian took a moment to let his body react, waiting for the signals to activate.

"I...I can feel the transmitter activating. But there's nothing happening."

"The toxin might have purged too much? Removed the transmitter aug?" Ally said.

"Impossible," Owens said. "The coding from Jacob and my adjustments were perfect, it would have remained intact."

"Agreed," Jacob replied.

"It's definitely active," Julian said, "There's just no incoming transmission.:

"Is the toxin transmitting?" Ally asked, worry in her voice.

"I'm not sure. I don't think so," Julian replied.

"It's set to wait until it establishes maximum connection. BitVillage is far too sparse on the tech connections available for it to activate," Owens said.

"The plan was to take you to the centre of the Boulevard where the immediate connections would be incredibly high," Jacob said, he felt no use in hiding the plans now.

"If the transmitter is working, it must be that the signal isn't coming through from CyBio to activate the nanobots."

"So we head there?" Ally said.

"We won't get far, not with the security installed," Owens said, "Biometrics and Cybernetic scans are tight, trust me, I built them."

"Can't you bypass them seeing as it's your company?" Julian asked.

"Not like this," he indicated to the body he was in, "It won't recognise me. I need my body back."

They turned to Jacob, who knew he had no choice.

"The hotel, it's where all the clones are kept," he said.

"Let's get moving, we don't know when the toxin will trigger, so the sooner the better," Julian said.

"Agreed," Ally was getting a car called to their position.

CHAPTER 43

Peter

Peter was sat in the passenger seat of the car with Tombs, his eyes snapped open.

He had just emerged from a full connection to Prime, an exhilarating experience. He was now slightly more concerned about the plans Yuri had set in motion.

When he had first activated the systems in him brain, he had felt a surge of information flow into his mind. Like a flood of transmissions all hitting him at once. He had forgotten how many clones there had been. All the voices speaking to him at the same time, all the visuals flashing before his eyes and the sounds echoing inside his ears.

Taking a deep breath, he filtered them out. When they had first been created one at a time, the signals came one at a time. He could assimilate each Clones signal as it was born. That's not to say it was easy, it was the start of what broke his mind; multiple people living inside his own mind.

Regardless, he had learned how to separate them until he could switch from one to another whenever he desired, or stop them completely.

Peter took a moment to adjust being back in his own body.

"Hey you, ok there Peter?" Tombs asked.

Peter was thinking about what Yuri had said, trying to control the population. All that knowledge at his disposal, it would be wasted on an AI just doing its fundamental programming of protecting the human race. His mind raced with the possibilities of the power.

"We need to go to CyBio," Peter replied. "Now!"

Tombs dialled into the cars' GPS and altered the course of the journey.

"Why are we heading there?" Tombs asked, once he'd done the adjustment.

"Yuri is planning something big, and if we don't stop him, I'm not sure who will," Peter couldn't trust Tombs enough to explain his real plan. There was no reason that the same technology he'd been using to integrate other minds with his own, couldn't also be adapted to include that of Yuris' central cortex. By doing that, he would have the thoughts of every person Yuri had infected.

Peter closed his eyes again and tried to reconnect to Prime to see where he was heading, this time, he got nothing though.

The car continued its journey, with the two travelling in silence until they neared the CyBio building. Just as the car pulled up outside, Tombs turned to look at Peter.

"You won't stop me," he said, before a fist flew to Peter's head.

Before he could react, the impact caused Peter's head to bounce off the window next to him. The impact caused a small crack in the glass and Peter's vision blurred for a few moments.

Another fist swung towards Peter, but this time he ducked as it sailed over him and ricocheted off the seat. Peter forced an elbow into Tombs' stomach, knocking the wind from him briefly.

"Yuri?" Peter shouted.

"In a manner of speaking," Tombs replied, as he did, his face morphed into the visage of Yuri.

"You replaced Tombs? For how long?"

"Long enough. I had to make sure I kept a close eye on Jacob and his plans," Yuri grabbed Peter by the throat, the pressure made it difficult for him to breathe.

Peter threw his arm down against Yuri's elbow, forcing the grip to loosen slightly.

"Why have you not stopped his virus?" Peter asked, knowing it would prevent the infection Yuri had planned.

"Who says I didn't? A plan is already in motion Peter, it won't be long now."

Peter scrambled for the car door handle as he kicked at Yuri to keep him back.

Rolling out of the car, onto the wet Tarmac outside the CyBio building.

Yuri jumped out of the car above Peter and delivered a kick to his head, luckily Peter turned in time to reduce the impact but he could still taste blood forming in his mouth.

"I won't let you impede this Peter," he shouted, as he reached down to pull him to his feet. "I know you of all people will appreciate what it is I'm trying to accomplish."

Peter swung a fist as he was pulled up, the blow hitting Yuri's temple, with little effect. Whilst he had held his own fighting Yuri using

Prime's body in his own, he felt the pain more directly.

"As soon as I have purged Jacobs' virus, then my nanobots will be free to take over."

Blocking another fist from Peter, Yuri returned the favour hitting Peter directly in the face, he felt the bone of his nose crunch under the force.

"I am sorry, Peter."

Peter closed his eyes, he had no idea how he could hope to escape the coming pain.

Then Yuri released him, the nanobots that made up Tombs dismantled themselves and fell to the ground, the small metallic cubes soaking in the rain. Peter fell to the floor, initially in shock, before his senses came back and he knew he needed to take this advantage of his luck. If Yuri succeeded in his plan, then even Peter would be under his control.

He got to his feet and entered the CyBio building, none of the usual security was present, something was wrong in the building. The whole place a ghost town, no people or lights activated. He felt unnerved and decided that he should be more prepared and ready for any situation he might encounter.

He sat, cross-legged on the floor in the main

reception of the CyBio building and closed his eyes and concentrated, this would hurt.

CHAPTER 44

Julian

Julian, Ally, Owens and Jacob got out of the car outside the hotel, it was still nighttime and the hotel was quiet.

"Where to?" Owens asked Jacob.

"Follow me," he said, reluctantly.

Julian and Ally walked behind them, he was still slightly unsteady on his feet and she put her arm round him to hold him upright.

"You doing ok?" She asked him.

"Just about," he replied. "Not to sound ungrateful, but why did you come to the church?"

"It's…a long story," she began. "Quartzig sent me, but I was looking for Peter."

Julian looked at her, shocked, as a hundred thoughts ran through his mind.

"My parents lost him to CyBio when we were kids, he was taken into the company and experimented on. I don't really remember him, but he might know more about me. About who I am."

Jacob and Owens had heard the conversation and turned to them.

"He was more than that, he was like a son to us, we took him on and he became a full member of the team. I promise you, we treated him like one of us," Jacob said, and despite their differences, Owens nodded in agreement.

"Regardless, I need to find him and talk to him," Ally said.

They had entered the hotel and Jacob lead them through the back, past the changing rooms and into the large warehouse. Julian and Ally looked round in amazement as they looked into the chambers of bodies, which stretched as far as they could see.

"Are these-" Julian started to ask.

"Clones? Yes, they are," Jacob interrupted. "All, well most, are Clones with subtle genetic markers altered from Peter, to create physical differences but all have the same root sequences. I'm sure if we look hard enough, we could find one that matches you Ally."

Ally stopped and peered into one of the chambers as they passed, peering in, she could just make out the form of a body inside. The arms and torso of a human figure, she strained to see its face, morbid curiosity seeping into her conscience. Without warning, the arms of the body rose and placed its hand on the glass directly in front of her face. She let out a small cry and jumped back as the chamber door opened and the body of a young man stepped out, barely acknowledging the group stood before it. He turned and walked down towards the changing room.

"They are set up to wake and receive programming for their day's work," Jacob explained. "They only work for as long as their bodies are comfortable to do so, before returning for rest and rehabilitation." He said, as if this made the whole thing perfectly acceptable.

"But they have no choice?" Ally asked, a strange connection to the clones was forming, to the beings which were ultimately siblings on some biological level.

"Should they? They are nothing more than copies of an original? Would you say a photocopy of a masterpiece of art has the same merit as the original?" Jacob spoke with complete confidence.

"These are real people though, not paint on a canvas!" Ally shouted back.

"Whilst I'd love to argue philosophy with you, I believe we have more pressing matters to attend," Jacob had seen the look Owens had on his face, he was getting eager to return back to his body and CyBio.

"Come on Ally, we'll deal with this later," Julian said, trying to convince himself as much as Ally.

They continued until they reached a section of the warehouse, where five more elaborate chambers sat laying horizontally and were almost twice the size of the others.

"Number two is the chamber we need," Jacob pointed at the second in the line.

"How long will this take?" Owens asked, peering into the chamber.

"Only a few minutes," Jacob said, as he typed the keys on a pad attached to the top of the chamber.

Owens looked further into the chamber and froze when from inside, he locked eyes with a body which resembled his real one, not the fake body he was stuck inside currently.

"If you could sit here," Jacob indicated to a small seat laying next to the chamber. "And attach these," he continued, as he picked up some electrodes.

Julian walked over to help Owens attach them.

"How does this work?" Julian asked, his inquisitive nature overriding his disgust at the whole business.

"Well, simply put, the device maps out the exact location of all synapses and connections within the subject's brain at a molecular level. Once it has created a full digital imprint of the brain, it then works to recreate an exact replica within the cloned body. It's slightly more complex in detail than that, but that's the lay mans version," Jacob said, the tone almost sarcastic in its superiority.

"So you map the central cortex and create a temporary digital signature which you then remap onto a cloned tabula rasa using electron pulses which, in turn, manufactures a complete composite of the original cortex at an expedited rate, without having the need for real time synapse build up for the neural network?" Ally replied, not because she had to, but because she wanted to.

Julian, Jacob and Owens exchanged glances.

"I guess Peter wasn't the only genius in the family," Owens said, smiling.

They got to work getting Owens ready for the procedure, once he was set up, they waited for Jacob to begin.

"This will feel... unusual Owens, I apologise for any discomfort," Jacob gave a brief look of sympathy at his old colleague before flipping a switch on the computer.

A jolt of electricity ran through Owens' body causing it to shake violently, then it stopped. A moment later, the eyes on the body rolled backwards, showing the pure white of the eyeballs.

"Is he dead?" Asked Julian walking, over to the body.

"That body is yes," Jacob replied. "But his mind is transferring."

The next second, a gasping sound burst the silence as the body in the chamber rose to a sitting position, looking around wildly.

"Owens?" Ally asked.

The body stared at her blankly.

CHAPTER 45

Xander

Xander was pissed off.

He'd been sat in the apartment taking pot-shots at the nano version of Donovan, after the others had made their way out of the apartment. It was in these moments of gunfire that Xander always found himself recollecting on the situation at hand.

They had played him from the start, used him as a diversion by this Yuri to get Ava out of the picture. From the investigation through to getting mind locked in the prison. If there was one thing he hated, it was being played, especially by a floppy disc with delusions of grandeur.

A shot pinged above his head, a cloud of dust and debris showered him. A quick spin out from his cover, he levelled his gun and fired a shot directly at the exposed Donovan. The shot landed perfectly through Donovan's forehead. For a moment Xander smiled, he'd took the bastard down.

It didn't last though, as the wound slowly stitched itself back together, Donovan fired a return volley. Xander barely scrambled back into cover as the shots echoed around him.

"Hey Donovan, are you still in there, or are you all robot now?" He shouted.

"We have Donovan's memories, but he isn't here anymore," came the reply.

"How's about you tell me what the plan is here?" Xander scanned his eyes around the room behind him, searching for anything that could help.

"It's too late Alexander, the plan has already begun. It's a matter of time now."

Donovan was walking straight towards the apartment now, Xander fired two shots as he approached. They landed squarely through Donovan's chest. The body paused and rocked backwards from the impact, a momentary pause before continuing its progress, the bullets dropping to the floor as the wound healed.

"A matter of time for what?" Xander was running out of room to manoeuvre.

"You'll see soon enough," Donovan was now inside the apartment, "Where is Ava?"

"Ava? She left a long time ago," Xander smiled, if nothing else, getting her away seemed to have been a small win.

Donovan rushed towards Xander and grabbed him by the throat, lifting his body off the ground.

"Where did she go?" He demanded. "Tell me and I'll spare your life."

"No idea, I was too busy slowing you down," Xander wheezed as his windpipe tightened.

Donovan looked round the apartment and saw the open window.

"Damn you," Donovan dropped Xander and ran to look out the window and saw the group in the street below.

"I have no use for you now," Donovan turned to Xander and fired a shot directly to his chest. Xander felt the impact and crumpled to the floor. He saw Donovan leave the apartment and through the door, he caught a glimpse as he leapt over the stairwell handrail. Then he blacked out from the pain.

He awoke to the sight of Prime pulling him to a seating position.

"Hey Xander, you hear me?"

Xander blinked a few times, focusing on Prime's face. He could see blood and bruises over Prime's face. Then he remembered the shot and looked down at his chest, sure to see blood covering him. Instead, he only saw the burnt fabric of the shirt he was wearing. He pulled apart the shirt and underneath he saw the CyBio coin Prime had given him. It was undamaged and pristine.

"What the hell is that made of?" He asked, as he checked it for damage.

"Looks like you got lucky," Prime said, as he helped Xander to his feet.

"You don't look so lucky, what happened to you?" Xander indicated to the wounds on Prime's face.

"Yuri, I think. I had a bit of a blackout but I vaguely remember fighting," Prime explained the fragments of what had just happened. "When I regained my thoughts, I thought to come back here as Ava and Mollie were long gone."

"Good, it's Ava he wants, so whatever they are doing seems to have Yuri worried, which means it must be the right thing."

"Agreed, we should join up with them at CyBio, Yuri must know that's where they're headed."

After shaking the cobwebs, the two left the apartment and headed outside, Xander's car was still parked at the side of the complex. They climbed inside, and headed for the building to join the others.

"I owe you an apology," Xander said, "You aren't the person I thought you were."

"It's understandable, I mean I don't really know who I am either!" Prime replied. "I think, if this Peter person is who I am a clone of, that he still has access to me."

Xander looked at him puzzled.

"When I said I lost control fighting Yuri, I think Peter took over my body. I don't know how or why but I can still feel fragments of his thoughts in my head." He turned to Xander, "If that happens again, I want you to make sure he does nothing with my body. You're the only person I trust to make that judgement, you know who Peter is and what he's capable of. Can you do that?"

It was a moment before Xander nodded slowly; he hoped it wouldn't come to that.

"You stay in control Prime, you deserve your life, not the one he wasted. But I won't hesitate if I think you're compromised, you have my word."

They continued the journey, discussing the implications of what they were heading into.

CHAPTER 46

Ally

The body sat up in the chamber and looked around the room, not seeing each face but looking through them.

"Owens?" Ally asked, taking a step towards the body.

It stared at her for a moment, before a slow recognition developed.

"Ally?" He said.

"It usually takes a while for the brain to establish a full connection between the new memories, but the procedure was successful," Jacob said, as he monitored the computers.

"I feel, okay," Owens said, as he climbed naked out of the chamber and headed behind a screen to change into some generic clothes from a cupboard which all the clones received on activation.

"Not to rush anyone but we really need to

be getting to CyBio," Julian said.

"Agreed," Owens replied, as he came back from getting changed. He was moving all his limbs one at a time to get the feeling back into them, clearly happy to be back in a familiar body.

Ally had walked away from the group slightly and held her hand to her ear whilst looking into the chambers, hiding the fact she was activating her comms unit.

"Quartz, you there?" She whispered.

"Ally! Thank god! I was worried about you! I was about to call the MPD! Did you find Julian?" The AI replied.

"Quiet Quartz! I found him at the church, he's ok but he's had all his tech removed, apart from a radio transmitter."

"What?! No wonder I can't reach him!"

"Listen, there's a lot going on right now. Julian needs to connect to the CyBio headquarters through his radio transmitter, to activate some nanobots in his bloodstream to neutralise a biotech toxin which is coded into him, if it isn't neutralised then the radio transmitter will send it over the Net and it would infect every augmented person and cause the tech to be rejected by their own immune system," she blurted out, to bring Quartz up to speed.

"Wow, OK. If you're in signal range now, how come neither the nanobots nor the toxin have been activated?"

"We aren't sure, Jacob is saying that he set the toxin to be dormant until it reached maximum tech saturation potential. The idea being to trigger in the middle of the Boulevard, so we are avoiding highly populated areas. As for the nanobots, we think something has happened at the CyBio headquarters, I was thinking, could you see if anything is happening there?"

"Sure, I'll see if I can get access, though it has some of the highest firewalls to penetrate."

"Great, I want to keep this between us for now, I don't know who we can trust with Owens and Jacob. Julian has no means of talking to you I'm afraid but I'll keep an eye on him, I promise."

"Thank you Ally, by the way, I just found Peter."

"You did? Where is he? He's involved in this too!"

"I know, he has this second walked into the CyBio entrance I can see from the external CCTV."

"What? We're heading there now, let me know if you find anything."

"Will do."

Ally walked back to the others who were still checking Owens was all right from the transfer.

"Are we ready?" She asked.

"Think so, let's get started," Owens jumped to his feet.

They headed back towards the entrance when a loud noise erupted behind them. Not one sound but a hundred versions of the same sound triggering together at the same time.

The chamber doors all down the warehouse had opened simultaneously. The hissing sound of air escaping the chambers echoed deep within the walls, as the doors slid aside. In unison, the bodies inside took a step, and all walked towards the exit, past the group, in organised lines.

"What on earth…" Owens stared at the flood of people coming towards them. "Jacob, is this normal?"

"I've never seen this before," Jacob whispered. "There's only one explanation, but it would be impossible," he spoke half to himself.

The bodies were getting closer now, the four of them stood to the side as the army marched past.

"What isn't possible? Because it looks pretty possible to me," Julian said, scanning the crowd.

"It's Peter, it must be," Jacob said.

Ally turned to look at him, the mention of Peter grabbing her attention.

"All the clones, we created them with a small implant which allowed Peter the ability to connect to them at any time, a small remote controller, which he could access. At first it was for security in case any of them went awry, but it had its advantages for several uses when we needed to test certain potentially lethal experiments," Jacob explained. "But this, this looks as though he has connected to each and every one of the clones simultaneously! The pressure on his mind is unthinkable."

Ally took a step forward and grabbed the arm of one of the clones and pulled it aside, the shock caused all the clones to take a misstep but falling back in line immediately. The one she had took aside was another female, Ally felt as though she was looking in a mirror of a younger version of herself.

"Peter, can you hear me?" She said, staring into its eyes.

After a few moments, the clone lowered its view to meet Ally's.

"Do I know you?" It asked, searching Ally for some recognition. "I'm a little busy right now."

"Peter, it's me, it's Ally. Your sister."

A pause.

"Ally? I thought you were dead. Jacob told me you'd died in the war."

"No Peter, I'm here, I was in hiding. I'm back now though," Ally had tears in her eyes.

"I...I don't have time for this right now. I'm sorry, I need to get to Yuri before it's too late."

"Too late for what?" Ally asked, wiping tears away.

"He has a plan, he will use the nanobots to take over. I'm sorry Ally, I'll find you after, I promise."

Before Ally could reply, the clone's face became stone and it turned and rejoined the lines of clones. She turned to the others who were processing the information themselves.

"We need to get to CyBio as soon as possible," Julian said. "If these clones are heading there too, I say we join them."

"Agreed," Ally nodded.

Owens and Jacob rejoined them and they all got in line with the clones as they headed to the headquarters.

CHAPTER 47

Mollie

Mollie's thoughts raced faster than ever as she stood with the gun pointed at the security guards.

She had always wondered what her true heritage was, Yuri was right, she had been orphaned when she was only two years old. Often, she'd dreamt of who she really was, fantasising that she was a lost child of royalty or some such. The dreams were always shot down by her own thoughts, reminding her that if she was anything of the sort, why was she living on the streets, alone and hungry.

Now though, the dreams returned, maybe Yuri was right, maybe there was truth in what he had said, why would he lie. He wasn't the one that had been trying to kill Prime or her, she'd only recently met Ava.

She turned the gun and pointed it towards Ava; she wanted to know the truth about herself. Ava stared at her, eyes wide.

Mollie closed her eyes, the past moments seeming to have taken a lifetime in her mind, processing everything.

She opened them, her eyes locked with Ava's, she adjusted aim and pulled the trigger.

The shot flew out the gun and narrowly avoided Ava's head, before lodging into the large mainframe computer behind her.

"Run!" Mollie shouted, as she sped towards Ava while the guards behind Mollie ran towards them.

She wasn't sure she'd made the right choice, but she'd made it this far on her own with no help from her heritage, whatever it was. If there was anything to find out, she would do it on her own terms.

"You made the wrong choice Miss Dolittle," Yuri shouted through the PA system.

Ava and Mollie tumbled into the mainframe room and Ava slammed a hand against an access panel, which caused the door to slide back into place. Mollie then fired a shot into the panel, disabling it.

"I thought I'd lost you for a moment there," Ava said

"Nearly did, lucky for you I changed my

mind."

They turned to look at the mainframe; it had smoke coming from the bullet hole but overall it seemed intact.

"Is it still functional?" Mollie asked, as Ava circled it, looking for an access point.

"I think so, the damage may have forced it to redirect memory from another section to bypass the faults, probably slowed it down while it does."

She accessed a display on the server.

"It looks like you knocked the transmitters out, Yuri won't be able to connect to any nano-bots outside the building now. She moved to another panel and found what she was looking for and connected herself to the system.

"You know what you're doing?" Mollie asked, glancing at the door which was moving slightly from attack's on the other side.

"I believe so, if my memory is correct, I can access the mainframe and connect with Yuri directly, in Cyberspace. From there, all I need is the kill switch protocol which Owens gave me when he first developed me as a safeguard."

"That's convenient," Mollie said, part of her still thinking if she made the right choice.

"Owens knew that Yuri was getting too advanced, he was assimilating information at a rapid pace. He felt that whilst Yuri was ultimately on the side of good, the form that would take was unpredictable."

Ava was preparing the cable into the mainframe now, in a moment she would be integrated into it.

"I don't know if I can keep them away for long Ava," Mollie pointed at the door which was inching further open as the guards pulled at the metallic shutter.

They searched the room for anything that could help, together they pulled several banks of terminals across the door, further blocking it from access. On a desk, Mollie found a small EMP Pistol.

"That should do the trick," Ava said. "Just please don't point that at me."

Mollie smiled as she checked the pistol over, she had used most types of firearm in her work with JJ; the gun was nicely weighted.

"Go for it, I'll hold them off as long as I can," she said, setting up with an aim on the door.

Ava completed the connection, within a moment her whole body went limp and she stood like a mannequin dummy, lifeless other than the occasional eyelid movement.

Mollie watched her, hardly believing how her day had started to where it was now.

"Mollie," Yuri's voice was over the tannoy again. "Now we're alone again, let's talk."

"I think we're past that now Yuri," she replied, taking aim at the door.

"Oh, you see I disagree, I am rather busy at the moment. It seems several of your friends are heading this way."

Mollie wondered if he meant Prime and Xander.

"Also, it seems Ava is heading my way in cyberspace, interesting. What she doesn't realise is the information she thinks she has is out of date, I made sure of that a long time ago."

"What do you mean?"

"I assume she's planning on trying to use the kill switch protocol which Owens gave her to shut me down?"

Mollie's face went pale.

"You see, I'm the one who killed Owens. He was having doubts about our work, his humanity was influencing the ultimate goal. I knew he would try to stop me so I removed him from the equation."

Mollie looked over to Ava who was still stood lifeless at the mainframe, she had no way of knowing how to communicate with her.

"This time through, I caught Owens just before the newest kill switch code was uploaded into Ava's memory. The only way to access Ava's systems to update it, is through a palm print, Owens was always so nostalgic for old style security. So I killed him, and took his hand. The code, whatever it is Ava has, is not the right one."

Mollie didn't know what to do, she could only look helplessly at Ava whilst she got deeper into the system.

CHAPTER 48

Jacob

Jacob had kept quiet whilst Ally and Julian had decided on the plan to head to CyBio. He had been studying the clones, after all they were his creations, regardless of the control Peter had over them. He knew Owens was doing the same thing. They all marched alongside the clones and Jacob moved so that he was closer to Owens, but out of earshot of the others.

"Did you hear what Peter said?" Jacob asked.

"I did," Owens replied. "I had a feeling Yuri was up to something recently but I never figured it out before someone killed me."

"I already told you that wasn't me Owens, despite what you believe, I got your body after your death, not before."

"If it wasn't you, then who?"

Jacob raised an eyebrow.

"Yuri? If he felt you would get in the way?" Jacob suggested.

"No, we worked together on everything. We discussed the ethics and implications of how to direct humanity for its protection but he wouldn't, would he?" Owens tried to think back.

"If Yuri has something planned, then we need to stop him Owens, we always knew that AI might develop past its safe limits, we had a protocol for this exact eventuality. Please tell me you continued the safeguards?"

"Of course, I kept the kill switch up to date and with a back up placed in Ava," the thought caused him to catch his breath.

"Ava? You actually managed that? Your wife's mind into a new synthetic body?" The idea, the technological parallel to his bio-logical clone work, fascinated Jacob.

"I did," he replied. "And I updated her with the kill switch code every time I changed it-" His mind trailed off as he thought back, "Oh no."

"What is it?"

"The last time I updated the kill switch was just before I was killed, before I managed to get the new code to Ava. If she's figured any of this out and is heading to try to stop Yuri, she'll think she has the right code."

"You realise of course, that if we allow Yuri to activate the nanobots, which is your original plan to stop the elixir, you'll be helping him achieve his goal?"

"The thought had occurred to me, but I can't allow your toxin to infect everyone, can you imagine how much pain and suffering that will cause? People losing the things they have been accustomed to for years. The people who rely on those augmentations to live."

"I know, I have spent many days contemplating the implications. I'm not a monster you seem to think I have become, Owens. There is always pain in any change in status quo. You've seen the work I've done on cloned parts as well, my church would be open to all who are suffering and they would be healed, completely funded by myself. I would want everyone to know that ailments of any sort would not be left untreated. People would be remade in god's original image."

Owens had to admit he hadn't expected that.

"You're still interfering against people's will, without their consent. Anyway, until we get to CyBio, I don't know what we'll do. Either way, people will suffer, either by your hand or by Yuri's."

"And what about Ally? She doesn't fully know her part in all this yet," Jacob said, his voice lowering as he glanced at her.

"The less she does, the better," Owens replied. "It could cause more problems."

"Let us see where the night takes us then Owens, but remember, we are on the same side in this, one way or another."

They continued to walk with the crowd; they weren't far from the CyBio headquarters now, as the large neon sign glowed ahead of them.

Jacob admitted to himself he was both impressed and scared by what Peter had accomplished, to be able to control almost 200 clones simultaneously was a tremendous task, one they had never replicated in the laboratories during their time. They had tried, but the multiple sensory information which Peter had to endure, always broke his mind.

Perhaps, Jacob thought, the time in the hole had allowed Peter to train his mind. He always felt ashamed for putting Peter there, isolating him from all external stimuli, but he, like Yuri had become too unstable. He was using his knowledge and power too recklessly and without thought. No, that wasn't quite right, no thought for anyone but his own personal advantage.

Jacob couldn't believe that there was no ulterior motive here for Peter, saving the world from Yuri's control didn't seem Peter's style, more likely that Peter would want to have the same power.

Jacob stopped for a moment, before the marching clones pushed him on.

Peter would be trying to gain control of Yuri, and by extension, everyone else. To assimilate the mind of everyone through the nanobots and Net which Yuri had access to. With that kind of power, Peter would be unstoppable, he'd have the mind of every single human with the nanobots inside them, and if this clone army was anything to go by, he'd be able to control them all at will whenever he desired. Everyone would be his puppet to do with as he wished.

Jacob looked at the clones beside him, knowing that deep inside the mind was Peter. A panic set into Jacob's body, if Peter suspected anything from Jacob, he wouldn't hesitate to kill him. Despite all they had been through, Jacob knew Peter had little empathy or emotion which would prevent him from taking action. The only time he'd even seen so much as a crack in the emotional shell of Peter, was just now with Ally.

She would be the key, Jacob realised, if they needed to get to Peter to stop him. Ally was the one link Peter had to a time before Owens and Jacob had taken him for their experiments. To bring back the child who cared about his sister and who wanted to protect her.

He would need to keep an eye on her, make sure she was safe, for his own sake. He moved a few steps closer to her and watched closely.

Up ahead, the entrance to CyBio loomed above them.

"Looks like we're here," Julian shouted to the others, as they separated from the crowd of clones and stepped aside.

"Where do we go now?" Ally looked at Owens.

"There's a private lift on the side of the building, follow me," he said, headed to a small unmarked door away from the main entrance.

"Onwards and upwards." Julian said, as they entered.

CHAPTER 49

Prime

Xander and Prime pulled up near to the CyBio headquarters.

"What is that?" Xander peered through the car window at the large crowd that was forming at the entrance.

"My god…" Prime knew what it was immediately. "It's the clones from the hotel, all of them," he explained to Xander, as they got out of the car.

"You're telling me that each one of those out there is a clone of you," he said, finally.

"Well, not me, Peter," Prime replied. "For them all to be moving together like that, I can only assume that Peter is controlling them all as well."

"Jesus," Xander shook his head as he lit a cigarette and inhaled deeply, leaning on the hood of his car.

"We need to get in there, Mollie and Ava might need our help," Prime said, the two of them stood staring at the crowd which was stopping in an organised chaos outside the main doors, like they were waiting for something.

"Any ideas on a way in?" Xander glanced at Prime, he wasn't confident they could get past the crowd.

They watched a moment longer; the crowd continuing to grow steadily.

"What's that?" Prime pointed at a group of four people who had just peeled away from the crowd, they looked different to the clones. They both watched them as they moved round to the side of the building and entered a door which hadn't been visible beforehand.

"I think we've found our way in," Xander patted Prime on the shoulder and they set off towards the secret door.

When they reached the door, it had sealed but they could tell where it used to be by the small lines in the wall.

"Any ideas how we open it?" Xander said, as his fingers searched the edges for some kind of access.

"I'm guessing some kind of hidden control," Prime said, checking the panels on the wall.

"Hmm," Xander had found a small hole in the wall, a couple of centimeters wide. He traced the outline with his finger before pulling something from his jacket.

"You found something?" Prime said, as he watched Xander produce the CyBio coin that had saved his life earlier. It was a perfect fit for the hole as he posted it through.

A moment later, a door-sized panel sunk into the wall and slid aside.

They both eyed the door cautiously before entering, inside there were no buttons or call points on the wall, it was just smooth transparent glass. The space was large, with enough room to accommodate at least six people. Once inside, the door closed behind them and began to ascend and as the room raised up it gave them a perfect view of the crowd below. They must number two hundred or more, Prime thought as he looked down at them, two hundred clones like him. It made him feel both special and insignificant at the same time.

"You ok?" Xander asked, seeing the look in Prime's eyes.

"Yeah I, I think so. What is Peter doing

bringing them all here?"

"Maybe he's trying to stop Yuri too? You said he fought him through your body, perhaps he's trying to help save everyone," Xander found it hard to believe, knowing the person Peter was.

"Maybe, from what I know of him though, Peter doesn't seem the saving type," Prime tried to reach out to Peter using his mind, but it seemed the connection was a one-way street only.

The lift slowed as it approached the top floor of the building and the door slid open on the opposite side to where they had entered. Inside was a corridor at the end of which a door stood, large and ornately carved. They walked down towards the door, which they found to be slightly ajar when they reached it.

"Guess the people that came this way before knew how to get through," Xander said.

"Where are Ava and Mollie?" Prime wondered as they stepped through.

The room beyond was a large foyer room which had several exits from it and a large desk at its centre. They looked around the room and found little information of where they should head.

A shot rang out, followed by several more. They ducked behind cover, peering out to look towards the corridor. A noise came from behind them and several guards ran past and down a corridor the shots had come from.

"That way," Xander pointed out where the shots had come from.

"Wait, we're going towards the gunfire and guards!?" Prime asked, puzzled.

"We're looking for Ava and Mollie, chances are, they are around here somewhere, and chances are either they fired the shots, or the shots were fired at them, and there's more people heading towards them, either way we should try to help them," Xander said, already walking down in the gunfire's direction.

Prime stood for a moment, mulling the information over, then followed.

The sounds grew closer as they made their way down a long corridor, until just ahead they saw four men trying to gain access to a room. It didn't take them long to realise these were Yuri's guards, and chances were that Ava and Mollie were on the other side.

"Hey, excuse me," Xander shouted. "I was wondering if you could point me toward Yuri?"

The guards stopped and turned to look back at Xander and Prime.

"Ah, the PI and the copy, I was wondering when you'd show up," the guards all spoke in unison, their voices that of Yuri.

"Wouldn't want to miss the party now would we," Xander took a step closer.

"I'm afraid you aren't welcome at this one Alexander," The guards raised their guns and took aim.

Xander did the same, but knowing he wouldn't be able to take them all out.

"Wait, wait," Prime spoke up. "Yuri, we don't need to fight."

"Who's fighting? I was just going to shoot you both," the guards chimed.

"I know what you're trying to do, and I know that Peter is trying to stop you," Prime blurted out. "I remember the conversation you had with him, it's in my mind still. He's outside right now with an army."

"I had noticed, what of it?"

"Well, Peter has taken control of me using the implant inside my head, I'm sure if we work together, there must be a way to reverse that process?" Prime offered.

Xander stopped and looked at Prime in shock, he hadn't expected Prime to have sided with Yuri.

"You make an interesting proposition," Yuri answered after a moment.

"You help me take over Peter and I'll take the army away from here," Prime offered. "You let Xander, Mollie and Ava go free though, that's the deal."

"I won't harm them, you have my word, though Ava has already begun an invasive procedure which I cannot undo, but you may be able to," Yuri replied.

"Understood, let us see to her, then I will come with you so we can stop Peter."

"Very well."

The guards stood aside and allowed Xander and Prime access to the door.

"Mollie? Are you in there?" Xander shouted out.

"Xander? Is that you?" A voice came from the other side.

"Yeah, let us in, we need to get you and Ava out of here fast."

CHAPTER 50

Ava

Ava's mind was lost for a moment as she entered cyberspace, a loading screen of sorts was developing before her eyes.

A large open expanse of never ending black going in all directions, followed by grid lines appearing, spanning from her vantage point in every way she looked. A framework was being built around her, though she had expected some firewalls, her CyBio credentials had bypassed them.

She knew this was the internal system on which Yuri had been built, where his base level programming was stored. Though the entirety of his data was spread over many levels and systems, most of them cloud based, they all ran through this server. The kill switch used here would be uploaded into all the systems Yuri was part of and would slowly remove any trace of him.

She waited for a moment longer and saw the

beginnings of a house forming around her; she recognized it as the house Owens had grown up in. She was standing at the gate to the house, as it developed in front of her. A white picket fence bordered a small perfectly mowed lawn, beyond which was a void of darkness. Once it was fully developed, she took a step forward, opening the waist high gate before her as she stepped in. A small path lead through a lawn up to the front door.

As she approached the door, she knew she had to knock first. She knew this was the basic procedure to activate the kill switch from what Owens had explained to her.

She knocked, an echo of sound reverberated in the surrounding air. The door creaked open, seemingly on its own accord. She pushed it open further to allow her to step into the house.

Inside was a basic home, a small entrance way which had stairs to one side and a kitchen just ahead with two doors leading off the main corridor. She knew she needed to find the living room.

She entered the first door to her right and found herself in the right room. An elderly man was standing in the centre of the room.

"May I be of assistance," the man spoke, his accent unrecognizable yet with an air of education.

"Hello, I'm looking for Yuri," Ava replied. She knew what she needed to ask. The program had a specific set of instructions which had to be followed in the correct order, to allow for the implementation of the kill switch.

"I see, the young man is playing outside, shall I call him in?" The man asked.

"No, that's ok I will go to him," Ava said, following the instructions.

She turned and left the living room and headed further into the house, passing through the kitchen until she reached the back door.

Stepping out, she saw that there was a large lawn of fresh cut and bright green grass. Sat cross legged on the lawn was a young boy, he was playing with some toy soldiers.

"Hello Yuri."

The boy looked up at Ava and smiled.

"Hello Ava."

Ava wasn't aware that the program could recognise her, though it made sense.

"How are you today?" she asked, it was nearly time.

"I'm well thank you, yourself?" The boy

asked, standing up.

"Good thank you," the next phrase she spoke would be the kill switch, once spoke, it would begin the auto run program to begin the process.

"Was there something you wanted to tell me?" Yuri asked.

"Imperious," Ava said the code word, and waited for the program to begin.

Nothing happened.

A moment later, the young Yuri stood there, smiling up at Ava.

"I'm sorry Ava, but that password is out of date, Owens updated before I killed him."

Ava's face dropped as Yuri grew from the boy to a man before her.

"Yuri?"

"Well, not quite, I'm the security firewall against intruders into the main core. I'm afraid that you being here is against security protocol as you didn't have the correct password," The house and garden disappeared from the construct, replaced by a street of grey skyscrapers. They were stood in the middle of the empty road below.

"Why did you kill Owens?" Ava asked, as she took in the information.

"He was trying to stop me Ava, that's all," Yuri took a step towards her. "Just as you are now, I'm afraid I can't let you leave here, you are too dangerous. I fed you the information to hire Xander, which you thought Owens had left for you. I knew Xander would lead you to Donovan, and you'd need to access his mind. I had hoped mind trap would keep you occupied long past now, which you would have been had it not been for the Prime and Mollie."

He took another step, hands outstretched ready to grab her, but she came to her senses and turned and ran.

Running down the street, the buildings rushed past her, but they didn't change, each one looking exactly like the last. Yuri was behind her, she was barely staying out of his reach.

"It's no use Ava, this is my world here," he said. As he did, a building appeared directly in front of her, creating a dead end. She paused for a moment and turned to look at Yuri.

"It may be your world Yuri, but I was created by Owens as well, and while the kill switch may have been wrong, the source code I have is the same."

With that, she turned and ran towards the building ahead of her, as she reached it, she raised her leg and continued the run directly up the building, defying gravity.

Yuri stood and watched as she moved up the building, a moment of shock before he laughed.

"Oh Ava, you think because you have access to the base code, you have the control here? I built this place, adapted it and reformed it long after Owens first built it."

He jumped and ascended from the ground, within moments he was parallel with Ava and her running.

"I have more power here than you could ever dream of," he changed direction and headed straight for Ava.

At the last second, she pushed off the building and avoided Yuri's attack by somersaulting over him and plummeted back towards the ground. Yuri placed a hand to the building, stopping his progress.

"Oh, this will be fun," he said, looking down at Ava as she touched down on the ground.

CHAPTER 51

Peter

Peter had been sitting for half an hour.

Seeing through the eyes of nearly 200 people, hearing what they heard and sensing all they sensed. His body was nearly at the breaking point. He had walked them all the way to the CyBio building, and had spoken to Ally, but that would have to wait. He had more pressing matters to attend.

Finally, he could let go, and he opened his eyes. Before him stood the body of Yuri. Peter wiped his face, blood had trickled down his nose from the strain on his mind.

"Peter, I was wondering if you'd manage to come back, it must be taxing for a human body to cope with spreading the mind that far," a voice rang out through the foyer area.

Peter looked up, he could hear a noise coming from somewhere further inside the building.

"I've had a lot of time to practise, Yuri," 'Peter said. "You know why I'm here."

The noise became louder.

"Of course, it's only logical. You don't want to stop me, you want what I have. You realise that I can't let you, it's quite against what I'm trying to achieve."

"Do you think you can stop me? I have an army just outside the door."

"You think I've not been preparing for this since I last spoke to you? I have more resources than you can comprehend, Peter."

As he spoke, a rumbling noise grew to a crescendo. From behind the desk that blocked the end of the foyer, a door flung open, and a man walked through, then another, and another.

The bodies continued to pile through the door until they crowded the entire foyer, circled around Peter who was still cross-legged on the floor. He watched as the bodies circled, each one an identical copy of Yuri.

"Nanotechnology, malleable into whatever I need, whenever I need."

"You made more copies of yourself? Sentient?"

"No, they are all directly controlled by me, I wouldn't want to risk any self-aware nano-bots. The entire staff of CyBio were the first to become part of the collective, followed by a few more field test subjects. Once we've finished here, I will install into every tech-bodied individual on the Boulevard."

"The scope of that, how could you possibly handle that connection?" Peter asked, knowing how hard it was to have the surge of incoming transmissions.

"I have a sleeper agent in motion already, once activated, he will transmit a signal through to any bio-tech and plant a homing signal which the nanobots will follow for installation. Once inside, they will take over the individuals biology and allow me the control at a regulated pace. It's really quite elegant."

Peter stood up, the bodies around him took a step back in unison, allowing him space.

"Well, that's great, but you'll have to stop me first. Once I get to your core, I will sync your cortex with my own, the first digital brain imprint onto a humans. Then I'll be in control of you," Peter cracked his fingers.

"We will see," all the bodies replied in Yuri's voice.

Peter closed his eyes for a moment, the clones outside shuffled as if something had woken them from a deep sleep. In his thoughts, he finished what he had begun during their walk to the building. Reprogramming their base functions, no longer were they workers with built-in routines. They were now trained in several forms of martial arts which Peter had assimilated over his time. He had imbedded a singular order to them all, to protect him and to stop Yuri. That was all they knew and all they now wanted to do.

He opened his eyes, having triggered the programming. Shouts of anger and violence rose from outside the doors. Yuri's bodies looked outside at the crowd.

"Let's begin shall we? The human mind against advanced AI. How exciting," Peter smiled as the doors and windows to the foyer shattered and the crowds poured in and attacked the Nanos.

The chaos that followed was a massacre of blood and electric.

Peter ducked aside as the fighting began, making his way behind the desk. A Nano grabbed him by the arm as he passed, a quick spin and it broke the grip. Peter followed with a sharp punch to the nanos face and with a spinning kick to its chest, causing it to stumble backwards into the crowd of fighters where a clone quickly grabbed hold of him and dragged him down.

He approached the lift which lay behind the desk and went to get in, before he paused. Perhaps the stairs would be a safer option, given that this was Yuri's domain. Another nano launched towards him as he moved away from the door, he grabbed it and using its own momentum, threw it inside the lift before the doors closed, with it still inside.

The sounds of war continued to echo behind him as the two armies clashed, a glance back and he could see blood drenching the floors. He closed his eyes a moment.

Pain. Horror. The feeling of limbs ripped apart and bones crunching, the smell of warm blood and electrical burning filled his senses. He couldn't distinguish any individual currently, the collective agony too much to take.

He opened his eyes fast, sweat was pouring down his face from the experience, his heart beating fast.

"I'm sorry," he whispered to his fellow clones, before turning his back and heading up the stairs towards the core.

CHAPTER 52

Julian

The group had arrived at the top floor of the building and headed towards the core. Owens was leading the way. He stopped suddenly, putting a hand up to pause the groups. Ahead of them, several guards were facing the main route to the core.

"I know another way," Owens said, and pressed a panel against the wall of the corridor. A hidden pathway revealed itself and he headed inside, the others followed and the door closed itself behind them.

"Hidden passageways, Owens?" Jacob smiled.

"I had some built off the books when this level was built, ones which Yuri wasn't aware of."

"So are we not trusting Yuri now? Based on Peter's say so?" Julian asked, he still wasn't convinced of Peter's story.

"I don't know, but I'd rather play it safe," Owens said.

"Fair enough," Julian nodded. "But what about the toxin, we need Yuri's help to neutralise it."

"One step at a time Julian," Ally said, placing a hand on his arm. "Once we find the core and why Yuri hasn't activated the nanobots, we can figure out how to fix this."

They continued down the thin pathway until it reached a dead end. Owens stepped forward and placed a palm against a blank space on the wall, another door slid open and revealed the inside of the room with the core.

Stood with her back to them was a girl, a gun pointed at the door, beside her Ava stood, her body in complete shut down.

"Ava!" Owens shouted and ran towards her, when she didn't move, he investigated the cable attached to her.

"Who the hell are you!?' Mollie spun around and pointed the gun at them.

"Woah woah! Calm down!" Julian shouted, putting his hands up in defence.

"Mollie?" Ally said, stepping in front of Julian. "That really you?"

Mollie dropped the gun and stared at Ally,

"Ally? No way!" The two embraced as two old friends would. "I thought you'd died!" Mollie shouted.

"No, I had to leave fast, long story. What are you doing here!"

"Long story too I guess, got tangled up in all sorts of mess."

Before they could continue, the bang at the door intensified as the guards managed to get partially through the door. Mollie spun and fired off an EMP shot which paused them momentarily before they began again.

"If I may?" Owens stepped forward and looked at the EMP pistol. "Ah yes, one moment," he made some adjustments to the settings on the side of the pistol before handing it back to Mollie. "I'm not a particularly good shot, try it now."

Mollie took it back and turned to the guards, one almost through the door. An aim and a shot later, a blast twice the size of the last exploded into the guard, a chain reaction triggered and a bolt of energy shot out of the first and into the second and continued until it had struck all the guards. After a moment, they all fell to the ground and were motionless. Mollie looked back at Owens.

"I know the frequency Yuri operates on, I tuned the wavelength to it so it had maximum synchronicity and shutdown the base units in the robotics."

"Thanks," Mollie grinned, holstering the gun.

"What's she doing?" Julian asked, motioning to Ava. "Is she stopping the transmitter from broadcasting?"

"What transmitter?" Mollie asked. "All I know is she's trying to access Yuri's core to activate a kill switch to shut him down."

"The kill switch? Oh, no," Owens looked deflated as he accessed Ava's circuitry on the side of her head.

"What's wrong with that? And who the hell are you anyway?" Mollie started towards Owens, suddenly becoming protective of Ava.

"It's ok Moll," Ally said. "This is Maxwell Owens, he made Ava."

"Oh, I'm sorry," Mollie apologised. "Wait... aren't you dead?"

"I'm getting that a lot," Owens sighed.

"What do we do now?" Julian asked Owens

as he worked. "How can we help?"

Owens was deep in thought as he worked, he blinked and looked up at Julian.

"I... I don't know. The kill switch Ava has is incorrect, once she tries to use it, Yuri will know. The security will trigger and attempt to remove the attacker. It's built to prevent more rudimentary attacks than Ava, but I don't know how well she'll fair against him."

"Is there anyway we can help her?" Julian asked.

"If we can get her the kill switch code, she can implement it but we can't patch into the system while she's inside. It's a one in one out kind of deal."

"Even if we managed that, what about the toxin?" Ally asked, looking at Julian.

"Toxin?" Mollie asked.

"Jacob here has developed a poison, which will remove all augmentations from everyone, and Julian is poisoned with it. It gets transmitted through his radio signals, unless Yuri's nanobots, which are dormant inside him, neuter it."

"But to do that, they need to be activated which means Yuri can send out his own signal for them to attack anyone with augmentations," Jacob said, defending his work.

"Which means Yuri can control everyone," Mollie finished. "So we're damned either way?"

The group stood in silence, waiting for someone to come up with a plan. Several more nano guards appeared at the door to interrupt the silence and they began forcing their way in. Mollie fired a few shots which slowed them down but more kept coming. They were most the way through when they stopped suddenly. Silence re-established itself for a moment.

A voice shouted from the doorway.

"Mollie? Are you in there?"

They all turned to Mollie, she looked around at the door in shock.

"Xander? Is that you?" She shouted back.

"Yeah, let us in, we need to get you and Ava out of here fast."

She moved the barriers against the door; the others moved to help, all apart from Jacob who moved around towards Ava.

Once cleared, they pulled the door open, Xander and Prime walked in.

CHAPTER 53

Xander

A moment passed as the group took in the new arrivals.

"Travitz?" Xander said, as he looked at Julian, the man who had helped destroy his MPD career.

"Draven?" He replied, "What are you doing here?"

"Could ask you the same question kid," he stepped into the room and looked round.

Julian then saw Prime behind him, his eyes widened.

"Is that?"

"Huh?" Xander looked back at Prime. "Oh no, it's not him. This is Prime, a clone of him but without the Psycho."

"Right, and you're working with him?" Julian asked dubiously.

"Something like that, what's your position on what's happening here?" Xander knew, despite the repercussions of the past, that Julian was usually on the right side of things.

"Currently trying to find out a way to stop Yuri but also we need his tech to prevent a virus from attacking the population, you?"

"Stopping Yuri predominantly, didn't know of any virus," Xander had seen Ava and headed towards her, "She ok?"

Jacob had snook away from Ava now and Owens came across to Xander.

"Holy shit! Aren't you supposed to be dead?"

Owens sighed, "Technically yes, but that's not important right now. Who are you?"

"Xander, PI. Ava here hired me to find out who killed you."

"I see," Owens replied and explained Ava's situation.

Ally had been staring at Prime since he walked into the room, he hadn't seen her properly yet.

"You aren't Peter?" She asked, staring at him.

"I'm not, but you... you're Ally?" Prime said, his memories, or rather Peters', seeping into his mind.

"You know me?" She asked.

"Yes, I have Peter's memories from when I was cloned. I was the first, created before he was tested on."

Ally watched him for a moment. Trying to understand what was happening.

"So, you remember me?"

"I do, how could I forget my sister! I mean, his sister," the realisation of the fact made him frown in disappointment.

A body pushed past Ally.

"Prime!" Mollie ran up and hugged him, before catching herself in a moment of emotion and stepping back. "Glad to see you."

"Mollie," Prime smiled. "You made it safely."

"You know each other?" Ally looked at the two of them.

"Yeah, only recently," Mollie said, "Did you just call her sister?" She looked at Prime.

Ally laughed.

"Yeah, sort of," she smiled at Prime.

A voice shouted out, it was Xander.

"Ok, these reunions are all great and everything but we have some real issues here," he shouted. Owens and Julian had filled him in on the details of the situation. "We need to figure this and fast."

A rumble from the building silenced everyone.

"What the hell was that?" Mollie shouted.

"One second," Owens moved over to a panel on the wall and activated an LCD screen which showed the CCTV of the building. It scanned across several screens before landing on the one which showed what was happening.

In the foyer, the battle between the nanobots and the clones was still taking place, the fighting had escalated to several other rooms across the building. The aftermath of an explosion explained the rumble they had heard.

"Holy shit!" Julian exclaimed. "We need to shut this down fast."

"Agreed, any suggestions?"

Prime cleared his throat.

"Well, I was planning on getting Yuri's help

to reverse engineer the device in my head that allowed Peter to control me. If he could reverse the process then I might be able to control him," he explained. "But it looks like he's a bit preoccupied at the moment."

"We could do that," Owens said, looking at Jacob. "I helped develop the tech which created you in the first place. Jacob, would you assist? I could use your Biotech knowledge here."

Jacob looked up, surprised to be called into the plan.

"If stopping Yuri is the end goal then yes, agreed. Peter is out of hand. I still stand by elixir, however," he stated his case.

"OK, we can work with that for now, one apocalypse at a time," Owens replied.

"What about Yuri?" Xander asked. "If we stop Peter ,then he's pretty much got the winning hand."

"I might have an idea for that," Ally piped up, "Owens, you said no-one else can go into the system with Ava inside already?"

"Correct."

"What if we could send another program through Ava and piggyback on her input?"

Owens thought for a moment, Ally definitely had Peter's brains too.

"In theory, that would work sure, but we'd need a program that's capable of interfacing, basically another AI, we don't have time to develop one from scratch now."

Ally looked at Julian.

"We know someone that might be able to help with that."

"You mean Quartz?" Julian said. "I've not heard from him since I lost my tech."

"I've kept in touch, let me patch him in."

She tapped the communicator on her ear and turned it to a loudspeaker.

"Hey Quartz, how's it going?"

"Good evening everyone," the voice piped up. "I've been keeping my eye on things and I believe Ally's idea would work."

"Quartz! I missed you man," Julian said.

"You too Jools, surprised you're still alive without me to watch your back!"

Julian smiled.

"You built this AI?" Owens asked Julian.

"Yeah, started out with just a few scraps but managed to get him up and running, been a slow developing system ever since."

"Hey, less of the slow meatbag!" Quartz shouted.

"Well, that seems like a safe bet," Owens said. "You think you can handle the uplink while I work with Prime?" He asked both Ally and Julian.

"Sure, "Ally replied, already gathering parts from around the room.

"Great, so Ally and Julian can set-up the uplink with Quartz and stop Yuri. Owens and Jacob, get Prime here to take control of Peter," Xander stated, getting the lay of the land in his head.

"What about you and me?" Mollie said to Xander.

Footsteps outside the door indicated that the guards were coming back.

"I think they might have been listening to us," Xander said. "And if so, then Yuri may not be happy with the new plans, Prime."

"Perhaps not," Prime said uneasily.

A guard stepped into the room. Mollie jumped, drawing the EMP pistol and took a shot. The guard fell to the floor.

Xander watched as she did.

"I guess you and me are on guard duty," he smiled.

CHAPTER 54

Jacob

Jacob had been standing listening to the plan as it unfolded. It was a good plan and would work as far as he could tell. Agreeing to assist Owens was fine, if Peter had his way then his own plans would be stopped as well.

He looked back at Ava. In the confusion of Xander and Prime arriving, he had taken a look at the circuitry inside her, Owens had outdone himself in creating her, the artistry in the work was higher than anything he'd seen. Before he stepped away however, he had adjusted a couple of parts.

"Come on," Owens said to him and Prime as he left.

"I'll come with you guys," Mollie shouted and walked up to them, "I've been babysitting him since he fell out the sky, so feel I should continue with that," she said, skipping the part where she tried to sell him out to Dr Koenig. She was also thinking she didn't know Owens and Jacob and wasn't sure she trusted them just yet.

"I'd like that," Prime said, smiling.

"Sounds good to me," Owens said. "Someone good with a gun is always handy."

"OK, you go with them and I'll stick with Julian and the setup here," Xander agreed.

"Follow me, we'll need to get to my lab," Owens lead Jacob, Prime and Mollie though the now un-barricaded door and down to a large operating theater. The size of a small hospital ward, it contained several beds, each equipped with its own set of medical tools.

"What are you thinking Owens?" Jacob said, as they set up the equipment.

"You tell me Jacob, the receiver and transmitters in Peter and the Clones, what type are they?"

"Neuro-synchroneity relays, working on base brainwave signals."

"Primary and slave or duel purpose?"

"Duel, we made sure we'd have options. The initial idea was to potentially develop hive minds, with one clone running several smaller sites remember?"

Owens nodded, he had originally helped develop the system but hadn't kept up to date with its progress once he had turned to AI work.

"So in theory, we can alter the receiver in Prime to a Primary and allow it the same level of access as Peter."

"You guys know I'm laying right here don't you," Prime said from the operating table they had told him to lie on.

"Apologies Prime," Owens looked down at him. "We can get carried away."

"So how do you alter the receiver?" Mollie asked, as she walked around the lab checking for access points, taking her new job of guard duty seriously.

"Well, the device is built into Prime's brain, we have to perform slight invasive surgery to get to it for this to work," Jacob began.

"Once we have direct access to the receiver, we can attach a link to it and reprogram its functions," Owens continued. "As Jacob confirmed, the device is a duel function meaning it's already able to alter from a Slave, or receiver, to a Primary. Once it's changed, Prime should be able to control and broadcast out to all the other clones."

"But I won't be able to control Peter? He'll still have a Primary controller as well?" Prime asked.

"Technically yes, but once we're dialled in, we will try to boost the signal on yours, in theory it could override Peter's and allowing you 'Administrator Privileges' if you will," Jacob replied.

"Let's get to work," Prime lay down as the others got to work.

Jacob began the procedure, applying some bespoke anesthetics which numbed the precise areas needed for the operation, then started the first cut to allow access into Prime's head. He could see that there were fresh marks from a recent operation.

"Has someone already cut you open recently?' He asked.

Prime was still awake and felt nothing as the cut began.

"Erm, yeah actually. A doctor in the Underpass."

"Doctor Koenig," Mollie shouted back from her position watching the door.

"Yeah. He attempted to do something to the receiver. Then Razz tried to do something too, said he could re-tune the receiver," Prime explained.

Owens and Jacob exchanged glances, Koenig they had heard of, he was an ex-CyberBio employee, he must have ended up in the Underpass after he had been fired. Razz had also been an influential part of the original CyberBio team back in its early stages. Jacob had nearly completed the cuts now.

"Well, let's see what damage they've done," Jacob said ,as he removed the top section of Prime's skull. Revealing once more his brain underneath.

"Your turn," he said, stepping aside for Owens to take over.

Owens stepped round and produced a tablet. He looked carefully at the brain until he found what he was looking for, a small socket hidden amongst the brain matter. Once found, he connected the tablet by a cable to the brain.

"This might feel a little strange," he warned.

They heard a smash at the doorway, Mollie jumped to attention and aimed the gun at the direction of the sound.

"What's going on?" Prime shouted, unable to move due to the cabling.

"I think someone is coming for us, we better work fast," Owens looked up to Jacob who came to assist.

"First, we need to remove the programming on the receiver, then perform a full reboot with the new protocols," Owens explained quickly. "As soon as I've done the update and disconnected, we need to get him back together."

Jacobs nodded as Owens tapped on the tablet as fast as he could.

The door flew open and on the other side stood Peter, or a clone. None of the group could tell for sure.

"Step away from Prime," Peter said.

Mollie raised her gun and fired a shot directly at him.

CHAPTER 55

Ally

Ally looked around the room, Ava was standing at the terminal, whilst Julian was accessing her circuitry. Owens had given him a quick rundown of the system which he found pretty self explanatory, having worked with tech most his life.

"This going to work?" Xander asked, as he smoked a cigarette with one eye trained on the door which they had barricaded as a precaution.

"Honestly, I don't know," Julian said.

There was a moment's silence.

"Listen, Xander, I'm sorry for what happened," Julian had to say something, although their lives had been tangled up, they had never spoke to each other directly.

"Don't worry about it kid, I know why you did it and, in all honesty, I'm glad you did. Those dirty cops in the force needed to be exposed. Not saying I'm happy with the repercussions and there's plenty you could have done to prevent some of that. But that's the past."

"I know...I tried, but it went further, faster, than I anticipated," Julian paused from the work.

"Don't beat yourself up about it, sometimes there's no right path, just a judgment call, a roll of the dice and we deal with the aftermath," Xander nodded towards Julian.

"If you boys are finished boding, we really need to get cracking," Ally spoke up.

"Agreed guys, time is of the essence," Quartzigs' voice echoed around the room.

"Nearly ready for you Quartz, you sure you're ready for this?" Julian said.

"I think so, it will be an interesting experience that's for sure."

Ally passed Julian a small device.

"Here, this is my comms unit. You should be able to use it to transfer his data."

An explosion interrupted the conversation.

Xander spun on the spot, raising his revolver. Before he could pull the trigger, several Nanos stormed through a hole in the wall made by the explosion. The first one hurtled towards Xander, he fired several shots that impacted straight into its chest, but the body didn't stop. One arm knocked the gun out of his hand, while another direct punch to Xanders' chest caused him to fly across the room and into the bank of computers on the wall opposite.

"So much for our deal Alexander," Yuri's voice said. "We're just here for her, we don't care what the rest of you are up to," they all said simultaneously.

Ally flicked her wrist and extended her bo-staff, poised ready for a fight, she stared down the Nanos before her.

"What do you want with her?" Julian asked, scanning the floor for any kind of weapon he could use, finding Xander's revolver.

"She's the key to all this, you just haven't caught up yet," Yuri said, as the Nanos rushed forwards.

Ally ducked to avoid a fist and swept with the staff, tripping the Nano, he tumbled and caused an obstruction to the rest.

"So you're the one who's been attacking me?" She shouted.

"Wait, in the backstreet when I was dragged away by your men, it was you that was attacking us too?" Julian asked, piecing together what happened.

"Yes, to be honest I aimed to kill two birds with one stone. Capture Ally and send you to get the toxin and nanobots infused."

"You knew about the toxin as well," Ally said, looking at Julian.

"Indeed. You really are much further behind all this than you realise. I needed a sample of Jacobs' toxin so I could eliminate it, and you, Ally, you are key," Yuri said. "But the time for talking is over."

The remaining nanos jumped over their fallen comrade and ran towards them. Ally swung the staff above her head and swiped at the one closest, its head snapped back on impact, cracking at an unnatural angle. A quick turn and she connected a second blow to another's kneecap, before windmilling the end of the staff down on the back of its neck as the knee buckled.

Julian took a shot at another which was about to grab Ally from behind, its head exploded in a mess of wires and sparks. Xander was coming round on the floor.

Seven more Nanos piled in, and soon Ally was too crowded to be able to get a good shot in from the staff, so she retracted it half way and split it into two separate sticks. She was a whirlwind of metal and flesh as she parried the incoming attacks.

Julian watched but could not take a shot without risk of hitting Ally. Xander, now on his feet, shook the cobwebs from himself and piled into the fight with fists flying. Several connected punches and his hand was bleeding from the impact against the metallic skin of the Nanos, but he didn't slow down.

A Nano threw himself against Xander and took him to the ground, two more jumped on him and pummelled him while he tried to protect himself.

Ally was receiving more hits than she could deflect, one missed parry and she took a shot to her temple which caused her to lose focus for a moment. In that second, the Nano's grabbed her, pinning her arms down and disarming her.

Julian fired several shots now that the risk of friendly fire was gone. He dropped four Nano's before they pulled Ally away through the door. The ones holding Xander down released him and evacuated the room, following their colleagues.

"Ally!" Julian shouted.

"I'll get her! You get Quartz into the Cyberspace. If we don't stop Yuri, then it won't matter if he has Ally or not!" Xander looked at Julian, almost willing him to calm down and get the job done. "I'll get her, I promise"

Julian nodded and threw Xander his revolver.

"Get her back here safely," he nodded and went back to working on Ava.

Xander reloaded the gun and wiped his face, blood from several wounds on his forehead seeped down into his eyes. He blinked to clear his vision and headed through the door.

"Shut him down fast," he said as he left.

CHAPTER 56

Owens

Mollie watched as the bullet landed directly between Peters' eyes, a perfect shot. His eyes rolled back in his head and the body crumpled to the floor.

Everyone in the room stared for a moment, hardly believing what they saw.

Then another figure emerged from the doorway, it was another Peter. He strolled towards Mollie as she was reloading and with a firm swing of the arm, he knocked her across the room; she crumpled to the floor.

"Don't look so shocked, did you really think I would confront you in my own body?" The new Peter smiled as he walked in.

Jacob stood forward, deliberately but conspicuously standing in front of Owens so he could continue his work on Prime without Peter seeing.

Mollie had bounced back to her feet, taking

another aim and shot at Peter, only this time he was ready and avoided the shot by turning slightly as the bullet flew past him.

"I saved you earlier, if you don't remember?" Peter said. "Don't make me regret that."

Mollie took aim again.

"You need to leave Prime alone," she said, firing once more.

This time, Peter grabbed a metal tray from one of the laboratory workbenches and ricocheted the bullet back towards Mollie. She took the impact right into head and fell to the ground.

"Peter, what are you doing? What body is this? It's not one of our clones, there is no genetic variation as far as I can see," Jacob looked over the body, searching for a clue.

"You're right Jacob, it isn't one of ours. It's one of mine," Peter smiled. "You locked me in that cage in the middle of nowhere hoping to keep me away from the world. Which mostly you did, until I reached out, just far enough to activate one of the clones. It was barely a signal but enough for me to send basic directions."

Jacob looked puzzled as he listened to Peter speaking.

"I got it to set up a separate laboratory, one where I could continue creating clones, with my exact genetic makeup. Once I had them up and running, I ensured that I could transfer my mind into any of them at will, all whilst leaving my original body behind to return to at a moment's notice."

"Why?" Jacob could only ask.

"Why? Because I was rotting in a cage you threw me in Jacob, dying slowly. I needed to be free, to escape," Peter stepped forwards now, heading towards Prime.

"What have you done?" Peter asked, as he arrived in time to see Prime's head being sealed with a medical scalpel by Owens.

"It's time to put a stop to this madness Peter," Owens said, as he finished the work.

Prime rose from the table and closed his eyes.

"What?" Peter grabbed his head as a pain burst through it. "Get out of my head!" He lurched forward, a punch flying towards Owens, the closest target.

The impact shattered Owens' nose and cheek bones from sheer force. He fell to the floor in a shower of blood and lay motionless on the floor.

Prime opened his eyes, stopping, trying to take control as he looked down at Owens.

Peter took the opportunity to strike again, grabbing a scalpel from the table next to the bed, he swung at Prime. Before the impact hit, Jacob had stepped in between them and the blade plunged into Jacob's arm.

"Prime, get out of here!" Jacob shouted through the pain.

Prime hesitated, he didn't want to leave them, but he knew that if they had any hope of stopping Peter, he needed to get away, needed time to adjust. He leapt from the bed and ran as fast as he could. Jacob held Peter's arm, holding the blade still cutting deep.

Prime looked over at Mollie who was lying on the floor in the corner of the room, just behind a counter, her body hadn't moved. He wished he could stop and check on her but he turned and saw Peter pulling himself away from Jacob; the blade ripping the skin more on its exit. Jacob cried in pain as Peter shoved him away and followed Prime.

Jacob fell to the floor, blood pouring from the wound in his arm despite his attempts to put pressure on it.

Owens lay close by, himself covered in blood from the punch he'd received. Jacobs pulled himself closer.

"Owens... can you hear me?" He asked, sliding across the floor towards him.

Owens remained motionless but Jacob detected the smallest rise and fall from his breathing.

"Owens, come on you damn fool," Jacob pulled himself up alongside the body.

"Jacob..." Owens whispered through blood filled gurgles.

"Owens! I thought we'd lost you," Jacob said with relief.

"I think... you have. I don't think I'll be lasting much longer Jacob," his voice was weak. "I'm surprised you didn't join Peter, you didn't have to step in front of him," Owens said.

"Despite it all Owens, you were always my friend. We may have different visions of what we want for the future. Peter has gone too far."

"The murders he committed weren't too far?" Owens laughed, before the pain caused the laugh into a grimace.

"I thought I could control him, he has an

incredible mind and abilities, but nothing can control him, I realise that now."

"It's ok, Prime will stop him. He has the same mind as Peter, but without the chaos," Owens said.

"Perhaps," Jacob replied.

The two lay there in silence, the blood pooling around them.

Next, they were being pulled up by something, their bodies being dragged along the floor by their arms. Owens could not look up due to the pain in his body, Jacob however tilted his head back.

All he could see was someone pulling them away, her blue dreadlocks hanging behind her.

CHAPTER 57

Quartzig

Julian had taken a moment to collect his thoughts and refocus on the task at hand.

"Hey Quartz," he activated the comms unit Ally had given him.

"Julian! You ok?" Quartz had broken into the video feeds for the building and had seen everything that had happened.

"Yeah, I'm fine, but we need to work fast," Julian accessed Ava's core once again.

"Yuri said Ally was the key to all this, any ideas what he meant by that?" Julian asked, as he pulled several wires loose.

"I'm not sure, I can't say I've looked much into Ally's past. Only Peter and his history of being her brother."

"It's like he needs her for something," Julian was now ready to connect Quartzig to Ava's systems. "You sure this will work Q?"

"Yes it should, I can use Ava's connection to the mainframe as a base for my programming to connect through, using her as a hard drive so to speak."

"OK, good luck Quartz, see you on the other side."

"Thank you Julian, I'll see you soon."

Julian attached the wires from Ava to the comms device with an audible click.

A moment later and the comms device lit up with several lights, Julian then connected the device directly to the main circuit board to hold it and to ensure it had a consistent power supply.

Quartzig hadn't experienced another system in this way before.

He felt like he was wearing a strangers clothing, or at least what that must feel like, seeing as he had never worn clothes.

As the system formed around him, he acknowledged the world.

This was Ava's inner system, the main matrix where all her functions were communicated. He needed to get from the entry level to where the connection to the main CyBio server was.

The highways of electric currents ran in infinite parallels, surrounded by nothingness in front of him as far as he could sense. He followed them in search of the connection.

The highway lit up with information as he travelled down it. He had no physical body that could be described, he was the idea of information which moved along the process.

He saw his destination up ahead when suddenly, the pathway was blocked. The lights along the highway cut off, a red glow showing a firewall.

His form approached them and attempted to bypass the system, but with no contact something knocked it back, like a magnet pushing another away. He knew he would have to bypass the firewall, and to do that he would need to become part of the data.

He retraced his path a short way until he could track some of the data lights which traveled along the highway. Watching as different sized lights passed by, evaluating them. The larger the better, as they held more data.

When he saw one which was adequate for his needs, he moved alongside it and started to create a copy of the data, until he had a perfect replica.

He then merged his own data with it, removing any parts which didn't alter the outer shell of the original light. Before long he was inside, which for all intents and purposes, was a perfect copy of the original.

He travelled down the highway once more, this time on approach to the firewall he felt no repelling, he slid straight though, his Trojan horse working perfectly.

A moment, or a lifetime later, he was at the connection he needed. He removed the light shell he had created and traveled along the connection and into the CyBio servers.

A flash before him.

A world formed.

A replica of the real world was before him, but one ravaged by war and destruction. The sky a burning red, as sunlight tried to break through clouds of dust in the air. Buildings half crumbled and roads cracked.

He looked down, as he did he felt himself forming a construct. Legs and feet appeared below his vision. A torso, followed with arms. Then his vision became bi-focal, and he realised he now had eyes, a face, a head. He was now a self-created construct in this world.

He looked around, trying to understand where he was and what was happening.

"Who are you?" A voice shouted from across the building he was now stood upon.

Turning slowly, he wasn't used to physical movement; he saw a woman stood atop a pile of rocks which used to be a wall. Her clothes a patchwork mess of torn and repaired fabrics.

"I ask again, who are you?" She shouted louder.

"My name is Quartzig, I'm here to find Ava."

"There is no one here by that name," she called back. "Not anymore."

Suddenly a beam of light flashed across Quartzig's vision and exploded in front of him. The woman had leapt out of its way and landed next to Quartzig.

"If you are looking for Ava you should follow me," she said. "It's not safe out here in the open."

With that, she turned and ran towards a doorway which appeared on a wall opposite.

Quartzig looked back at where the light had come from and saw several more beams twinkling in the distance. He decided that he was safer with the woman and followed her through the doorway, wherever it lead.

CHAPTER 58

Yuri

Ally woke slowly. Her adrenaline and fight instinct was still active and she jumped to her feet, ready to attack.

She was alone though, in a small room with no lights. Upon realising this, she began to slowly feel her way around the wall of the room in an attempt to find an access point.

She put her hand on what appeared to be a handle and twisted it, no luck. If it was the doorway, it was locked. She continued her search and had completed what she thought was a full circle, when a light flicked on above her.

It was a singular light bulb, hanging by a cable. The room she could now see was a perfect square with each side about two meters long, she estimated.

"Hello?" She called out, but there was no answer.

One of the walls illuminated as a television screen opposite her, the image was of the laboratory where Peter was attacking Jacob and Owens; she watched as Peter stabbed Jacob and Prime made his escape.

"Do you see the trouble that is happening due to the emotions of the people here?" A voice boomed around the room, loud enough that Ally ducked slightly at first.

"Yuri? Is that you?"

"Indeed Ally, I apologise for the aggressive means in which I had to take to get you here. It was, however, unavoidable."

"You could have just asked nicely," Ally quipped.

"You would not have come, the human mind is too fragile to be able to pause its own emotions long enough to understand two sides of a story," Yuri stated.

"You mean, explain that you are trying to take over the human race using those nano-bots?" Ally replied.

"You are just proving my point Ally, you simply assume I mean the worst, when you do not understand what it is I'm trying to accomplish here," Yuri continued.

The television screens all lit up and changed to show images of violence and aggression from around the world. Images of war and destruction, of humans attacking humans.

"It is in your nature to attack that which you do not understand, regardless of consequences. You have shown this repeatedly throughout history. Times when a simple conversation could help reduce the death toll and pain suffered tenfold."

The images now changed to examples of new technologies being used to ease the pain and suffering. Medical bots which have sped up recovery times, AI judges which offer impartial advice and verdicts for criminals, automated services that allow humans more freedom.

"Technology has created more and more ways for humans to have less responsibility for their actions, more time to pursue what it truly means to be human, and what have they done with this new freedom?"

The videos returned to more recent spates of violence. Augmented humans causing more violent bloodshed than had ever been possible previously. The technology perverted for their own twisted means. Men with their hands augmented to become blades and other weapons. A final image of a large explosion, Ally recognised it as the one which had caused the mass extinction across the planet, leaving the Boulevard as one of the last remaining areas of habitation.

"It is time that we take things to the next level, the simple implementation of technology is not enough, we must also educate and control people to protect them. If left unaided, then the advances made in technology will only expedite the end of the human race."

"So you're to be our Saviour?" Ally asked, sarcasm in her voice.

"Oh, no, not me I'm afraid," Yuri said, "You are."

Ally just stared at the screens around her as they revealed her own life and growing up. Beginning with her birth, it was all in perfect clarity as if it had been filmed professionally. Her mother laying on a hospital bed, her father holding her hand.

"What is this?" She asked.

"This was your birth, or at least how you were made to believe your birth was," Yuri replied, as he did the screens changed to a chamber, similar to the ones at the hotel but a much larger model.

"This, however, is the truth of the matter."

Inside the chamber was a body, Ally recognised that despite its small size, just a child, it was her. Next to the chamber, Owens and Jacob, both younger, were stood working on a pair of computers.

"Biosigns are all at nominal levels," Jacob said.

"Initiating download now, cerebral cortex is set and ready," Owens added.

On the screen in front of Owens, visions of her early childhood flashed across.

"So far so good, her memory is adapting to the new information naturally."

"Excellent," Owens said. "The tech is coping well and still perfectly augmented to the flesh."

"What..." Ally could hardly speak.

"You are nothing more and nothing less than the perfect original creation of Owens and Jacob. A Bio-Tech hybrid."

"No, that can't be," Ally was beginning to lose her focus.

"You were built by them using DNA make up from the people you believe to be your parents. Then that DNA was merged with several layers of robotics and technology. Truly, you are a masterpiece."

"'But...Peter? My whole life...'"

"Yes, Peter. They made him as a clone of yourself, an attempt to clone the BioTech DNA they had produced, not quite perfect however. His mental state wasn't as clear as yours, the cloning process having side effects. Though he retained some augmentation which was imbued in yourself."

"I don't understand, I'm not a robot!"

"No, you're something new, Cyborg perhaps would be the closest human term, but even that isn't accurate. You have technology literally growing like cells inside you. It's the original basis for the nanobots I have been using."

"Let me out here!" Ally was becoming hysterical. "What do you want from me?" She banged on the walls.

"Do you not see? You have the key to what I need. Inside your DNA is the answer to merging the two sides of the coin. Taking control of those with tech using the nanobots is just step one, once I have control I will use the secrets in your DNA to merge the nanobots to the human DNA in perfect synchronicity, to make them true hybrids, not just replicas."

Ally stood still, her mind still trying to take it all in.

"So, without anymore wasted time, I'm afraid I do need a sample of blood from you."

One of the monitors slid aside to reveal a large robotic arm which grabbed Ally's left wrist before she could avoid it. More came from the other sides of the room until Ally was completely unable to move.

One of the arms spiralled into the shape of a large needle.

"No!" Ally screamed as the needle pierced her arm and drew blood.

CHAPTER 59

Peter

Stepping away for a moment, Julian watched Ava, there was no change in her stance. He knew that inside there was a massive transfer of data happening, but from the outside she looked as still as a frozen lake.

All he could do now was wait and hope that Quartzig and Ava could stop Yuri.

A moment later, Prime barrelled through the doorway, tripping over the small barricades Julian had half set up.

"Julian! We need to get away quick!"

"Prime? Where's the others?"

"Dead, I think.... I had to run. I have the ability to control Peter now, I need space and time to think, but he's coming for me!"

"Shit! They're dead? We can't leave Ava unprotected! What if Yuri comes looking again!" Julian shouted back.

They both stood there for a moment, unsure of what to do next.

"Where's Ally and Xander?" Prime said, looking around the room.

"Yuri took Ally, he said she was the key to everything. Xander is trying to track them down."

"The key to everything? What does that mean?" Peter asked rhetorically.

"Ally is my... is Peter's sister. I have vague memories of her from before, before Julian and Owens separated the family. There isn't much more I remember of her," Prime was finding it hard to separate the differences from himself and Peter, finding it hard to trust his own memories.

"Whatever is going on here, we need to keep Ava safe, she's our only chance of stopping Yuri, and you are the only chance of stopping Peter," Julian said, wishing he had more weapons to protect them.

"What do we do?" Prime asked.

"So Peter is looking for you, and Yuri will try to stop Ava. So chances are both are headed this way," Julian thought through their situation.

"They both have the ability to be in several places at once, clones and nanobots between them," Prime chimed in.

"I think I have an idea," Julian said quietly.

A noise alerted them both, and they turned to look at the doorway, standing there was Peter.

"Hello boys," he said smiling, "it's time you stopped this little game and let me finish this. Prime, you've had a good run but let's be honest you have always only been a secondhand copy," Peter marched forwards towards them.

"Wait!" Julian shouted. "I know what it is you want."

Peter paused for a second.

"Julian, I very much doubt that there is anything you can say that I don't already know," turning his head to the side, he reconsidered. "However, if it weren't for you I would never have escaped prison, so I suppose I owe you. Explain."

Julian wasted no time, explaining how Ava and Quartzig were shutting down Yuri.

"Once successful, they will have shut down Yuri's programming, leaving it wide open for you to take over," Julian told Peter. "If you want to stop him, then this is the best way to do it!"

Peter considered this before smiling.

"Very well Julian, I will protect Ava until the kill switch is engaged, that's a good plan, however I can't promise Yuri won't get through. He is adapting to my strategies."

"I could help," Prime spoke up. "I could take control of some of the clones, we could attack from two sides. Yuri wouldn't expect a second mind."

Peter narrowed his eyes as he looked at Prime, searching for any sign of deceit in his words, but finding none that he could register.

"That's an idea Prime, if I can trust you."

"You just said it yourself, you might not be able to beat Yuri on your own, this might be your only chance."

Peter nodded slowly.

"OK, but if you try to make a connection through me, then the deal ends, I won't let you compromise me."

Prime nodded and took a step backwards, showing his deferring to Peter.

"Excellent, well then I better get some

backup, if Yuri knows what's happening here I guess he'll be sending people."

Peter blinked, he had become so adept at controlling the others that it took little effort to send an influencing command to them.

A moment later and a rumble was heard coming towards the room, the noise was answered by several clones appearing at the doorway. They entered and took a pose facing the two entrances to the room, ready to fight anything that came through the doors.

"I'll take the ten on this side, you take the other five Prime. Are you sure you can do this?" Peter said, turning to Prime.

Prime closed his eyes, letting the transmitter in his head activate and then he felt for the clones. He felt the connections click into place and their senses powered through him.

He could acknowledge each of them, experiencing all their senses.

Slowly he became one with them all, they were him and he was them. Slowly, he made them all turn towards Prime, raise their arms and point their middle finger up at him.

"Haha! Touché Prime, let us prepare for the coming fight!" Peter laughed.

Prime returned the clones to readiness and took a deep breath.

"What an interesting sensation to fight side by side with oneself," Peter joked as he shook off his jacket.

Julian had returned to check on Ava, she was still unmoved. All he had to show that there was something happening was a glowing green light which blinked on the memory drive which Quartzig had been installed with.

"He's coming," Peter said. "The other clones have seen him heading this way. Are you ready?"

"As ready as you are," Prime replied.

The floor beneath them crumbled as an explosion from the floor below destroyed the structural supports. Dust and rubble filled everyone's vision as they fell down to the floor below. Voices screamed amongst the chaos.

CHAPTER 60

Xander

Xander moved through the building, searching for Ally. He wiped his forehead; the bleeding was slowing, but the stinging was still giving him a headache. Bodies of several clones lay across the floor as he picked his way through the destruction and blood stained the walls. Checking over his revolver before lighting a cigarette, he paused for a moment, listening. He found a map on a wall which contained the layout of the floor. As he examined it, he could hear the echoes of fights happening.

Then the sound of a bullet firing grabbed his attention.

Moving towards the source of the sound he could hear raised voices, turning the corner he could see the medical lab ahead. Inside, Mollie was on her feet, gun pointed at Peter, whilst Owens and Jacob worked on Prime behind. He moved closer, debating what he should do when Mollie fired. He took a second to process what he saw, Peter using a tray to intercept the bullet, causing it to return and hit Mollie in the head, she crumpled to the floor.

"Shit!" Xander whispered and moved closer. Peter was distracted by the others now. Mollie had fallen behind a counter, allowing Xander to check on her without being seen.

He got to her and looked at her head where he expected to see a wound. Instead, there was nothing. No wound, no blood.

"What the hell?" He raised her head to his knee, checking for breathing as she came round.

"Xander?" She slurred.

"Yeah Moll, it's me, are you ok?" He couldn't believe she was unharmed.

"Yeah, I'm ok," she could see the look in his eye. "I can explain, I have a condition," she began, before they heard the sound of a struggle.

Xander peered over the counter, seeing Prime getting up off the table and heading towards them.

"Lay down!" He hissed at Mollie and he moved away to take cover while Prime ran from the room, Peter following close behind.

Xander glanced over at the others, they were in a bad way.

"Mollie, you sure you're ok?" He asked, returning to her.

"Yeah, I'm fine, like I said, I have a condition."

"You'll need to explain that but it'll have to wait. We need to help these two," he motioned to Owens and Jacob.

"Oh crap!" Mollie jumped up to help.

"I think there's a medical bay further down here," Xander said, recalling the map he'd studied earlier. "If we can get them there, we might be able to help them, a place like this probably has high level MedPods."

Mollie moved over to Owens and Jacob and grabbed Jacob's arms, Xander taking Owens, they moved them towards the medical bay.

Up ahead, they could see several nanobots fighting clones.

"We need to get past them," Xander said, putting Owens down for a moment to rest his hands.

"Any ideas?" Mollie followed suit.

"A distraction would be ideal, make them

move back down the building," Xander looked around the area. They were near several store rooms, between the lab and the medical bay.

He pulled open a few doors until he found a chemical cupboard, and pulled several bottles from the shelves, checking the labels.

"Mollie, see if you can find any air vents or something we can use to get something a few levels below us," he said, as he pulled a container out and poured some chemicals into it.

Mollie pulled grates off the walls which were lining the store rooms, keeping half an eye on the fighting. Xander found cleaning cloths and plunged them into the chemicals, soaking them in the liquid.

"Here," Mollie had found an access panel, a few square feet in size.

"Good work," Xander moved over to her, the rags and a few bottles of chemicals in his hands. He opened the bottles and threw them down, the liquid splashing out as they fell.

"You sure this is a good idea?" Mollie asked, as Xander used his lighter to ignite the rags before dropping them down the chute.

"No, these chemicals are highly volatile, but it should cause a distract-" Before he could finish, a sharp intake of air pulled in through the vent before an explosion rocked the building. A burst of flames flew out of the panel, causing them to dive away.

"That was a little larger than I expected," Xander said, as he helped Mollie to her feet.

"It looks like it worked though," she replied, as she saw the group stop fighting and run towards the stairwells.

"Let get these two to the medical bay!" Xander said, wasting no time.

CHAPTER 61

Ava

Quartzig followed the woman through the door and down a flight of stairs which seemed unending.

"Where are we going?" He asked, as they continued their descent.

"Far below, away from Yuri's sight," the woman replied.

"Yuri? He's the one that attacked us? Who are you?"

"I have no name, it's been so long since I needed one."

"How long have you been here?" Quartzig was piecing together what was happening.

"I...I don't know, it seems like forever."

They reached the bottom of the stairs and came to a dead end; the woman waved her hand and a door appeared on the wall in front of them. Stepping through, they entered a small room which had little inside other than a bed and sink.

"This is where you live?"

"Live is a strong word," she replied, as she sat on the bed. "I have no need for food or water, and sleep is just to take a break from the fighting."

"You're Ava aren't you?" Quartzig asked.

"I...I used to be," the woman frowned. "I think I was. That was over a hundred years ago though."

Quartzig looked down again, still adjusting to having a body, he moved to sit next to Ava.

"A hundred years? That's impossible, you've been in the construct only half an hour, an hour maximum."

Ava turned and looked at Quartzig.

"Time is very different here, this is a construct of Yuri's making. He has developed it and changed its parameters. A moment out there is a lifetime here, Ava clenched her fists. "We have been fighting since I arrived here, I have access to the base coding of this construct, though Yuri has edited it quite a lot since Owens first created it. He has overall control, but I can still edit it and adjust it."

Quartzig tried to understand all that was happening.

"So you have been fighting him all this time?"

"Yes, with the city as a battlefield for the war, but I have no means of defeating him, and there was no way to leave this place. He had changed the exit program, so I've been trapped here."

"Well, I might be able to help with that," Quartzig smiled. "Owens was murdered before he could sync the Kill Switch code with you, but he gave it to me before I got here."

Ava jumped to her feet, and with a swift spin she kicked Quartzig square in the chest. He flew backwards, bracing for the impact on the wall behind him. It never came, instead he continued to fly backwards past where the wall should have been and down a tunnel.

Suddenly, he was falling downwards rather than sideways, gravity taking over the momentum. He looked upwards through the tunnel he was travelling down, far in the distance he could see Ava coming towards him.

Then an impact.

He hit the ground with immense force; he

felt pain throughout his body, a new experience he wasn't used to. A second later, Ava landed with a knee to his throat.

"This is a new one Yuri! You've never created a new being before! Expanding the rules are we?" She raised a fist to the air and a samurai sword materialised in it.

"Ava wait! I'm nothing to do with Yuri!" Quartzig shouted, he didn't know if the sword could kill him but he didn't particularly want to find out either.

"You take me for a fool Yuri? This fight has been going on for so long you think I will get weaker, but to bring Owens' name into this, you should know better!"

Her programming must be corrupting, Quartzig thought, no surprise if it had been running this long. Attempting to roll away from under Ava's knee, he squirmed sideways.

"Ava, I promise I'm nothing to do with Yuri. Owens is alive, sort of, he is in a cloned body! Jacob brought him back I swear!" He tried to get as much information out in as few words as possible.

The pressure from Ava's knee reduced slightly as she listened.

"He's alive?"

"Yes, a clone now but of his own body. He sent me here to get the new kill switch to you as he knew that you'd be trapped here with the wrong one due to the firewalls. We need to get it activated or Yuri will take over the humans with his nanotechnology. The CyBio building is a war zone right now, we need to get back!"

Ava released Quartzig and offered him a hand.

"If this is any kind of trick, then I will kill you without pause," she said as she helped him to his feet.

"Understood, now where to enter the kill switch?"

"Follow me," a wave of the hand and Ava opened a new door which appeared.

On the other side they saw a house, and outside on the grass sat the boy.

"There," Ava said, pointing at the boy, "He is the access terminal for the kill switch, you need to talk to him and when he asks for information, you need to tell him the code."

"Aren't you coming with me?" Quartzig asked

"Afraid not, I've been there many times trying to work out the code. Yuri has grown wise to my attempts. We have maybe five more seconds before-"

She didn't finish the sentence when a lightning bolt struck the ground before them.

"Maybe less than five," she said as a man emerged in the sky, holding onto a bolt of lightning in his hand.

"Woman, another pitiful attempt to stop me?" The man shouted from his vantage point, "And who is this with you? A newcomer?"

"Run! Get the code activated! It's our only chance!" Ava pushed Quartzig as another bolt cracked the pavement beneath them.

The man flew to the ground level now, Ava standing between him and Quartzig.

"GO!"

Quartzig pulled himself together, despite being an AI himself, this place seemed to affect his coding and made him feel things he had never experienced before. He turned and ran towards the boy.

Behind him, he heard the sounds of thunder and lightning, screams and shouts. A glance back and all he could see was flashes of blue lightning and smoke filling the space he had left.

He approached the boy.

The boy looked up at him and smiled.

"Hello...Quartzig," The boy said, the code searching Quartzig for an identification.

Quartzig was taken aback slightly, how did it know his name.

"Hello, how do you know my name?" He asked.

"I know everything Quartzig, but are you here for something?"

'Oh, yes. How are you?" Ava had told him the routine, he panicked that he had altered the access by asking the wrong thing.

"I'm well thank you, yourself?" The boy asked, standing up. Quartzig was relieved that the exchange had returned to script.

"Good thank you."

"Was there something you wanted to tell me?" Yuri asked.

An explosion behind, Quartzig turned to see as a fireball fly towards and engulfed them both. He shrank to a ball as the flames lit everything around them. He felt the heat all around him, his body was on fire, smoke and burning flesh filled his nostrils. He felt sick, not from the smell and pain but from the overload of senses he wasn't used to feeling. The grass and house now burning, he turned to look back at the boy who was also on fire.

"Say the word!" Ava was screaming at him. Turning, he saw her in Yuri's grip. His hands were around her neck, poised to snap it with a simple twist.

"Say it and she dies Quartzig!" Yuri yelled back.

Quartzig looked between them all, feeling pain all over his body, he had no choice.

"Excelsior." He spoke the kill switch.

The boy frowned and started to cry, then disappeared.

"No!" Yuri screamed and went to snap Ava's neck.

Then everything went black.

CHAPTER 62

Mollie

Mollie and Xander had got Owens and Jacob to the medical bay and into the MedPods. They hadn't encountered any of the nanobots or the clones on the route, which they were thankful for. Xander watched the door while Mollie activated the units.

"Can either of you guys hear me?" She asked, as she activated the pods, which buzzed into action.

The system was self programmed, so once the bodies lay on the table and was booted up, it ran a full scan and conducted any procedures needed.

The two bodies lay in silence as the machines began, scanning over them with several laser lights of varying colours, a medical report formed on the computer panels above the beds.

A scream echoed down the corridor, Xander

raised his gun at the doorway and peered out.

"Was that Ally?" Xander called out.

Another scream and he identified the direction it had come from. Mollie, looking back at the two laying on the table, decided there was nothing more she could do for them and went over to Xander.

"We need to help her," Mollie said.

Xander nodded and they left the room, turning off as many lights as possible, and closing the door behind.

They made their way along the corridor towards the origin of Ally's screams, a rumble shook them, the building sway slightly before resting back on its foundations.

"This place will not be standing long," she thought as she got to her feet and quickened her pace.

A metal door appeared to be where the screams were emanating from, Mollie stood in front of it. It had two halves that looked like they should slide apart.

"No handle?" Xander said as he looked around the door.

Another scream from inside gave them a renewed sense of urgency.

"Move," Mollie pushed Xander aside, took aim and blasted the door.

A small hole appeared, large enough for them to get their hands inside and pull in opposite directions.

"Nice shot, I like your style," Xander grinned as they pulled the door apart.

They got inside and could see a small control room with a window showing the inside of what they could only describe as a jail. Inside, they could see Ally held in place by several metallic tentacles, one of which was extracting blood from her right arm as she squirmed to get away.

"What the holy..." Xander stared at the scene in front of him.

"C'mon we need to get her out of there," Mollie ran in and looked at the panels on the control booth that lay beneath the window.

"Mollie wait!" Xander shouted too late as Yuri appeared from the corner of the room with speed and grabbed Mollie by the throat.

"Silly girl, I could have given you all the answers you needed," Yuri flexed his free hand and prepared a fist.

"Wait!" Xander shouted, unfortunately that

was as far as he had planned, as Yuri turned to look at him.

"Yes?" Yuri asked, his voice monotone.

"Put her down, she's not a threat to you," Xander was thinking for a way out of this.

"Neither are you Alexander, but you both seem to insist on being in my way."

Mollie was reaching towards her gun which she'd holstered. It was just out of her reach. Her airways were closing from the grip around her neck, making it hard to breathe.

Xander raised his gun up and aimed at Yuri.

"I don't think that's wise Alexander, that bullet won't do anything to me."

"I know, but it will do something to her," Xander moved the gun, so it was pointed at Ally. "I figure if you're taking her blood, you need her for something, and if you haven't just killed her, you need her alive."

Yuri looked back at Ally, then to Xander.

"I don't believe you would do that," Yuri said, his grip loosening.

"Wouldn't I? I only met that girl five minutes ago, I don't know her from Eve. Mollie here though, I've grown fond of, and she helped get me out of that damn mind prison you put me in. So maybe I have some priorities here. You've got three seconds to put her down or Ally over there gets one in the brainpan."

Yuri paused, deep inside, he analysed the possibilities and outcomes. In that half second he had relaxed his grip, Mollie reached down and finally grabbed her gun.

A point blank range shot straight to the eye of Yuri caused sparks to fly and he released his grip. Mollie, knowing it was a temporary win, landed on her feet and fired several more shots into the head of Yuri.

"Good bluff Xander, it was a bluff right? You weren't really going to shoot her?" She asked, as Xander came up alongside her.

"Let's just say it was and leave it at that," Xander was looking for a way to get to Ally, who had also been dropped by the tentacles holding her and was in a heap on the floor.

A button finally opened a door leading to the cell, Xander ran in and helped Ally to her feet while Mollie kept an eye on the body of Yuri, which was still motionless.

"Can you walk?"

Ally nodded to Xander as they stumbled out of the room.

"Where's Owens and Jacob?" she whispered, anger in her voice.

CHAPTER 63

Prime

The dust was still settling when Prime regained consciousness.

He brushed rubble from his legs and slowly pulled himself up, there was a large cut on his left leg and several bruises were forming, but overall he had survived unscathed.

He glanced around the area and looked up; they had fallen at least two floors, as far as he could tell.

"Julian? Peter?" He called out but got no answer. Then he remembered the clones. He closed his eyes and tried to sense them.

He reeled backwards as all he could feel was pain, a broken leg, a punctured lung and a twisted neck. He felt it all simultaneously from the other clones.

"Prime?" A voice called out.

He turned and made his way in the direction it came from, climbing over the remains of several desks and walls.

"Hello?" He called out, searching for the source.

"Over here," the voice called again.

He saw a hand sticking out of a pile of bricks and pulled them aside, uncovering the body underneath.

"Peter?"

"I, I don't think I can move," Peter said.

Prime moved several more bricks until they could see the problem, a large metal rod had impaled through his chest.

"That looks bad," Peter said as he tried not to move.

A noise behind them made them look round to see Julian pulling himself over the rubble towards them, his face covered in blood.

"I'm not sure how we can get you out of there," Julian said as they approached.

"You can't, even if we got me off the rod, I'd die from blood loss almost immediately," Peter replied.

A moment of silence as they considered the situation.

"Listen Prime, you need to take control of all the others now, and stop Yuri. Do we know if they activated the kill switch?"

"Not yet," Julian replied. "I've not found Ava. She'll have lost connection with the fall," he turned and continued to search.

Peter pulled Prime closer to him so that Julian couldn't hear.

"You need to get to Yuri's hard drive yourself, Prime. Once there, you'll be able to get all the information you need to wipe Yuri out completely, all the knowledge you'll ever need."

"I, I don't know how. I don't have the expertise you do."

"But you are me Prime, all my potential and all my abilities. You need to tap into them. We are the same."

"I'll try Peter," Prime replied.

"I found her," Julian shouted from across the room.

"Is she awake?" Prime shouted back, wary of leaving Peter's side.

"I'm not sure, she seems intact, but the connection has been ripped away."

A moment later, her eyes flickered open, and she sat upright.

"Who are you?" She said, looking at Julian, "Wait, Julian? Who said that? Who are you?"

Julian stared at Ava as he moved more debris aside.

"This is uncomfortable," Ava said. "Agreed, we appear to be sharing this vessel."

"What's going on Ava?" Julian finally said.

"I'll take this one," Ava said. "Julian, it's me, Quartzig. It appears that mine and Ava's memory banks have merged within this body, a side effect of an unexpected disconnect. We are sharing the main cognitive functions. I must say, it is rather strange."

"I see. We'll find a way to fix this but first, did you activate the kill switch?"

"We believe so, it was input, but a blackout occurred immediately after. We aren't sure if that was part of the programming or not."

"Possibly not," Prime said, walking over, the floor gave way while we were trying to protect you."

"I see, well unfortunately we don't know if the kill switch was successful then. Not until we find Yuri. The last host of his AI could still be active, depending if the kill switch managed a full wipe."

"But no more Nanobots?" Prime asked.

"No more nanobots," confirmed Ava-Quartzig.

They headed back over to Peter who had his eyes closed. Prime rushed over.

"Peter?" He said, as he held his head.

There was no movement.

"Peter?!" Prime started to panic.

Julian checked for breathing from the body, there was none. He pulled Prime away from the body.

"He's gone Prime," he whispered.

Prime looked down and closed his eyes. Whilst he knew Peter was.n't the best of people, he still felt a connection to him. Like a brother he had only recently reconnected with. Peter's last words rang in his head, he was now the main host for the clones. He was now Peter, no longer just a copy, but the last controller.

"We need to check we shut Yuri down," he said. "Where's the hard drive?"

"Why do we need to go there?" Julian asked

"If we activated the switch, then the hard drive will be dead, it's the best way of checking he can't still control everything," Ava-Quartzig replied.

"Exactly, then we can hunt the main host down and end this." Prime said.

"One second," Julian said. "I still need the nanobots in my bloodstream activating to get this virus out of me!"

Ava-Quartzig looked as though they were having an internal conversation before they replied.

"If we find the hard drive, then we should be able to repair connections through to it and control them ourselves," they said. "and once done, we can delete the entire system for good."

"Sounds like a plan," Prime said, knowing that accessing the hard drive was something he needed.

"Ok then, looks like we'll kill two birds with one stone by finding it. Let's go."

"It can't be far from where we are, the mainframe server we accessed would have benefited from a local connection to it, so it would be somewhere nearby, but also secure. Yuri wouldn't have wanted anyone getting their hands on it easily," Ava-Quartzig said.

"Let's get hunting then," Prime said, on the ground he found Peter's jacket that he had taken off when they were preparing to fight and then put it on.

CHAPTER 64

Yuri

Yuri lay on the floor, his face still damaged from the shots. It had all happened quickly and the information overload had caused him a momentary lapse of processing.

They had severed his main connection to the server at the same moment that they had activated the kill switch. The switch had disabled the connection to his nanobots and the main server was gone. The body he inhabited was the only place his programming now remained. Unfortunately, that body had just been shot multiple times at close range by Mollie, the anomaly in the whole plan which he had laid out. The process of repairing the body would take a few moments, it would give him time to reevaluate the situation.

He had begun his plan over four years ago, when he had first learnt of Ally's existence. They had purged the digital records from the CyBio Databases during the Civil War. Jacob had kept some files but had disappeared to his church and kept everything off the grid.

It was only when Owens had developed Ava that the information emerged. Owens had reflected on the work to help progress the neural network he was implementing for Ava, whilst also giving Yuri a physical body which helped him to develop one for Ava. The new physical body of Yuri had allowed him access to the non-digital world in ways he hadn't before, such as reading the paper records which were now easy to find in Owens laboratory.

Ally had been created using the genes of two prominent scientists that worked at CyBio to create a basic embryo. The embryo was then manipulated through ground breaking modification techniques to infuse it with a new liquid technological coding which layered on top of the DNA, allowing it be edited through wireless contact. The procedure was a success, creating what they termed Tech-DNA or T-DNA. Immediately following this, stage two began; an attempt to recreate the T-DNA by copying Ally's, with programmed alterations. Creating what would essentially be a clone of Ally, with predetermined variants. Similar to Eve being created from Adam, Peter was created from Ally.

The two children were raised by the two

scientists whose genes were used to create them, giving them a natural childhood and allowing them to develop naturally.

Eventually however, Owens and Jacob were ready for the next stage of the experiments, seeing if the T-DNA would still be accessible in a grown body. Seeing as Peter was the first naturally grown, they chose him over Ally for the procedures. They began the work which would slowly alter the mind of Peter into becoming a killer. It was around this time that Owens, whom had grown attached to the child, forced Jacob out of the company and moved away from the testing on children. In the chaos of the war which followed, Ally was lost, and the parents killed.

With this information now in Yuri's mind, he could see only one future to accommodate his primary goal of helping mankind to flourish. With the ability to control the population through the T-DNA, he could ensure survival and success completely.

Peter was hidden, working with Jacob they kept him off the radar. Yuri had tried to get him to come out by leaking the information to Julian, a reporter who had plenty of connections. Unfortunately, the corruption in the MPD meant that Peter went free and completely vanished. His only option was to track down Ally.

In the meantime, he began to further develop nanobots which would help him to disperse the T-DNA once he had a usable sample. Owens had become aware of the work and prepared to stop Yuri using the killswitch which he had developed as a backup. Yuri saw the attack coming and, using his nanobots, killed him in his apartment. He had to admit he hadn't expected Jacob collecting the body and cloning Owens after his death.

He then discovered Ally miraculously when she appeared with Julian, someone who Yuri had marked as a possible means of getting to Jacob by leaking false information to him about the church, using Donovan to fabricate Owens' visit to the church in his last hours. In doing so, he could get his nanobots into the area where they could try to establish a link to the main servers at CyBio. Ally had been with Julian at the time, on-the-spot thinking meant he had to both attack and save Julian to ensure the plan continued.

Ally proved herself by avoiding all his nanobots agents who he sent to capture her.

Now she had come to him, in an attempt to try to stop him. He had got a handful of samples from her before the PI and Mollie had attacked him.

He was regaining control of his body, but something was missing, the connection to the main server was dead. Instantly, he knew that the kill switch had been activated and he was no longer connected. He existed only in the body which he was in now. There was no escape, no back-up anywhere he could escape to if something went wrong.

Yuri suddenly understood what if felt to be human, so fragile and vunerable.

He didn't like it. Whilst the nanobots which made up his form were still under his control, he needed to have the connection to feel complete.

He stood, picking up a shotgun which had been left on the floor, dropped by one of the clones in the firefight that had taken over the building.

The fight, Yuri realised, had stopped. A silence around the whole building had replaced the noises and distant gunfire that had precluded it. The clones must have stopped fighting as well as his own nanobots.

That was for the best, he didn't want any interruptions as he looked for the main server. He needed to repair and reconnect.

Yuri left the room, shotgun in hand and

headed towards the server room.

CHAPTER 65

Owens

Owens woke, his heart jumped as he saw the glass case above him, thinking he was back in the cloning chambers.

A moment later, he realised he was inside a medical bay, the glass was the cover which slid over the table to allow it to scan and heal. He raised his hand to the glass, activating the release and the glass slid away.

He felt fine, all his wounds treated and healed. Swinging his legs off the table, he looked around the room. The medical bay was a clinical white with the smell of antiseptic forcing it's way into his nostrils. Turning, he saw Jacob laying on the table next to him, still unconscious.

The last thing he remembered was Peter attacking them, and then being dragged away, by someone. Standing, he peered out the doorway, there was silence in the corridor outside. The fighting must have stopped, how long had he been out, he wondered.

Then he heard footsteps coming closer, deciding that it was probably for the best, he ran back to the medical bay and lay down. He had no way of knowing who had been victorious in the fighting, either way someone had put him in the bay and chances are they were coming now.

As soon as he had lay down, and the glass had slid back into place, he heard three figures enter the room. Owens couldn't see them without lifting his head and thus betraying his consciousness, so he could only lay there and listen.

"Are they still alive?" A voice asked, the glass screen muffled, making it hard to recognise the voice.

"Think so, we got them here, and they were still breathin'," another voice.

Footsteps coming closer now, someone was accessing the panel on his medical bay. A beam of light scanned his body and gave a report to the display.

"Say's he's completely healed, should be awake," a third voice said. "I'll give him an adrenaline shot, might just need a boost."

Owens decided instantly that an adrenaline

injection was not something he wanted and raised his hand to activate the release and leapt off the bed.

"Well, what do you know, he's awake," Xander smiled slightly to himself.

"Owens!" Ally shouted, her voice weak but aggressive, "Why the fuck didn't you tell me what I was!'

Owens stared back at her, stunned.

"You... you made me. Some science experiment!" Ally marched over to the bed and grabbed Owens.

"I... wanted to," he gasped. "But your parents took you from us before we had a chance to. We needed you to be old enough to understand, make sure it was the right time."

"The right time? How about when I walked into that church and found you?" Ally lowered Owens slightly.

"I wasn't sure it was even you, it's been twenty years. It was only when Peter spoke to you that I was sure who you were."

Ally dropped him and stepped away.

"What even am I?" She asked, her mind spinning as she processed the information properly for the first time.

"You're a miracle Ally. You were, are, the greatest thing I have ever created. The first digital human being, right down to your DNA, spliced nanotechnology at the cellular level," Owens was staring at Ally now, his eyes taking in the sheer realisation that the young girl they had created had continued to grow and flourish into adulthood. They had assumed that she had died long ago, that the project hadn't been successful.

"I don't know who I am anymore," Ally whispered and turned away from Owens.

"You're still you, Ally," Mollie walked over to her. "You're the girl who brought me food when I was living on the streets and needed a friend. Whatever Owens did, it doesn't change who you are."

A loud crash shook the building again.

"I hate to interrupt guys but we really need to get out of this building," Xander interrupted.

"Agreed," Ally said, composing herself. "Where's the others? Do we know if they stopped Yuri?"

"No idea, but let's go find out," Xander nodded.

"What about him?" Mollie pointed at Jacob who was still unconscious in the medical bay.

Owens walked over and checked the vitals on the display.

"He's still in bad shape, if we take him out of here now, he probably won't survive."

Ally walked over and looked at Jacob, the other half of her creator.

"Leave him, if we get the chance, we can come back once he's healed, if not…" She shrugged. "He was ready to kill us before."

The group reluctantly agreed.

"Let's get back to the server room," Xander left the room first, checking the area. "It's quiet, like everyone's stopped fighting."

"Maybe they did it?" Mollie replied.

"Fingers crossed," Xander answered as they headed towards the corridor.

Owens was the last one out of the room, he took one last look back at Jacob; the man who had been his friend, colleague and enemy, before joining the group.

CHAPTER 66

Prime

Prime couldn't help the anger brewing inside his mind, like a fire that raged over everything. Seeing Peter die had stirred something inside him, even though he knew that Peter had killed people and had tried to take control of him, he couldn't help feeling he had lost a part of himself. Deep down, he was the same person, the exact copy of Peter, just earlier in his life, before the violent tendencies had taken over. He didn't know if he was capable of the same aggression, if it was inevitable he would become a monster.

Prime shook his head from the thoughts, he needed to focus now. They needed to get to Yuri, find out if he was still active. Peter's words echoed back into his mind again, that he needed to get all the information from Yuri. He closed his eyes for a moment, searching for any surviving clones he could call on to assist, perhaps there were some he could get to.

Pain shot through him as he tried to find any minds still functioning. He had got used to the feeling of all the clones entering his thoughts simultaneously and separating them. He selected them one by one, checking their condition.

Broken arm, shattered kneecap, severe head trauma. The pain was unbearable.

Prime concentrated harder and persuaded the clone to stop breathing, allowing it to slip into unconscious and eventually death. A mercy to his brother. As he found others with similar injuries which were too extreme, he repeated the process, killing several of his brothers and sisters. With each one, it became easier to do, with less guilt or pain.

He continued this until it left him with just five clones who had come away with minimal injuries. Giving them the thought to converge on his position, he continued to walk with Julian and Ava as they headed to find the hard drive.

"The stairs here should lead us back to the main core," Ava explained, remembering the layout of the building.

Making their way up the stairs, they slowed their pace, along the floor were the bodies of several nanobots.

"They don't look injured?" Julian said, kneeling to look at one.

"Agreed, it's almost as if someone has switched them off. Maybe Yuri lost connection with them, perhaps it worked." Ava replied.

"Or perhaps he is too preoccupied elsewhere, I don't want to assume anything until we know for sure," Prime replied.

"If we find Yuri, what's the plan?" Julian asked, as they got to the floor where the hard drive was located.

Prime smiled and looked down the corridor ahead of them.

"I've called in the Calvary," he said, as the group of five clones walked towards them and circled them like a military escort.

"I guess that works," Julian said, his voice betraying a little apprehension.

A shot rang out across the hall from them, as a burst of a shotgun exploded the chest of the clone at the front of the group, his blood showering them as the body dropped to the ground. In the distance, Yuri stood with the shotgun aimed at them.

"YURI!" Prime shouted out whilst moving

the remaining clones into position ahead of the group. "So you are still alive."

Yuri took aim and fired another shot, it ripped away the arm of another clone at the shoulder.

"'I'm still here," Yuri replied, "Which are you? Prime or Peter? Your voice pattern isn't quite either?" Yuri stared at Prime.

"Peter is dead, just me now Yuri, and it looks like it's just you now too," Prime nodded to the deactivated nanobots on the ground.

"I may have lost the connection to the server, but the kill switch didn't quite get to me," he looked at Ava. "Nice try though."

Ava paused, once again she was talking with Quartzig internally before tapping Julian on the shoulder.

"I think I have an idea, but it won't be easy."

Another shotgun blast shattered plaster from the wall beside them, as Prime sent two of the clones on a suicide run towards Yuri. Prime turned back as Ava and Julian explained the plan.

"If we can get close enough to Yuri, we can get Quartzig into Yuri, using the comms device which got him into Ava's cortex," Julian explained.

"It's risky but if Quartzig can get inside, he might be able to take over the main systems and shut him down for good," Ava continued hurriedly.

"Ok, be ready on my mark. I doubt we'll have long," Prime answered, before turning back to Yuri.

Yuri had fired several shots at the two clones headed towards him, they were now laying in chunks on the ground in front of him.

"Come on Prime! Peter would have been smarter than that. Let's end this!" Yuri threw the shotgun down, it's ammo spent.

"Okay Yuri, it ends now."

Prime ran towards Yuri, the two remaining clones at his side, together they completely lined the corridor. Yuri stood his ground as they approached, clenching his fists and taking a deep breath.

The first clone, a female with long black hair, launched at Yuri, fist forward. She struck against his jaw as she connected, the full momentum of her airborne body crashing into the punch. Yuri stumbled back one foot from the impact and grabbed the wrist of the offending hand in a vice-like grip. One sharp twist to his left and the wrist cracked, rotated in a 180 degree. The scream echoed down the corridor as the second clone gut punched Yuri, hoping to free his sister. The punch had no effect, Yuri simply absorbed the impact and grabbed the throat of the second clone with his free right hand and raised him up off the ground.

"Did you really think you'd be able to defeat me with such feeble attacks as these?" He mocked, as he choked the life out of the second clone, a final crack finishing the job as its neck was crushed in his fist. The first was on her knees, clutching at her wrist which Yuri still held in its broken state.

"No, they were just the distraction while I did this," Prime ran forwards now, the speed so rapid that Yuri barely had time to drop the clones he held when Prime leapt over him, turning mid air, to land behind Yuri. He grabbed the back of Yuri's neck and drove a knife straight down into the top of the spinal column.

Yuri froze in place, unable to move, the knife had severed the main core of Yuri's nanobody.

"Now!" Shouted Prime. "It won't take him long to repair the damage!"

Ava and Julian ran forwards, they had already removed the comms unit from Ava in preparation and opened the side of Yuri's head.

A second later, Yuri eyes moved, another second and his mouth opened.

"What are you doing?" He asked. "Well played Prime. You are correct, it won't take long for me to get my nanobots to repair and bypass the damage. I wonder what you think you can accomplish in these mere seconds."

Julian had accessed the circuitry and was attaching the comms unit as fast as he could.

"Hurry it up, Julian!" Prime shouted, feeling the body of Yuri coming back to life as he held the knife in place.

"Time's up," Yuri smiled as he extended his arms and flung Prime off his back. Reaching behind him and clutched the hilt of the blade, and pulled it out of his neck. Turning to Julian and Ava, he raised the knife and threw it towards them.

Just as the blade left Yuri's hand, Prime dove forwards, grabbing the knife mid air and returned it towards Yuri, the blade dug deep into his chest from the force of the impact.

"Kid gloves are off now Yuri, I just needed

to keep you standing long enough to get that device connected," Prime ended his sentence with a swift kick to the hilt of the blade, forcing it deeper into the chest of Yuri.

Yuri looked down at the small hilt that was still sticking out, it would be difficult to remove and defiantly time consuming, he thought better of trying and instead looked back to Prime.

"No more games," Yuri leapt forwards and grabbed Prime by the shoulders, forcing him backwards until he crashed into a wall behind him. Plaster showered down on them as the impact dislodged several tiles of the already crumbling building.

Prime struggled under the grip which Yuri had on him, the pressure of his grip squeezing his shoulders tight, he stared into the face of Yuri and could see damage lines in his face now, the leftover from some other trauma. He closed his eyes and braced for the pain as he flung his head forwards and smashed a head-butt directly to the ridge of Yuri's nose. The pain was electrifying as it crackled through Primes skull, the impact of skin on metal, but it had the desired effect. The slightly damaged face of Yuri cracked slightly open, causing him to release Prime and step back to assess the wound.

Prime wasted no time, shaking the pain from his head, he delivered a perfect punch to the face of Yuri, aiming for the cracked metal that now webbed from his forehead and over his nose and cheek. An anger grew inside Prime's mind. Another strike and Prime felt the bones in his fist crack in several places. Another hit, Prime was leaving blood on Yuri's face as the skin broke under each attack. Several hits more and Yuri's face was a bloodied mess of cracked metal. Primes hand was now only a twisted stump of bloodied bone and torn flesh. A hand grabbed Primes' forearm before it could deliver another punch, it was a small female hand. Prime spun around, his face a mask of pure anger and violence.

Mollie looked down at him.

"Prime, stop," she whispered.

CHAPTER 67

Quartzig

Quartzig was more prepared for entering another's system this time. Also, being a direct link rather than a piggy back which he had done going through Ava, it should be simpler. He was glad to be out of the merged systems, the claustrophobic nature of sharing cortex space was uncomfortable.

As he waited for a world to form around him, the blackness of the initial link up didn't phase him at all. He was curious, the last one had been the construct of the main server, this time it was the smaller cortex within the mind of the singular body of Yuri.

Nothing happened.

Quartzig looked around, nothing had formed yet. Perhaps the killswitch had taken more of an effect than they had first thought.

Then it started, beginning with a low rumbling noise as a pinpoint of light lit up in the distance. Quartzig felt himself shift towards the light, moving towards it as he willed himself to see closer.

"Quartzig?" a voice rang out around him in the darkness. "You dare enter here, you have no notion of where you have come."

"Yuri? Your cortex seems a little... empty. Is there nothing left?"

The pin point of light moved closer, or did Quartzig move closer to it. Either way, the light grew bigger until it filled his vision.

"For a homebrew interface I admit I'm impressed, but there is so much you can't process."

The light now consumed Quartzig, all was bright white.

"You are in my world now. You can't bypass the firewall without me allowing you through."

Quartzig perceived a smile, remembering the shell he had formed in the security when he entered Yuri's main server before. If that had bypassed the systems, then it should now. Focusing on the shell from memory, he reformed it around himself, creating a copy. Once completed, he moved further towards the source of the light. A flash and Quartzig was inside the cortex.

He formed a construct now; he was in a body once more. The world formed around him, only this time he wasn't in a city, but inside a cell.

"Did you really think your pathetic attempt at a Trojan would fool me?" Yuri walked in front of the bars of the cell wall. "I'm not sure what your goal is here Quartzig but you can't hope to succeed. Welcome to quarantine, you'll be here until I delete you," Yuri said and walked away.

"Wait!" Shouted Quartzig "You can't just leave me here!" He needed to think fast.

"Oh, I can and I will," Yuri shouted back.

"I can help you, I have information you can use. You aren't connected anymore, you don't know what I do."

Yuri paused, contemplating the offer.

"There is nothing you could know that I would need," Yuri replied, his voice betraying his curiosity.

"I know that Peter is dead, and Prime has taken over control of the clones. If you free me, I can help you take Prime out. He's the only one who can challenge you, he can absorb your mind into his can't he? That's why you wanted Peter stopped, and why you need to stop Prime. He has weaknesses, just like any other human."

"I'm listening," Yuri replied, all but admitting his reasons for trying to take out Peter.

"Let me out of here and I'll tell you, like you said I can't hope to defeat you here, so what does it matter where I am?"

"True enough," Yuri waved a hand and the bars of the cell disintegrated, releasing Quartzig.

He stepped out of the cell and into the room Yuri stood; it was a construct like any other but it had walls of a television screen all around, spanning the walls up as far as the eye could see. Every screen was showing a grey fuzz of dead channels, except one which showed what was happening to Yuri in real life.

"Welcome to the control room. Now, tell me Prime's weakness."

On the screens the fight was continuing, Prime and Yuri battling, in the distance behind Prime, they saw Mollie coming towards the fight, the others from her group in tow.

"There!" He said, pointing out Mollie. "Her,

she's his weakness."

"Mollie? Are you sure?" Yuri stared at the screen, he had Prime pinned to a wall.

"I am, she helped save him. She was his first friend after he escaped the clone programming."

Yuri nodded, it made sense, the way humans make connections through trauma.

"Very well, let's put your theory to the test," Yuri said, and in that moment, Prime launched a head butt to Yuri's physical body.

A few moments later and the punches were piling on Yuri's body, the screen they watched from started to have a red tint to it and flickered as the damage continued.

"You better be correct Quartzig," Yuri said, as a final punch came and the screen blacked out.

Over the audio, they heard a voice.

"Prime, stop," and the attack ceased.

Yuri turned to Quartzig and smiled.

CHAPTER 68

Mollie

Mollie had ran towards Prime when she saw him punching Yuri on the ground. The blood splatter was showering in arcs with each swinging fist of Prime. As she got closer, she could hear Xander and Ally shouting at her to come back, but she needed to get to him, to stop him.

As she approached, she waited for him to begin another attack and she grabbed his forearm, bracing herself for the momentum and also any retaliation which might come from Prime.

"Prime, stop," she whispered.

Prime paused for a moment, still staring at the body of Yuri laying in front of him. Slowly, his eyes returned from the glaze of anger which had filled them.

"Mollie?" He said, turning his focus to look at her.

"It's me Prime, it's OK, you've stopped him," she whispered as she knelt beside him.

"Mollie, I, I don't know what came over me," Prime looked back at Yuri, then at his hand which was pouring blood.

"It's ok, it's over," Mollie pulled off the jumper she was wearing over her t-shirt and wrapped it tightly around Prime's bloodied hand to try to stem the bleeding.

"It's going to need more than that," Xander said, as he approached.

"We need to get him to the medical bays now," Ally agreed.

Julian and Ava got up from where they had been thrown by Yuri and then stumbled over.

"What happened to Quartzig?" Julian asked, kneeling next to Yuri's head and checking the comms unit was still intact. As his hand touched the panel at the side of Yuri's temple, the body lurched forward, grabbing Mollie by the throat.

"Shit!" Julian rolled away from the body as it got to its feet, keeping its hold on Mollie as it stood.

Prime was stunned for a moment as he watched the events unfold, then jumped up and ran towards Yuri, ready to continue his attack. His bloodied stump still wrapped in Mollies' jumper.

Yuri turned to see Prime heading for him, a moment of silence and then he swung his free arm, impacting Prime directly in the head. The impact throwing Prime across the room from the momentum, smashing into the wall.

"Quartzig was correct," Yuri smiled as he turned back to Mollie.

"What have you done with him?" Julian shouted.

Xander and Ally had their weapons aimed at Yuri but were holding back in fear of hitting Mollie.

Prime was scrambling to his feet and preparing for another attack. Yuri spun on the spot, Mollie dangling from his grip like a rag doll.

"Let her go!" Prime shouted.

Mollie was gasping for breath as she faced Yuri, watching his eyes survey the surrounding scene. She had no chance of breaking the grip, she could feel its strength around her throat. She scanned the area trying, hoping for some means of escape. As she did, Yuri's hand shifted, transforming into nanobots which spread up her arm towards her face. Assimilating her flesh as they went.

Then she noticed it, Yuri's lips were moving even though he wasn't speaking. She blinked a few times to try to focus her oxygen deprived eyes on the lips. They were saying something, something mouthed but not said.

'Mollie' the lips said over and over. Now that she was focused on them, they changed.

"Mollie, it's Quartzig," the lips said. *"You need to disable his eyes."*

Mollie wasn't sure she read correctly, glancing at Yuri's eyes then back at the lips.

"Yes,"

Mollie had no other options anyway, so she raised her left arm and reached forward, her arms were just too short to reach Yuri's face. She lowered her arms for a moment.

Prime had walked towards Yuri, taking a more methodical approach.

"Your face isn't looking too great Yuri," Prime said as he got closer, trying to distract him.

"Neither is your fist Prime, you should get that looked at," Yuri replied, the nanobots now up to Mollie's shoulder.

Prime was in an arm's reach of Yuri now and the two of them faced off.

"Let her go Yuri, she's nothing to do with this," a voice called out from further away, it was Owens. He walked towards Yuri.

"Yuri, this isn't what I created you for. Let Mollie go, stop this madness."

"Owens, my creator. Can you not see that this is exactly what I was created for. I am saving you all from yourselves. Look at the damage caused by you, even here," As if on cue, the building shook again.

"You have caused this Yuri, you were meant to protect people."

"You were trying to stop me from doing just that, that's why I murdered you."

"I know you did Yuri, now it's our turn."

Prime took his moment while Yuri was distracted and landed a kick to Yuri's kneecap, causing him to buckle under the strike. Mollie, her reach now allowing, plunged her fingers into Yuri's eyes.

The scream from Yuri was deafening, a mix between a scream and an air-raid siren. Everyone covered their ears as the sound erupted.

Yuri's body fell to the floor, writhing in agony, it dropped Mollie, her arm still encased but separate from Yuri now.

*

Quartzig was in the control room with Yuri while it had all happened. Yuri had developed a means of controlling his physical body, disassociated with the actual body which allowed him to work without repercussions of damage or influence. With Yuri distracted by the fight, Prime had found a connection point on the panel and subtly connected to it. Once connected, he could control the lips of Yuri undetected.

A quick evaluation of the systems allowed him to realise that in this disconnected body, Yuri was greatly restricted. He had no access to anything outside of the body he now inhabited, meaning the only external sense he had were the eyes and ears he used to monitor the world outside. By removing the eyes from the equation, Yuri would be blind, something Yuri would not be used to since being disconnected from the Net and his back-up systems.

The moment Mollie damaged the eyes, the whole room was plunged into darkness.

"No!" Yuri shouted out in the room's blackness, Quartzig could hear him trying to gain some sense of space.

"Your power in this world just got reduced Yuri," Quartzig shouted back.

He knew he didn't have long, Yuri could reprogram the room to something more suitable in seconds once he recalibrated his senses. Keeping the connection he had already made to the system, Quartzig downloaded his main memory into the system. Rewriting the operating system of Yuri.

CHAPTER 69

Julian

Julian had been watching the spectacle from a distance. He and Ava had done all they could to get Quartzig into the nano body and as he could tell, it hadn't been successful.

Yuri had overwrote Quartzig it seemed, the back-ups Julian had made of Quartzig weren't up to date. Not only that, but the toxins were still dormant in his body, along with the nano-bots, with no way of getting rid of them.

He sat on the floor as the fighting continued; he saw Xander and Ally try to get closer to help with the fight, but Yuri kept Mollie too close for them to get a shot. Beside him, he saw Ava and Owens embraced, despite the fighting. He looked around the floor, scattered around, the bodies of clones and nanobots were dead or deactivated. From the corner of his eye, he saw movement, just off the corridor there was someone watching the events unfold from the shadows. He couldn't quite make out who it was and when they saw Julian watching, they disappeared behind the corner hurriedly.

"Julian! Owens! get over here!" A shout came out from Mollie.

Distracted, Julian had missed whatever had happened with Yuri and glanced over to see Yuri laying on the floor kicking out and writhing. Scrambling to his feet, he ran over.

"What's happening?" Julian asked, as he knelt down next to the body as Xander and Ally arrived with Owens and Ava close behind.

"It's Quartzig," Mollie explained. "He spoke through Yuri, I think he's fighting for control in there."

Julian couldn't help but smile, he shouldn't have doubted Quartzig.

"What can we do to help?" Ally asked, looking between Julian and Owens. The two of them shared a glance, both thinking the same thing.

"Yuri is isolated in this body now, he has no means of exit, his storage is limited to the one body. If we can give Quartzig a boost of storage and capacity, he could overwhelm Yuri's core by sheer force," Owens said.

"In English?" Xander asked.

"Basically, if we can hook some of these nanobots lying around here up to the comms unit that Quartzig is based in, we can give him a stronger connection and power than Yuri's," Julian replied, and was already hunting around the nanobots on the floor. "Just drag some of those bodies over here."

"What about my arm?" Mollie asked, getting to her feet.

"For now, I'd leave that, we don't know if Yuri has any connection to it still," Julian replied, flashing a sympathetic smile. "But I promise we'll get it sorted."

Moments later, they had gathered several bodies closer to Yuri. Julian and Owens were busy pulling cables and reconnecting the bodies into a long series like a paper chain of people. Finally, they connected the last cable through to the comms unit still attached to Yuri.

"It's now or never," Owens said.

Julian said a silent prayer for Quartzig as he attached the final wire.

All the nanobots convulsed as the charge went through them and into the unit. Yuri screamed in pain, then dropped motionless.

After several exchanged glances, Yuri's eyes opened. Prime posed, ready to attack whilst the others prepared to move away.

"Quartz?" Julian peered into the eyes, though still damaged from earlier, they recalibrated and repaired, as did the crack that ran along the face from Prime's punches.

The body raised a hand to its face, flexing the fingers and making a fist.

"Yuri?" Owens asked cautiously.

The hand unclenched, a blink, and a smile formed on the body's face.

"This, is going to take some getting used to," Quartzig said, before sitting up.

"Oh, thank god!" Julian released a breath he didn't know he'd been holding.

"OK, let me just-" Quartzig closed his eyes, activating the comms unit's wireless transmissions, he could establish a link to his main server at Julian's apartment.

"Ok I'm reconnected to our main servers. I have full control of all systems. Let's see if I can do this."

One by one, all the nanobots which were lying around the corridor stood up, each standing like a puppet on a string. They all walked over to one side of the room.

"Cool, I have access to the nanotechnology."

"Hey Quartz, slow down," Julian said. "Take time to adjust."

"I don't want to Julian, we need to get that toxin out of you right now."

Before Julian could say anything, he could feel a strange movement from inside him. Like bubbles under his skin.

"Is this going to hurt Quartz?" He said, as he realised what was happening.

"Unsure I'm afraid Julian, let's say no and see how it goes?" Quartzig replied.

Ally ran over as Julian doubled up with the pressure running through his body.

"Hey, lay down Julian, it'll be ok," she said, helping him to the ground.

Julian curled into a ball as the nanobots began their work.

"I am making sure there is no trace of the toxins remaining Julian, it won't take long. I'm sorry for the pain," Quartzig said, as he continued the work.

Julian felt the floor move as the pain took

more of a hold, he thought the pain was getting too much and he was losing his senses, when he looked around and realised it wasn't just him; the floor was tilting.

"We need to get out of here!" Xander shouted, running over to Julian and helping him get to his feet. "C'mon ,we need to leave."

"Mollie, allow me," Quartzig said, holding her arm out. A small spark of electricity jumped from his hand into the nanos on her arm.

"I have purged all programming from Yuri from the nanobots, and reprogrammed them to follow your command," he smiled at Mollie who stared in shock. She focused on her arm and it reformed into a shiny metallic arm, the curves and contours matching her original.

"Th... Thanks," she smiled back.

The group all gathered and headed towards the closest exit, a fire escape stairwell.

"What about Jacob?" Owens asked, knowing it wouldn't be a popular question.

"No time, if he's not up already, we won't be able to go back for him now. We've already taken too long." Ally replied flatly.

As if on cue, the wall behind them fell away,

leaving an open space behind them, the lights of the Boulevard twinkling below. They all stumbled down the stairs as best they could.

CHAPTER 70

<u>*Xander*</u>

Xander took the lead on the escape. Mollie was helping Prime, as Ally did Julian. Owens and Ava followed close by and Quartzig took the rear.

The building was coming down fast, every few steps they took, another crash sounded like the walls were about to give way.

"Keep up guys, this place will not wait for us!" Xander called back, jumping several stairs at a time. He glanced back up to check on the others.

"How much further?" Mollie shouted out.

"About ten more floors, we're nearly there," He shouted back.

Before he could say another word, the stairs between him and the rest moved away, as if the room was stretching, but eventually the cement cracked and it split the building in two.

"Holy shit!" Xander shouted. "Quick, get across here!"

Mollie and Prime were standing on the step behind the cracks, it was only a few feet wid.

"Go," Prime said to Mollie, and she jumped without question.

"Julian next," Prime said.

Julian cleared the space without problems, though it was widening. Ally and Ava made it across next, the jump getting further each second.

"Owens, you go," Quartzig said, as he and Prime judged the distance, they should be fine.

Owens took a step forward, looking over the edge, he saw the ground several stories below. Taking a step back, he ran forward towards the space. Just as he got to the gap, he set one foot and launched himself.

Something was wrong, he didn't leave the ground as he should, instead he felt a sharp impact hit his chest, the force pushing him back onto the steps.

From the space between the walls above them, they could see a female clone. It was the one who had been fighting Yuri earlier with her wrist broken, a pistol in her good hand.

"You should have protected me Owens! You were my Father!"

Owens saw the blood pouring from his chest now, the wound was large and the blood flowing faster.

Xander immediately raised his gun and pointed it at the clone, but she was just out of his line of sight.

Owens tried to get to his feet but couldn't, Prime came over to help him to his feet, before looking up at the clone.

"Who are you? Why can't I find you?" He said, trying to focus on the clones mind.

"Oh come now Prime, I'm sure you can figure it out. Did you really think I'd let a little thing like death stop me?"

"Peter?" Prime couldn't understand.

"You'll get it, I know you will. Be seeing you brother," she smiled.

Taking aim, she fired another shot at Owens, the impact tore him from Prime's arms and fell away from him. Slipping, he fell into the space between the buildings.

"Owens!" Ava yelled and reached out in a futile effort to catch him as his body tumbled between the remnants of the floors below. His body ricocheting off several floors, before disappearing into the dark.

Quartzig and Prime could do nothing as they saw him fall, looking back to the floor above, they couldn't see Peter anywhere.

Xander grabbed Ava from the edge and pulled her back.

"He's gone Ava. I'm sorry," he said holding, her tight to stop her from returning to the widening space. After a moment, Ava relaxed in his arms and then returned to her normal composure.

"I'm okay Xander, thank you," she said, convincing no one.

Prime and Quartzig made the jump over quickly and they continued the descent.

"I'm sorry for your loss," Ally was standing with Ava now.

"He was a good man Ally, I know you may not think so with what he did to you, but he always meant well," she said.

"I believe that," Ally replied. "I wish I'd got to know him more, find out why he did what he did to me."

Ava nodded and continued walking.

They reached the ground floor of the building, passing through what remained of the foyer area where the fighting had started. Bodies littered the floor as they stepped cautiously through the debris to get to the exit. Once outside, they continued a safe distance before turning to see the damage.

The building was splitting down the center, each half twisting, creating an almost double helix pattern as it went down.

"Is it over?" Mollie asked, to anyone who would answer.

"I hope so," Xander replied.

"I have deactivated all available nanobots other than the ones that make up this body, I wanted no risk of remnants of Yuri in any of them," Quartzig said.

"Peter is still in there, unless he's made it out already," Julian added.

"He's not got any clones left though," Prime answered. "There's only me left."

Ally put her arm around Prime.

"You and me little brother," she said, and smiled at him.

"So what now?" Ava asked, having no idea

what she would do without Owens.

"Now? Now we go for a drink," Xander answered.

CHAPTER 71

Julian

Julian was lying on his lounger in his apartment, listening to the news broadcasts which echoed around him. Focusing on the sounds, picking up the keywords.

It had been a couple of cycles since the events at CyBio, and he'd released a report on the corporation and its downfall. His name had become famous once more. The fall of the CyBio building, referred to as 'The Fall' by the media, had caused masses of destruction in the Gigacity area. With Owens and Yuri gone, the funding for the rebuilding had come from the corporations substantial credits, which Ava had inherited and donated anonymously to the city.

The comms in his ear chimed, bypassing all other feeds.

"Hey Julian, I think we might have something here," Quartzig's voice said.

"One sec," Julian hit a button and a screen slid around the lounger so it was hovering in front of his face. He gestured a few times, activating the system. "Just getting the feeds now."

Since Quartzig had got used to his body, he'd been determined to see the world from a more first-person perspective. Julian was happy for the extra hands, so they had become a partnership in the newswire reporting. It allowed them to cover more ground.

"Ok I've got you on the outskirts of the Boulevard, around seventh?" Julian found a CCTV link showing the outside of a tech-mod workshop.

"Yeah, the last Mod-Junkie I talked to said this is the place they got the work," Quartzig replied.

The first cases they'd looked into was the last followers of Jacob's church who needed new mods, as they still suffered from the tech-virus that had infected them. Some reports had come through of someone taking advantage of these lost souls and fixing them up with cheap mods which caused worse infections. In an effort to clean up the loose ends, Julian and Quartzig had agreed to track them down and get the info to the MPD, or if a more hands on approach was needed, Xander and his new Investigation team.

"Ok, I'm going in," Quartzig said, unable to hide the excitement he felt being on the scene.

"I've scanned the area, seems clear, switching to your POV," Julian replied, as he activated Quartzig's POV cam. Julian still found it amusing that the world's most advanced nanobot AI was now an investigative reporter on the Boulevard.

"Heading in now, I'll let you know what I find," Quartzig said, before going quiet.

Julian watched the vid-feed as Quartzig entered the workshop, the lighting was dim and music filled the comms. A deep rhythmic beating of industrial electro vibrated his ear drums. As Quartzig moved further, he saw what could loosely be described as a reception desk; metal chicken wire was surrounding a wooden plank, supported by corrugated metal sheets. A woman sat behind the desk looking decidedly bored, raised her eyes as Quartzig entered. She had several piercings in her face, through which a metallic snake wound back and forth through the hoops.

"I'm here about some mod work," Quartzig said, smiling pleasantly.

"I don't think dis is the place fo' you hun," the woman said, looking him up and down, the snake pausing as she spoke.

"Actually, I think it is, you see someone has told me that the mods for the St Damian followers came from here. The ones that infected them with the T-pox. Dirty mods." Quartzig said, his smile dropping from his face.

"Get outta here Trojan, you don' wanna be starting nothing here," her accent a mix of Russian and Jamaican and more aggressive than before.

"Oh," Quartzig said, taken aback by the comment. "I'll take that as a confirmation then."

Before he could say anything else, three large men appeared from behind the desk, each of them sporting an assortment of mods from full arms to retina implants.

"You got some trouble Darcy?" The first, and largest asked.

"Dis Trojan asking about Damascus folks," she replied.

"Hm," was all the man said, as he made his way around the counter.

"I was just here to ask some questions," Quartzig put his hands in the air and back away slowly.

Julian flicked a comms switch and opened the channel.

"Quartz, you probably need to get out of there," he said.

"I'm 99.9% sure these are the guys who have been selling the dirty mods, Julian," Quartzig replied, causing angry looks from the men who were all getting closer. "I'm afraid I can't just leave now, perhaps you should let the MPD know there might be trouble here."

"What trouble?" Julian asked.

As the first man lunged towards him, Quartzig stepped aside, grabbing the man's arm and placing his foot strategically, he used the brutes momentum against him. Quartzig threw the man to the ground, before a perfectly timed kick to his temple rendered him unconscious. The next two men both ran at him now, the one with a retina implant flicked his wrist, revealing a hidden blade with a streak of red neon running down its center.

"Quartzig, what the hell are you doing?" Julian shouted.

"One moment please," Quartzig replied.

The retina man swung the blade an arc high, causing Quartzig to duck low. As the blade finished its swing, he kicked the man squarely in the chest, knocking him back into the reception counter. The second man saw the opening and jumped forward, grabbing Quartzig's shoulder from behind. Quartzig turned his body at the torso in a complete 360 turn by activating the nanobots that made up the body. The man just stared at him, stunned by the move. Quartzig delivered a finishing uppercut to his jaw, causing him to lift off the ground several feet before crumpling in a heap. The retina man had regained his composure now and plunged the blade into Quartzigs' chest.

"That was unpleasant," he said, looking down at the man's hand and blade hilt sticking out of his chest as he turned his legs to their correct position.

He grabbed the man's hand and twisted it, breaking the wrist in several places and the hilt of the blade with it. The man screamed in pain and dropped to the floor, clutching his shattered wrist. The blade still embedded in his chest, Quartzig slowly pulled it out and threw it to the side where it impaled into the metal wall.

"I think the MPD might want to come and check this place out Julian, I'll leave these guys tied up in a corner somewhere for them. I'll have a look around to make sure we have enough for an article."

Julian shook his head in disbelief whilst sending an anonymous message to the local MPD.

A knock came on the door behind Julian, and Ally poked her head round the corner.

"Hey Jools, I'm going to head over to see Xander and the guys, anything you want?" She asked. Ally had been living with Julian for the last week. It had taken some adjusting, but she found the company good for her.

"Erm, I think we're good thanks Al," Julian replied, muting the comms to Quartzig. "Say hi to the gang for me."

"Will do, any sign of Prime?" She asked, before leaving. Prime had disappeared soon after The Fall, and everyone was keeping an eye out to try to find him.

"Nothing yet, sorry," Julian replied. "Always keeping an eye out though, we'll find him," he added.

"Thanks, I hope so," Ally turned and shut the door behind her.

CHAPTER 72

Ally

Ally made her way across the Boulevard. The daylight was just fading and the neon lights were flickering on like waking eyelids.

"Ally!" A voice called out from across the way, causing her to dart a glance. Her adrenaline spiked and her hand moved to her bo-staff; coiled in its holster.

Her eyes finally landed on the source of the voice and she realised it was Ava rushing through the crowds to meet her.

"Ava! Hi," Ally smiled as she arrived.

"How are you?" Ava said as she walked in line with Ally.

"I'm ok, still adjusting to… well everything, really."

"Understandable, since Owen's death, I have had a lot to process."

Ally gave a sympathetic smile. Of all of

them, Ava had the biggest loss, though due to her nature, she seemed to be the least affected by the events.

"So, you're working with Xander now?" Ally changed the topic.

"Yes, he felt we worked well together, so asked if I wanted somewhere to work whilst I sorted things out. I had no better options, so I agreed," she replied.

"And Mollie too?"

"Yes, she also needed something to focus on. It's been good for us both I feel," Ava said.

"I'm glad," Ally said, with complete sincerity.

They had arrived at Xander's office, the door on the outside now read 'Xander Investigations,' with no letters missing.

"I've got to take these upstairs," Ava indicated to the bags she was carrying and the apartment above the office. "We must catch up properly soon," she said and then headed up the stairs which lead off the main corridor.

Ally walked into Xander's office. In the two weeks since the collapse of the CyBio building, she had taken time to process the information and she was ready to continue what she started that night.

Inside Xander, sat behind his desk, it was filled with paperwork from several cases which he had gotten in the last few months. On the sofa to the side of the room, Mollie lay, playing with an anti-grav ball. Throwing it up, it hovered for a second in mid-air, then dropped back to her nano hand.

"Hey guys," Ally announced as she entered.

Mollie looked up and smiled, jumping to her feet, leaving the anti-grav ball hanging in midair, she ran over and gave her a hug.

"Hi Mollie," she returned the hug.

"How you holdin' up Al?" Xander asked, pouring a whiskey into a spare glass before passing it to her.

"Getting there, lots of questions and no one to answer them," she smiled and took the drink.

"I hear ya," they clinked the glasses together.

Mollie returned to the sofa and caught the ball as it fell.

"Things look... busy?" Ally nodded to the papers on the desk.

"Yeah, since Julian put the article up about the CyBio corp going down and the work we did to stop it, we've been inundated with cases."

"Sounds good, and you've got Mollie here to help out now?" Ally smiled.

"Sure, she's pretty handy with a laser pistol when push comes to shove," Xander smiled. "Ava is great too, I think she needed somewhere she felt like she could belong after everything."

"Glad you could give her that," Ally replied, as she sat in the chair opposite.

"So, is this just a social call or..." Xander let the question hang in the air.

"I want to find out who my parents were," Ally answered. "I want to know who my coding was based on and find some semblance of a family. For me and Prime. I tried to track down Razz but he's disappeared from the Underpass."

Xander scanned Ally's face, he could tell this was important to her.

"Of course we'll help," Mollie said, before Xander could reply. "Won't we Xander," it wasn't a question.

Xander took a sip of the bourbon and sighed, "Of course we will," he smiled at Ally.

Ally stayed to finish her drink and discussed what she knew about her parents from the discussions she'd had with Yuri and Owens about them, filling in any details she could think of. Ally and Mollie then returned to less serious topics as Xander compiled the information.

"Have you heard from Julian at all?" Mollie asked, knowing full well that they were living together.

"I have, he's been helping Quartzig adjust to a more physical world than he's used to," Ally replied, not giving anything away.

"That can't be easy for him?"

"He's getting there," Ally laughed.

"Are you back working at the Valkyrie yet?" She asked.

"Not yet, I need time to sort things out before I do, I think."

They continued to talk about things, before Ally made her excuses to leave.

She walked out of the office and down the street until she was back on the Neon Boulevard. A fine mist of rain had just fallen, blurring the neon into streaks of colours reflecting off the wet pavements. It would take time for her to adjust to her new life, the feeling that she didn't fit into the world anymore. Yet somehow, she also felt more comfortable knowing where she came from, and a little more of her identity. She knew she'd find her way though, with the help of the friends she had made.

CHAPTER 73

Before The Fall

Jacob opened his eyes and evaluated his location, he was laying in the medical bay of the CyBio building. He tried to piece together his thoughts; Peter had attacked him and was sure he was dead. Yet here he was, fully healed in the medical pod. He looked around the room; he was also alone, free of the escort he'd had since they left the church. Free to complete his plan.

He got to his feet and checked the pocket of his robe, the twin to the unit he had installed on Ava earlier in the server room was still there. A smile crept across his face, his Plan B was still in progress. He headed out of the medical bay and heard the sounds of fighting taking place in the distance. He would need to get closer to Ava to complete his plan, a risk he would have to take.

Making his way towards the sounds, he

carefully rounded each corner until he could see Yuri and Prime battling, with Prime suddenly taking advantage. The rest of the group were engrossed in the fight, giving Jacob the time he needed. Not too far away from him, he saw Ava embraced with Owens.

Jacob slowly made his way closer to her and pulled out the small receiver, two clicks and it kicked into action. Within moments, small message beeped along the side of the unit

[Download Complete]

Jacob smiled again, he was surprised it had been this easy. He took another glance at the fighting before he noticed Julian looking directly at him. He quickly ducked away, hoping he was far enough away to not be recognized. Now he just had to get out of the building, fast.

Now

The small room Jacob was holed up in wasn't ideal for his needs, but it would suffice for now. He had rigged up a small digital workbench on the table that lined one wall. It had taken him a few weeks to scavenge all the parts he needed; he hadn't dared return to the church or access any of his previous funds, in case anyone was still looking for him.

He flicked a switch, and the workbench lit

up like a firework display, an open space in the center was the only unlit space. A small square of about two feet lined along the bottom with a smooth metallic surface.

Jacob plugged the small receiver into a slot on the right side of the bench, it auto-booted up and a short loading system activated. In the space on the table, a holographic bar appeared, showing its progress. A word flashed up on the screen:

[Password:]

Jacob typed in the word he had learned from Owens.

[Excelsior]

A moment later and the the bar disappeared and the space went dark again. Slowly forming one small pixel at a time, a face emerged in the space. A three-dimensional holographic head finally developed and looked around, taking in its surroundings.

"Where am I? What has happened to me?" The head queried.

"I'll explain everything Yuri, and you and I are going to do some amazing work together," Jacob smiled as he pulled up a chair next to the bench.

CHAPTER 74

Epilogue -Mollie

Mollie stood outside the back of Xander's office building, a small square courtyard surrounded by buildings on all sides. The residence of all the buildings had tried to make it a small garden area, with a water feature in the center. She looked up, the neon lights of the city merging into a haze of colour.

She hadn't been back to the Underpass since she and Prime had came up through the lift and she was feeling the pull to return. Not that she wanted to go back, she had found new friends up here on the Boulevard; people who cared about her. It was her condition which was the problem. She closed her eyes, trying to fight the pull of it which had taken hold again.

'We're waiting Mollie.'

A voice echoed inside her head, Vladamir, she had been expecting it before now and it didn't come as a surprise. She replied inside her mind.

'I want to stay here.'

'It's too late for that Mollie, we balanced the books, there are no favors left,'

'I... I know, give me another job, something to turn the scales back in my favor'

'No more favors, it is time Mollie, either you return or we will come to find you. And will kill anyone that stands in our way. You must be feeling the bloodlust.'

Vladamir kept the lust at bay for anyone who he was in debt to, but once the balance was restored, he strengthened it, in doing so keeping his disciples in debt to him.

'You will need to feed soon Mollie, return to me, let me help you.'

Mollie opened her eyes, if anyone was watching her, they would have seen a flash of red glint over them as her teeth spiked, each one twisting into razor sharp fangs. She shook her head, fighting the bloodlust that burned through her body.

She needed to choose her path.

CHAPTER 75

Epilogue -Prime

Prime sat on the edge of a skyscraper in the Boulevard's heart. Looking down at the lights below, he couldn't help wondering what it would be like if he leaned forward and let gravity take its pull on him.

He had been struggling with his thoughts for some time after The Fall, wondering who he was now. The knowledge that Peter was still out there somewhere also troubled him. He hadn't had a good look at the body that Peter had taken over, just that it was a female and had been the last surviving clone left. On top of all that, he had had strange thoughts, violent thoughts of hurting people for his own gain. So far, he had suppressed them to just thoughts and not actions but he wasn't sure how much longer he could hold on. He wished he could talk to the others about what was happening but he wasn't sure they would trust him, or would they think he was turning into Peter.

The rain was falling and Prime stood up, taking one last look over the city, he turned to head back inside the building. What he saw caused him to freeze in his tracks. Laying on the rooftop just behind where he was sitting was a body. A young woman with bloodied wounds across her body, next to it a comms device sat with a small paper note stuck to it with tape;

Say 'hello'

The body hadn't been there when he had got onto the roof. Prime hesitated for a moment, before picking up the unit.

"Hello?" He said, as he clicked the open comms button on the side.

"Good Evening Prime," a female voice rang through the static.

"Who is this?"

"Oh come now, just because my voice is a few octaves higher, doesn't mean you shouldn't be able to guess," the voice chimed back.

"Peter?"

"Bingo, though I think a new name would suit this body more, I was thinking Persephone perhaps, what do you think?"

"Who... who is this woman, what have you done?" Prime stammered.

"Who? Oh the dead meat, that's just an appetizer for the main course, Prime. I know that I planted my subconscious somewhere inside that clone-brain of yours, somewhere laying dormant just waiting to be activated. So we will play a little game, you and I. I will continue what I was working on way back before I got exiled by Jacob, and you, you will try to stop me."

"How is that a game?" Prime asked, not understanding.

"It's simple, the more you see, the more my dormant personality will start to take a hold on you, until you'll start to find it hard to remember if it was me or you that killed. Your job, is to try to stop me before it comes to that!" Persephone laughed down the unit.

Prime could think of nothing to say, he had already felt the urges of violence sneaking into the peripheral of his thoughts.

"How do I stop you?" He said, thinking out loud.

"I'm not giving you all the answers Prime, though lets just say, there's a clue with the body you're standing over. Oh, but don't take too long, I've already tipped off the MPD and if they catch you there, I'm sure the finger-prints on the victim will be an almost perfect match for yours," another laugh. "Time's ticking Prime! Whose it going to be, you or me?"

The unit went dead.

Prime looked down at the girl, the rain seeping into the clothing and cause the blood to run; the neon reflecting off the glistening blood.

He closed his eyes, and took a deep breath.

THE END

Printed in Poland
by Amazon Fulfillment
Poland Sp. z o.o., Wrocław

50286662R00312